Her entire body was buzzing like a swarm of bees eager to get to a big ol' pot of honey.

"Tell me kissing you would be a mistake," Harry said, his voice low and sexy as hell.

She swallowed. "Okay. If that's what you want."

A smiled teased his lips. "What do you want?"

"You don't want to know."

That heat flared again as if he were reading Jaimie's mind. "I really think I do want to know." And he brought his mouth against hers, and she let out a sound he cut off with his lips, firm and soft and very, very nice. No tongue, not yet, just his mouth, pressing hers, moving against her lips, and oh, those swarming bees were definitely headed for the honey. Jaimie let out a little laugh and he raised his head in question.

"Private joke," she mumbled then pulled him to her again and kissed the living daylights out of him.

BOOK YOUR PLACE ON OUR WEBSITE AND MAKE THE READING CONNECTION!

We've created a customized website just for our very special readers, where you can get the inside scoop on everything that's going on with Zebra, Pinnacle and Kensington books.

When you come online, you'll have the exciting opportunity to:

- View covers of upcoming books
- Read sample chapters
- Learn about our future publishing schedule (listed by publication month *and author*)
- Find out when your favorite authors will be visiting a city near you
- Search for and order backlist books from our online catalog
- Check out author bios and background information
- Send e-mail to your favorite authors
- Meet the Kensington staff online
- Join us in weekly chats with authors, readers and other guests
- Get writing guidelines
- AND MUCH MORE!

**Visit our website at
http://www.kensingtonbooks.com**

A HARD MAN IS GOOD TO FIND

Jane Blackwood

ZEBRA BOOKS
Kensington Publishing Corp.
http://www.kensingtonbooks.com

ZEBRA BOOKS are published by

Kensington Publishing Corp.
850 Third Avenue
New York, NY 10022

All Kensington titles, imprints and distributed lines are available at special quantity discounts for bulk purchases for sales promotion, premiums, fund-raising, educational or institutional use.

Special book excerpts or customized printings can also be created to fit specific needs. For details, write or phone the office of the Kensington Special Sales Manager: Kensington Publishing Corp., 850 Third Avenue, New York, NY 10022. Attn. Special Sales Department. Phone: 1-800-221-2647.

First Printing: December 2004
10 9 8 7 6 5 4 3 2 1

Printed in the United States of America

Chapter 1

Jaimie McLane stared at the headline—"Man Loses Cock"— for the tenth time wishing somehow it would disappear and wishing just as hard no one would notice it.

"Did you see this?" Nate Baxter asked, handing her that day's edition of *The Nortown Journal* and trying not to grin. The assistant editor had thought the headline was a real hoot the night before when Jaimie had gleefully typed it over the story about a local farmer who lost his prize Rhode Island Red rooster. It had been a joke, it was not, obviously, meant to run over the story.

"I'm screwed. I can't believe we let this through. Harry's going to be shitting bricks over this." Jaimie buried her head in her hands. "I'm so dead. Dead, dead, dead," she moaned, beating her head against her fists.

"He won't fire you," Nate said.

He being Harry, her new boss and the man she was quickly growing to dislike intensely. She knew herself well enough to know she could never fully hate something as beautiful as Harry Crandall. Perhaps she could loathe him instead. When he'd walked in two months ago her heart had actually done the oddest thumpety-thump, something that hadn't happened in . . . well, it had never happened quite that way. Her cheeks had flamed, her ears turned red, and the neon sign on her forehead that flashed "hottie alert" whenever she saw a man who made her lungs compress buzzed on. He was a juicy combination of Matthew McConaughey and Paul Newman in his prime with a bit of a young Cary Grant thrown into the mix to give him that stand-offish better-than-you air she found so unpleasant in Harry and so pleasing in Cary. Except he didn't have any of their boyish charm or lazy smiles. Jaimie grimaced at her thoughts. That's what came from watching too many movies late at night—most of them black-and-white relics in which every star was either now dead or suffering from Alzheimer's.

He might be eye candy, but Harry had managed to throw a big ol' bucket of cold water over her head after he fired three reporters the first week. Fine, they were dead wood, but they were *her* dead wood. Everyone in the newsroom was walking around as if the slightest mistake would end with him or her out on the street. And now she had the awful feeling he was about to turn his ax on her.

"He should fire me. I would." Jaimie peered up through her fingers. "I'm not sure if I should tell him I don't get the sexual connotation or admit to fooling around on deadline and being too stupid to remember to change it. I can't believe it got through."

Nate skittered away suddenly, moving so fast his skimpy comb over blew in the breeze, and slinked around to his desk that sat opposite Jaimie's.

He had arrived. Mr. Pulitzer-prize-winning Harry Crandall. Mr. *GQ New York Times*. As he had done since he took over the paper precisely sixty days ago—Jaimie had the date marked with a black X on her calendar at home—Harry walked in without looking at a single person in the newsroom, went straight to his office, and shut the door. Mr. Personality. If the guy smiled, his face would probably crack, Jaimie thought grumpily.

"How long before he sees it?" Nate whispered.

"Five minutes." Jaimie glanced nervously at the clock before booting up her computer and pretending to work. "I'm so dead." Far sooner than five minutes, she saw his office door open but didn't look up as she stared intensely and blindly at the screen in front of her.

"McLane. Get in here."

"Shit," she whispered, feeling the noose tighten around her neck.

She walks toward the door, her heels clicking on the hardwood floor. Right before she enters, she smooths her skirt and checks her lipstick on the doorknob. "Don't tell me to apologize, chief, 'cause I won't. You and I both know that was the best story this paper has ever seen." He stands and glares, smoke from his cigar swirls around his head. "I oughta fire you, but I got a thing about firing dames." He throws down his cigar in disgust. "Especially dames that look like you," he says so she can't hear.

"Jaimie, you going in or what?" Nate asked.

Jaimie closed her eyes, briefly wishing her life were really a black-and-white movie instead of this very sucky reality. "Oh, God. I'm dead," she croaked. And Nate, supportive friend as always, began to whistle "Taps." Jaimie gave him the bird behind her back right before walking into Harry's sparsely furnished office. It held only a large antique oak desk, Paul's old couch, and a water cooler that chose that moment to burp up a bubble. And it was so cold Jaimie wondered if she'd be able to see her breath, so she hugged her brown sweater more tightly around her. Other than his irascible nature, the only other thing she'd noticed about her new boss was that he kept the air conditioning in his office so high, his windows fogged up. The Ice Man Cometh.

Harry's desk was clean but for that day's edition of the *Nortown Journal*, folded in half, front page showing. He looked at her with an unyielding gaze, his dark gray eyes boring into her making Jaimie want to squirm. He didn't look exactly angry, more . . . impatient. He had been pushed back in his chair, but he moved slowly forward until he was standing and leaning over his desk, his large hands laying on either side of the paper, the tips of his fingers pressing into the wood. And now, to Jaimie's growing fear, he did look angry. She watched, in curious fascination, as a bead of sweat moved down his lean face, over his hard jaw, and dropped silently onto his well-starched white dress shirt. How on earth could the man be sweating in air this frigid? Unless he was so angry he'd broken out into a cold sweat.

Jaimie swallowed and tried not to look as terrified as she felt. "Before you say anything, would you rather I be stupid or incompetent?" *Please, please laugh.*

"I'd rather you not be here at all," he said with horrible calmness.

Oh, shit. "Are you firing me?" she choked out. She kept waiting for the ax to fall, an ax wielded grimly by a stone-faced man in a perfectly tailored suit.

"I'm putting you on probation." He sat down, looking remarkably less angry than when he'd stood up, his movements slow and measured.

Somehow, probation was worse, far more humiliating, than being fired. If she'd been fired, she could have gotten all indignant, vowed to find a better job at a better paper for more money. Seasoned journalists got fired, greenhorns got probation. It would have been difficult to decide which burned brighter, the red on her cheeks or the anger in her eyes. Jaimie took a breath to calm down. "I understand you are angry, but . . ."

"I'm not angry and there are no 'buts', no excuse for what happened. And you know it. For the sake of clearing the air, let me tell you what happened. It was late, near deadline, and you and your pal Nate came up with this very funny headline. It wasn't meant to run, am I right?"

"Yes," she ground out.

"And yet it ran anyway." He looked at her expectantly.

"Obviously, yes." *You arrogant son of a . . .*

"I can tell you one thing. I bet it was the most well-read story in the paper today." His eyes flickered down to the paper, and Jaimie thought she detected the slightest bit of humor in their cold depths. He gave her an assessing look, a completely asexual look, and Jaimie curled her fingers around the cuffs of her too-long sweater as she fought a shiver.

"You're a damned good editor, Jaimie, and I'm certain something like this won't happen again."

She could almost hear the unspoken *or else* in his tone. While she knew she deserved more than he'd given, Jaimie couldn't stop the deep resentment churning in her gut. Maybe it would be better if she did leave. That thought left her colder than Harry's office. "I've been editor here for five years and there's never been this kind of screw-up. It won't happen again."

He nodded, an agreement and a dismissal, and Jaimie left the office feeling relief and slightly less loathing. She was at her desk for two seconds before Kath Kopf came over, a wide grin on her face.

"So, are you fired?"

"Don't sound so hopeful," Jaimie grumbled. "No, I'm not fired."

"Did he ask you out?"

"No, we just had sex on his desk. He's got a small dick."

"Really?" Kath asked in mock dismay. "When I had sex with him on my desk, I thought it was rather large."

"We all have different standards," she said dryly. "He put me on probation. All in all, I got off easy."

Kath's smile disappeared. "Probation? I didn't think we had anything like that here." She gave Harry's office a worried look. "Do you think he's done firing people?"

Jaimie was startled by the real concern in Kath's voice. Kath, short for Kathleen, had been at the *Nortown Journal* nearly as long as Jaimie. She was a hardworking, fast-writing, tough-as-nails reporter who should have moved on to another, better paper years ago. "Kath, you have nothing to worry about. You're safer than I am."

"But I heard he's hiring a couple of Columbia University hotshots."

Jaimie hadn't even heard that—something that made her feel even more impotent. "You're not seriously worried, are you?"

"We all are," Nate said, unabashedly eavesdropping on their conversation. "He fired three reporters already."

"I'm pretty certain he's all done firing." Her two friends looked uncertain, which made her unsure about Harry's plans as well. "Do you want me to talk to him?" she asked, praying hard and fast they'd say no.

"We want you to sleep with him then use your body to gain favors for us," Nate said, as Kath nodded.

Jaimie gave them a withering look. "Thanks for the vote of confidence, guys, but I really don't plan to use this body as an instrument of extortion. Anyway, sexual harassment is illegal."

"When did you get all politically correct?" Nate said, smiling evilly.

Jaimie let out a beleaguered sigh so her friends would know exactly how much she hated to confront Harry with their concerns. "I'll talk to him, but I really doubt I'll find out anything. And I'm not going to talk to him today. I'm already on his shit list."

Kath gave Nate a look. "We think you should, um, make friends," she said.

"I am not sleeping with that man," Jaimie said, blown away by her friends' suggestion and the fact they'd met and discussed this at length, coming to the astounding conclusion she'd have any influence over Harry.

"Who said you should sleep with him?" Kath said. "We just want him to get to know us, like us. It's easy to fire people when you don't know them. He won't be able to fire people he likes."

Jaimie shook her head in confusion. "What are you suggesting then?"

"For starters, you could invite him to the softball game. Have him join the Dead Pool. Tell him about Duffy's Bar. Use your imagination."

Jaimie gave her friends a sick look. "Why me? Ted's way more friendly with him than I am."

Nate rolled his eyes. "Ted's sports editor. He doesn't have anything to do with the newsroom," he said as if talking to a simpleton. "It's got to come from you, our hallowed leader. Otherwise, he's going to slowly and methodically replace us with new college grads. They get paid less, they're eager, and they'll kiss his ass."

"So you are making me the official ass-kisser? Is that it?"

Kath grinned and gave Nate a nudge with her elbow. "Finally she gets it."

Jaimie made a sick face. "You do realize what you're asking me to do. Play nice with a guy I can't stand."

"He's not that bad," Kath said. "Plus I wouldn't kick him out of bed. Wink, wink."

"You still think Ted Bundy's innocent," Jaimie said, dismissing Kath's assessment of Attila the Hun. "Just because he's okay-looking . . ."

"Okay-looking?"

Jaimie narrowed her eyes. "Just because Harry's . . ."

"Gorgeous."

"Is he?" Nate asked looking over at Harry's office with pure puzzlement.

"Yes. He is. But he's a jackass," Jaimie said with force.

"And you're going to invite that jackass to the softball game, right?"

Jaimie looked Nate in the eye. "To save the newsroom, I'd do just about anything."

From his new office, Harry could look out over the newsroom, a large seemingly endless room of desks and computer terminals. At the far end of the room was the production section, where the paper was laid out before being shot and brought downstairs to the printing press. Anyone could tell when the paper went to press because the ancient three-story building shook whenever the paper rumbled through the outdated printer. The *Nortown Journal* was a fitting newspaper for this broken-down old mill town that straddled the Connecticut River. Harry was fairly certain he'd never seen, never mind lived in, a more depressing city. Like so many old New England cities, it had once been a bustling city, a huge center of manufacturing and the arts. Now, those graceful old mills that once employed thousands were vacant hulks. In the Eighties, a couple of entrepreneurs made a valiant effort to rehab the old places. A few were turned into condos, another into a biotech company, but most now housed only large, fat rats. Perhaps most depressing—other than the "downtown"—were the grand old mansions that lined Empire Boulevard. A town common, now a dirty, garbage-strewn "park", once separated the boulevard and its rich, powerful mill owners. Now, the owners' mansions that were still standing had been broken up into apartments. The last century had not been kind to Nortown or its inhabitants.

The newspaper was housed in a run down building built at the turn of the last century whose only renovations were the partitions that separated the editorial offices from the newsroom. He'd only been working as publisher for two months, and not a day had gone by where he didn't think, if only briefly, that his life sucked far worse than he ever could have imagined. God, he hated his life.

Was it only a year ago he'd been a top reporter for the *New York Times*, only three that he'd gotten a Pulitzer Prize for a series of articles on the World Trade Center? Only three months since he'd woken up next to the woman he'd thought he'd spend the rest of his life with? When things went to shit, they went hard and fast.

His eyes rested on his city editor and he almost smiled. He had to give her credit for being extremely pissed and keeping her mouth shut. The truth was, the headline was damn funny and he really didn't care that it had run. He should care. But didn't. And he knew this noncaring was a symptom of the rest of his lousy life. Probation. What a joke. He couldn't fire her but he wouldn't let her know that. Jaimie McLane was as close as a person can come to being irreplaceable. She'd been at the paper for years, she knew every politician, every major story and all the main players that had graced the pages for more than a decade. She grew up in Nortown, poor thing, so her friends were now emerging as lawyers in big cases, as cops who got into trouble, as politicians running for office. The former publisher, Paul Mayer, had filled him in on Jaimie, talking so highly of her Harry thought maybe the old guy must have had a crush on her. Jaimie didn't know just how vital she was to the success of this paper, but Harry knew. She was a bit rough around the edges, editorially speaking. Her training was lacking, but her news instinct almost gave him shivers. What she was still doing here, at this cash-poor paper, was a mystery. He figured maybe she'd just dug a rut so deep the thought of climbing out of it was too much to face.

Jaimie McLane was, to Harry, a strange, foreign being. He was used to New York, fast-paced, upwardly mobile, backstabbing, intense and so damned exhilarating his blood would sing every time he walked into the *Times* newsroom with a kickass story in his notebook and a great lead in his head. Jaimie was intense, that was for certain. She held her editorial meetings as if she were listening to the most interesting story ideas ever to grace the pages of a paper. She offered suggestions, she canned certain ideas, and she had, in that strange head of hers, more information about this lousy little city than Harry would have thought possible. She knew when stories had been written, down to the week they appeared in the paper.

Harry was used to being around career-driven women. In fact, nothing was sexier than a successful woman in a business suit rushing to her computer to write a front-page story. That was when he'd first noticed Anne, beautiful, driven, cold-hearted Anne. She'd had a look of determination, almost a fervor in her eyes, as she sat down and wrote her first page one story for the *New York Times*. Damn, she was hot back then.

And still was.

Harry's gaze again took in Jaimie. She looked more like a ditzy artist than an editor. Even though it was mid-August and hotter than hell outside, she wore a baggy, too-big sweater to work every day. She must have a closet full of big, frumpy sweaters and shapeless pants. He found himself slightly curious about what she was hiding beneath all those clothes. Whatever her body, she hid it well—curiously well. Her straight reddish blonde hair was, every day for the past sixty days, pulled back into a sleek ponytail. She wore no makeup. Her nails were unpainted and clipped short.

He noticed because he was so used to women like Anne—put-together, sharp-tongued, and eminently desirable. Harry felt another drop of sweat make its way down his neck and he swore. He took out a handkerchief and wiped roughly at the moisture.

That life is gone now, Harry, and you'd best just get on with this new one.

If Harry were a man who cried, he would have curled up in a ball and sobbed his heart out.

Chapter 2

It wasn't a very nice thing to do, but in a newsroom, sicker things than betting on your boss's affliction happened all the time. Like the Dead Pool. Every news reporter and sportswriter in the newsroom put five dollars in a pool then named the public figure who would die next. The only rule was that you couldn't pick someone who was already dying. Sure, it was sick, but kind of fun, too.

So the Harry Pool wasn't so bad, Jaimie told herself. Everyone in the newsroom was dying to know why Harry was stuck in Nortown, Connecticut. As cities went, Nortown wasn't especially attractive. On a map, it looked like someone took a blob of slime and slapped it over the Connecticut River. So why would Harry, a Pulitzer Prize-winning writer, a senior reporter with the *New York Times*, end up here? She knew enough about the business to know the *Nortown Journal* was mediocre at best, and this small city she'd grown up in was about as vibrant and exciting as, well, a blob of slime. Guys like Harry maybe started in Nortown, but they didn't end up in it.

It was this mystery that had Jaimie thinking way too much about her new boss. And if there was one thing reporters didn't like, it was mysteries. It was driving her crazy.

Jaimie sat across from Paul Mayer, her old boss, at Duffy's where they'd eaten nearly every workday since she'd been promoted to city editor. Duffy's was quiet this time of day, but at night when most of the newsroom and half the police force ended up sitting at the bar, it was far noisier. Single businessmen grabbing a quick lunch occupied only two other tables. Roger, Duffy's owner, came over wiping his hands on a clean towel that was perpetually jammed into the front of his jeans.

"Paul. How've you been?" Roger asked, slapping the older man on the shoulder so hard Paul winced.

"Good. Retirement's great." His cheer sounded forced. Paul, whose slightly thinning white hair was tinged with yellow from the high blood pressure medicine he took, had newsprint-stained hands before he'd retired. Now, Jaimie noticed his hands were clean, and frighteningly old.

"Are you really enjoying retirement, Paul?" Jaimie asked after Roger left.

"Can't say that I am. But I suppose I'll get used to it. Too much time on my hands."

"I don't know what I'd do if I retired. Go nuts. But I am thinking of leaving," she said, amazed at herself that she'd actually said the words aloud. The fear that instantly coiled in her stomach told her thinking about leaving was likely as far as she'd ever get to walking out the door. Still, it felt good to gripe to her mentor about all the changes, her probation, her general antipathy toward Harry. She'd thought she'd have an ally, but Paul disappointed her.

"I consider myself lucky to have found a man like Harry Crandall to run this paper. I know it's not easy,

Jaimie, but I'm going to tell you something. I thought about firing Jake, Chrissy, and Maxine years ago. Hell, I thought it was a mistake to hire them."

Jaimie's jaw dropped. "Why didn't you say something?"

"Lost interest, I guess." He looked out the window, his eyes studying the dirty street outside. "I never wanted to run this paper, Jaimie."

If Jaimie's jaw could have dropped off completely, it would have. She'd always thought Paul lived and breathed the *Nortown Journal,* and here he was telling her he never wanted it? "What would you have done instead?"

"I wanted to go to law school." Paul shrugged. "Maybe I will now."

"This is all I've ever wanted," Jaimie said. "And now I'm afraid it's being taken away. What's his story, anyway? What's he even doing here?"

"He was looking for a job and I hired him."

Jaimie narrowed her eyes, searching her old friend's face for any guile. "You didn't ask him why he was leaving the *Times?*"

"Nope."

"Did he say?"

"Nope."

Jaimie rolled her eyes at Paul's Yankee reticence. "Are you going to tell me you don't think it's strange for someone like Harry to take a job here? No offense, Paul, but this isn't normally where Pulitzer Prize-winning *New York Times* reporters end up."

"I'm sure he has a reason. He assured me he was leaving the *Times* in good standing. I did call. I'm not an idiot. According to his former boss, Harry is just short of becoming a journalistic deity."

Jaimie had the distinct feeling Paul was leaving

something out. "I just don't get why a guy like Harry would want this job."

Paul, good-natured as always, chuckled. "Don't know his story and don't care. He knows the business almost better than I do. Maybe better, thank God, 'cause financially things aren't very rosy. Harry just might turn things around. I'm not going to look a gift horse in the mouth." He took a bite of his burger, pointing his finger across the bun. "And neither should you."

"I know. I know." She pulled a face. "But he's such an autocratic jerk."

"That may be. But he's the best damned newsman I've ever seen. Bar none. I think he's going to take this paper places I never could." Paul looked sad all of a sudden, and Jaimie felt selfish and mean.

"I'm sorry all I've done is bitch. I'm sure it'll just take some getting used to. If not, I'll look for another job."

Paul shook his head. "Your feet are embedded in cement."

Jaimie felt herself bristle even as she acknowledged to herself that he was right. "No they're not. I could leave. If I wanted to. I just don't want to."

Paul smiled gently. "You sound like an alcoholic saying he could give up drinking."

Jaimie frowned and took a bite of her BLT. "The other guys think we should all make friends so he won't be able to fire any more of us. What do you think?"

"I think you're spending too much time thinking about your new boss," Paul said. "You're beginning to sound obsessive."

Jaimie wrinkled her nose. "I am not. Just curious, like a good reporter ought to be."

Paul leaned back bracing both hands on the scarred wooden table, and had a look on his face that told Jaimie she was in for a speech. "Jaimie, just leave it be. Sometimes a man has to do things that aren't pretty and that he doesn't want to do. Sometimes life isn't fair. You're right. Harry Crandall has no business being here. But he's here and from what I can see, he's trying to do something with this paper. I don't know what happened to him personally and I don't care. Cut him some slack, will you?"

"I'll try."

"And one more thing I want you to know. I considered making you managing editor and publisher." He held his hand up to stop Jaimie's wide-eyed response. "But I didn't want you chained to this place your entire life. When was the last time you took a vacation? Hell, when was the last full two-day weekend you took?"

"I like my job."

"When was the last time you went out on a date. You're not a dyke, are you?"

"Paul," Jaimie said, embarrassed and appalled and slightly amused. "No, I'm not. I just haven't had time . . ."

"Take the time, Jaimie," Paul said. "Before you know it, you'll be seventy and alone and wondering what the hell you did with your life. You're already, what, thirty?"

"Thirty-one," Jaimie admitted. "Paul, don't worry about me. I'm not you. I'm doing what I want, I'm living my dream."

"Dreams change."

"I'm sorry you're so unhappy. But I'm pretty content. I've got a house and a nice car, a job I love."

Paul just shook his head. "A job can't love you back."

Twenty minutes later, Jaimie trudged up the two-story flight of stairs that led her to the second-floor newsroom feeling depressed and angry. She'd have to thank Paul for

making her feel like a failure in life when all along she'd
felt pretty damn good about herself. He was just bitter and
alone and full of regrets. But he wasn't her. She was still
young and hadn't sworn off marriage. She just hadn't
found the right guy yet. So what if she hadn't gone out on
a date in more than two years. Okay, four years.

"Oh my God," Jaimie said softly to herself just before
reaching the second-floor landing. "Four *years?*" She remembered vividly the last time she'd been out with a man,
the last time she'd had sex. With someone. Dennis Bailey,
used car salesman extraordinaire, married, two kids,
claimed he was single and looking for love in all the right
places. Jaimie hadn't sworn off dating after that bitterly
embarrassing situation, but it seemed dating had sworn
off her.

When Jaimie got to her desk, she found two folded
pieces of paper with five dollars paper-clipped to each.
She opened each one and laughed aloud. That made
eight people who had joined the Harry Pool so far. For
the past two days, reporters and sportswriters had
furtively approached Jaimie and handed her a piece of
paper, along with five dollars, with their guess as to
what the hell Harry was doing in Nortown.

The reasons were as follows: He was a drunk. He was
a druggie. He's insane (Jaimie's contribution). He's suffering a broken heart (Kath's guess). He killed someone.
He plagiarized and got fired but the *Times* covered it up
to save the paper's reputation (Jaimie thought that one.
from Ted the sports editor, was pretty good). He's secretly
from Nortown and is returning to his roots. He actually
wants to be here and has no ulterior reasons (from a reporter, Beth, who obviously has a crush on Harry).

Jaimie had the damning list safely locked in her drawer,
but it bothered her to have it there, like the telltale heart

in Edgar Allan Poe's story. The pool bordered on mean-spiritedness, not just clean good fun, and Jaimie was beginning to feel more than a little guilty about it.

"Why don't we just call the *Times* and talk to someone," Jaimie suggested to Kath when her friend returned to the newsroom. The newsroom was nearly empty but for Jaimie and Kath; Harry was in his office in some sort of meeting.

"I'll call," Kath said, jumping away toward her desk.

"Are you sure about this?" Jaimie called.

Kath waved a dismissive hand. "It was your idea. Don't worry about it." Knowing Kath as Jaimie did, she probably already had on her desk the name and extension of a reporter who knew Harry.

Jaimie watched Kath furtively as she made the call, studying her expression in an attempt to gauge the direction of the conversation. Kath nodded a few times, looked up at Jaimie, and frantically waved her over. On her reporter's notepad she'd written: "Fired for sexual harassment."

Jaimie couldn't have been more stunned. And doubtful. Her expression showed it. She grabbed the notebook and scribbled a question.

"Were charges filed?" Kath asked. "Mmm hmmm. Wow. Well, I appreciate your talking to me. Thanks."

Kath hung up. "Oh. My. God."

"Looks like no one won the pool," Jaimie said dryly. "Who'd you talk to?"

Kath smiled knowingly. "The guy who replaced him. He was very forthcoming. No charges were filed, but they made that a condition of his firing. You know, you're fired and we won't press charges."

Jaimie shook her head. "It seems hard to believe,

doesn't it? I mean, he doesn't seem the type. At all."
And why hadn't anyone told Paul about the charges?

"What, just because he hasn't come on to you?"

Jaimie gave her friend a look. "No. He doesn't seem the type to dredge up enough emotion to harass someone. Sexually or otherwise." She looked over to Harry's office where he was still in a meeting. "The guy seemed like he was telling the truth?" she asked doubtfully.

Kath shrugged. "I don't know why he'd lie."

Kath had a point. Why would someone lie about something like that?

Harry's cell phone rang just as he was wrapping up his interview with the *Nortown Journal's* new cop reporter.

"I'll see you on Monday, Ryan. Come in a little early and I'll introduce you around."

After four rings, Harry answered his phone.

"Harry, it's Dan Partington. How the hell are you?"

"Shitty," Harry said to his old buddy.

"Yeah, I bet. Listen, I just got a call from one of your reporters. Kathleen somebody or other." Dan started laughing and Harry furrowed his brow. "Get this, she called to find out why you left the *Times.*"

"You're kidding."

"No." He could hardly talk for all his laughing.

"I don't want to know what you said, do I?" Harry asked dryly.

"Sexual harassment."

Harry let out a sharp bark of laughter. "You prick."

"No, according to the story, you're the prick."

"Very funny, Partington. They already hate my guts, now they're going to be afraid to be in my office alone. More than half the reporters are women." He looked up and saw Kath talking earnestly with Jaimie, and let out a curse. It bothered him that anyone would believe such a thing about him, particularly his thorny city editor.

"Come on, I couldn't resist." He paused before lowering his tone. "How have you been, Harry? Really."

"I think I told you."

"I'm so sorry, man. You know I'm in your court."

Harry swallowed. "I know. Thanks." *Don't ask, don't ask, don't . . .* "How's Anne?"

The hesitation was clear. "I don't know. The same. I don't see her much."

"No?"

"I think she might be dating someone."

An invisible hand must have punched Harry in the gut because he felt as if a strong and brutal fist had just plunged into his stomach. "It's someone I know, isn't it."

"It's not common knowledge."

Harry could picture his friend's indecision.

"Bob Porter."

"Jesus Christ, he's *married.*"

"He's supposed to be separated or something."

"He's fifty fucking years old. She's twenty-eight."

"I'm not one hundred percent sure," Dan said quickly. "Actually I am pretty sure. Sorry. Bob's had a thing for Anne for years. You know that."

Harry closed his eyes briefly. "Yeah. I know that. She didn't wait long, did she? I've only been gone eight weeks. Eight fucking weeks and she's screwing another guy." He'd been gone for two months, but he and Anne had parted ways intimately months ago. Even though he still loved her. Even though she'd claimed to still love him. What bullshit. "How's Amy and the kids," he said, changing the subject abruptly.

"They're great. Katie just started walking and Emma's

learning how to swim. Oh, and Amy's going for her masters this fall at Columbia." Dan stopped, as if realizing how much better his life was compared to his friend's.

"That's great."

"Hey, I'll talk to you soon. I just wanted to let you know your reporters were snooping around looking for some dirt on their new boss. You should have a little fun with them. Act like a letch for a day."

"Just a day?" Harry said, laughing. "Thanks for the heads up. Talk to you." He punched off the phone and looked out of his office, his eyes searching for Jaimie. He'd bet his salary that she put Kath up to it. The merest hint of a smile touched his lips. Maybe he should give Jaimie something to think about. It would serve her right.

Chapter 3

Nope. Just couldn't picture Harry propositioning a woman for power. It didn't make sense. A guy like Harry Crandall couldn't charm a squirt of mustard from a hot-dog vendor, never mind flirt with someone to the extent it could be interpreted as sexual harassment. She looked up from her desk to see his back to the newsroom as he typed on his computer, and shook her head. It couldn't be. Why would someone with Harry's looks have to harass someone into going out with him?

Not that she would. No siree. Uh-uh. But Harry, she suspected, would be able to ask any female in this newsroom for a date and they'd likely jump up and squeal, "Yippee." Some women actually liked cold, handsome men. Jaimie liked big ol' puppy dogs, the kind that looked at her and fell in love and got all hurt and teary-eyed when she dumped them because, God, she *hated* saps. Other than the used car salesman, they all fell too hard too fast and got real boring. But a guy like Harry, the strong, silent type, the type that could make your toes curl when he finally looked at you as if he saw you. Now that was a guy she should avoid. Right.

Ugh!

Clearly, Jaimie thought with disgust, it was time to break her four-year drought. Four years without sex had her thinking things she had no business thinking. Like Harry in the shower, steam clouding around him, around his hard . . . stomach, his firm butt.

He turns around, surprised to see her there watching him as he slowly soaps his beefy chest. Steam rises around him, obscuring any details of his lower half. She stands as the room fogs around her, staring, staring . . .

"Jaimie. Will you please come in here?"

His voice, sounding irritated and definitely real, shocked her out of her ridiculous movie fantasy. No more film noir festivals on Bravo, she thought. She gave herself a fierce mental slap before walking into his office.

She marched in, still a bit flushed from the shower scene, and sat down in front of his desk. He was looking at her weirdly. Maybe it was her imagination, but it sure as heck felt as though he'd given her the up-and-down scan she'd hated as a teenager.

Harry knew he was looking at her weirdly and it was all Dan Partington's fault. He'd inserted sex in his mind while he was looking at Jaimie and there it was, juxtaposed indelibly. Sex. Jaimie. Sex with Jaimie. Hmmm.

He looked down at a stack of resumes on the desk in front of him and tried to banish those thoughts from his head. Jaimie was not the kind of woman who ever made him think of the hot sweaties, so he knew he could place the blame fully on Dan's shoulders for doing this to him. Frumpy just didn't do it for him—until now.

"We have two new reporters starting Monday for the cop beat and the Colchester town beat. I'd like you to have a list of stories they can work on, features, follow-ups, et cetera for our editorial meeting. They're both young, recent grads, so they're going to need a bit of direction. But they're both good writers, got some great clips." Harry chanced a look at her, this woman he could suddenly picture in a Victoria's Secret pose lounging on his desk. What the hell. Except she looked like a pissed-off lingerie model wearing a baggy sweater.

"We usually don't hire reporters without daily experience," Jaimie said.

"They worked at a daily in college. Columbia."

He could almost hear the "ahhh" in her frigid expression. Harry wouldn't even bother telling her that just because the two graduated from his alma mater didn't weigh all that much. They both had strong clips and excellent recommendations.

"Okay. I'll have the lists," she said, and Harry would swear her lips didn't move over her clenched teeth. "Is that all?"

He thought about asking her out—as a condition of her probation—just to freak her out, but stopped himself. He'd let her wonder a bit longer about those harassment charges before he let her off the hook. "That's all."

Then she closed her eyes and grimaced. And, strangely, she smiled, though she looked anything but friendly. "Next Saturday we're playing softball against the *New London Day*. Do you think you'd like to play?"

The invitation was so obviously forced, Harry decided now *would* be a good time after all to make his nosy editor squirm a bit. It had been a while since he'd flirted overtly with any woman, but he figured he still remembered how. If he recalled, he'd been pretty damned good at it.

"Play?" he asked, moving around to the front of his desk and sitting atop it directly in front of her, his knees splayed so if she stood up she'd be standing right between his legs. He leaned forward, as if whatever she was about to say would be the most erotic, sexually charged words a woman ever uttered. She flushed, deep red, and he barely stopped himself from smiling smugly. "What, exactly, did you have in mind?"

At the moment, all Jaimie's mind could think about was sex. That was bad. Very bad. Because Harry was her boss and she liked the word "jerk" next to his name as in, "That jerk Harry." She did not like placing the word sex anywhere near Harry's name, as in, "I'd really like to have sex with Harry."

"Wh-what?"

He gave an innocent, almost aw-shucks-ma'am boyish shrug that was incredibly charming. "I just wanted to know what you'd like to play?"

She swallowed. "Softball."

"You like to play with balls, do you?"

Jaimie's mouth opened a bit, too shocked, too horrified, to speak. She looked up at him, into those cold, cold gray eyes, and saw a warmth there she'd never seen. To her panicked brain, she saw raw heat, and she stopped breathing. He got off the desk and braced his hands on each armrest. She could see each bristle of his beard poking through his skin, each of the varying shades of green and gray in his eyes, each long, straight lash, his lips, curving up in the smallest of smiles. Jaimie swallowed, knowing deep down inside he wasn't sexually harassing her, he was sexually entertaining her.

Very, very bad.

"What are you doing?" Jaimie choked out, trying to sound affronted.

"Why, Jaimie, I'm sexually harassing you," he said, so slowly her eyes drifted down again to his mouth, his smiling, smirking, you're-such-a-little-idiot mouth.

"Oh," she said, closing her eyes in mortification. "You found out."

In a heartbeat, he was back on his own side of the desk, looking ridiculously pleased. "Frankly, I'm surprised that a newswoman of your caliber accepted the word of a single source. And such an unreliable one."

"So it's not true." At his look of disbelief, she shook her head. "Of course it's not true. I didn't really believe it, you know."

He let out a disbelieving laugh. "You were scared to death. Admit it."

"Okay, I admit it, the thought of you coming on to me was terrifying," she said, glad to turn the tables on him a bit. "I should be mad, but I guess I deserved it. So, are you going to be on the softball team?"

He smiled and sat down, relaxed and very un-Harry-like. "I haven't played baseball in years, not since college."

"You played in college?"

"I actually played double A for a season before I ruined my back. Believe it or not, I started out as a sports writer for the *Hartford Courant.*"

Jaimie was delighted. A ringer! The friendly rivalry the *Nortown Journal* had with the *Day* almost always ended the same way: The *Day* would win with humiliating ease. Jaimie was the only woman on staff who had actually played organized softball. It was supposed to be a "friendly" game, so Jaimie couldn't exclude anyone, but she sometimes wished a few people—Kath, for instance—would opt out of the game. "But you can still play?"

"I can try," he said, suddenly sounding put out by the light conversation. It was as if an alarm had silently rung in his head telling him to stop acting like a normal person. His face, just moments before relaxed and warm, was now tight and about as welcoming as a pissed-off rattlesnake. Maybe that injury left him jaded and bitter, one of those glory-days guys who lived on the past and all those what-ifs.

"Okay. The game's next Saturday at Nelson's Field. I'll post directions on the bulletin board."

"Fine."

Jaimie stared at him a moment, wondering where the hell the nice guy she'd been talking with went. "Harry, I'm sorry about that call. It was out of line."

He nodded and Jaimie left his office feeling more confused about her new boss than ever. She'd seen a glimpse of a nice guy, a guy she could joke with, could maybe even like. Then, within the span of a few seconds, he turned back into Harry. Maybe he was the kind of person who didn't believe in getting too chummy with his underlings. She had been sitting at her desk working about twenty minutes when his nail-gun voice called her back.

"What is this?" He held that day's edition in his hand.

Her heart slammed down to her toes. *Oh, no, not another mistake.* Ever since she'd let that headline about the lost cock go through, Jaimie had been a fanatic about checking every headline. "Is something wrong?"

"You wrote this?"

He pointed to a feature story she'd written herself. "Yes." Oh, God, it stunk. It was rife with bad writing, clichés, overused imagery . . .

"When do you find time to write?" He didn't seem mad, just curious.

"Sometimes I'll work on a story on the weekend, something I want to do. Is there something wrong with it?" Her heart was slowly making its way back into its proper place. The story was about an old man who'd lived in a once-grand hotel that over the years had become nothing more than a flophouse. He and his brother, both in their seventies, died in a fire that turned out to be arson. They were found in their shabby little room on the eighteenth floor. Turns out the old men, both bachelors, had been millionaires and a genealogy firm had been trying for more than a year to find their heirs.

"This fire was a huge story a year ago, right?"

"One of the biggest we ever covered. The only thing bigger was Joshua Tate's murder."

"This," he said, jabbing a finger at the story, "should have been on page one. Don't lose your news sense just because you wrote it. Did Nate edit it?"

Jaimie took a deep breath. "Yes."

He was silent for a while as he stared down at the story, and Jaimie was struck, hard, by how handsome he was. Just out-and-out gorgeous, fantasy stuff, *Men's Health* cover boy stuff. "Next time, let me have a look at it, okay? He missed a couple of things. Minor things. But a story like this deserves better than it got."

"Thanks."

He looked up, his eyes just as cold and hard as ever, boring into her. "You want to know what I'm doing here, right? That's what that phone call was about."

She nodded, guilt flooding her again.

"Well I want to know what the hell you're doing here."

"I like it here," she said.

He narrowed his eyes. "I don't buy it. The *Nortown Journal* is a way station. You and I both know it."

"You sound like Paul. He told me earlier today that I should leave. But . . ."

"I know all about buts," Harry said, then surprised

them both by raising a salacious eyebrow at the double entendre.

Jaimie let out a small laugh. "I'm going to get back to work." She turned, and smiled. "Pig."

When he chuckled, she knew: beneath all that sober, hard-as-nails exterior was a real guy, a guy who could laugh at her even when she was being obnoxious. She wasn't holding her breath, but Harry just might turn out to be not such a bad boss after all.

Chapter 4

Ted Buckner didn't make enough money at the *Nortown Journal* as sports editor to afford a spread like the one he had, and he wasn't at all shy about telling Harry how he got it.

"Married into money," he'd said, a grin on his prizefighter face. Ted wasn't a good-looking guy, but Harry supposed he had his charm. He must have, because how the hell did a guy like Ted, a jock with a mug that would have looked better on a bulldog, end up with a wife like Sharon? She was classy and funny, thin and pretty, and obviously and mysteriously loved Ted to distraction. When Ted had introduced her to Harry a week ago at a casual dinner at their house, he'd said, "I really think she's got a screw loose." And Harry would have agreed if he hadn't seen how great the two of them were together. Ted was one of those guys that everyone liked instantly, a big balook with a heart the size of a watermelon hidden inside the body of a linebacker.

Ted and Sharon shared a four-bedroom contemporary in Nortown's only posh neighborhood, a house complete with indoor gym and heated outdoor swimming pool. Harry stood beneath a green market umbrella, holding an iced water, looking at a pool no one was swimming in.

"Why don't you take a dip?" Sharon asked.

"Not hot enough yet," Harry said, feeling uncomfortable when her eyes darted to the sweat pouring off him. The truth was he had a nasty scar on his back from his baseball years and he didn't feel like explaining it to the half dozen people who were sure to ask about it. At that moment Ted did a nice cannon ball off the diving board.

"He's such a boy," Sharon said, amused and slightly exasperated.

Ted heaved himself out of the pool, shook his head like a dog, and swiped a hand down his hairy body before walking over to the pair. Then he pulled Sharon to him and she pretended to get mad even though she was laughing.

"Look at me," she said, looking down at her now-wet T-shirt.

"I am," he said, and growled like a hungry bear.

She gave him a peck on his cheek, which, at two in the afternoon already sported a decent beard shadow. "I'm going to change. Be right back."

"She loves it when I torture her," Ted said. "You all set with that drink?"

Harry nodded, noting that Ted had invited his entire sports staff, mostly young single guys probably talking about the fact that the Red Sox were taking yet another tumble from first place—as usual. They all wore cargo shorts and all but one a baseball cap, and they each held a beer. Just then, as if pulled by the same string, all five sports writers turned toward the house. Harry followed their gaze, felt his jaw drop, his blood burn, his heart stop. She was the most beautiful woman—from the neck down—he'd ever seen in the flesh. Breasts. Oh, man, those were the most glorious breasts he'd ever laid eyes on. Her stomach was smooth and sexy and taut. Her hips wonderfully rounded, her legs long and firm.

She wore an anklet and a toe ring and Harry was making an ass of himself staring at her and he didn't care. He especially didn't care that he hadn't seen the woman's face yet because that didn't matter at the moment. Those breasts, however, high and luscious and, God, who the hell was she? His forced his reluctant eyes to her face, to the stupid straw hat she had on her head that hid her face. A body like that just had to have a beautiful face.

She turned, a graceful tilting of her head, and spotted the drooling throngs, put her hands on her hips and laughed. One of the punks must have said something because she struck a pose. She walked over, arms outstretched, and gave one of the baseball hat-wearing kids a hug, laughed again, and stood there, beautiful back to Harry, chatting away as if she weren't some goddess descended on man to make him very, very happy.

"Who's that woman?" Harry asked, trying to sound as if he were asking about a brand of beer and not a woman he'd already decided he just might ask out. Why not? One date with a gorgeous woman would go a long way toward making him feel a bit more human.

Ted grinned knowingly and shrugged his massive shoulders. "Must be one of Sharon's friends," he said, but he was smiling way too much and Harry suspected he knew her. Maybe she was in advertising? He mentally ticked off every woman at the *Nortown Journal* trying to come up with one who might look like that in a bathing suit, but came up blank.

Then she turned, looked up, saw Ted standing across the pool, waved and . . .

"Jesus," Harry whispered. "Jaimie." The owner of that body, that drop-dead gorgeous, I've-got-to-have-sex-with-you body, was Jaimie.

"Those big sweaters hide a lot, huh?" Ted said, taking a finger and forcing Harry's mouth shut.

"Wow," he said, before he could stop himself. He gave himself a mental shake and tore his eyes away from her, feeling weirdly betrayed and disturbingly angry. He was her boss, the same guy who'd *pretended* to be sexually attracted to her. "I didn't recognize her without a sweater," he managed to say through a throat gone dry. It was impossible the woman he was trying not to gawk at was his frumpy, slightly attractive city editor. Jaimie was drab, unspecial in nearly every way.

"Are you kidding me? She's a centerfold."

Sharon, wearing a fresh T-shirt, hurried over to them, looking extremely pissed. "Would you guys stop staring at poor Jaimie," she hissed.

Harry lifted an eyebrow. "Poor Jaimie?"

"Oh, so you think it's fun to get stared at by a bunch of drooling apes."

"I wasn't staring," Ted said. "Harry was."

"She doesn't seem to mind," Harry said defensively with a knowing look to the sports writers.

"This is a pool party. She's wearing a bathing suit. A *tank*ini, not a bikini. It's not like she's got a thong on or anything. Ugh!"

Great, now all Harry could think of was how nice Jaimie's ass would look in a thong. It was there, stamped indelibly, and he knew that errant thought would attack him at unexpected moments for a very long time: Jaimie in a thong. He should not have come to this cookout, he thought viciously, or at least asked whether Jaimie was planning to attend. Hell, he hadn't known what she looked like beneath that ugly sweater of hers. It wasn't his fault she had the kind of body that made men do stupid things—like stare and drool.

"She's coming over here, do you think you two can behave?"

"You know I can," Ted said, and Sharon gave him a playful elbow jab. Harry heard him whisper, "Why don't you go put on your thong?" He got another jab.

Sharon was right, Jaimie was on her way over, walking with the confidence of a woman who knows she's beautiful and doesn't care if people notice or not. *Look at her face, look at her face, look at her face.*

God, she had beautiful breasts.

"Hi guys," she said, sounding chipper and completely unaware Harry was beginning to feel things he didn't want to feel. Anger was the safest of those emotions so he decided to tap into that one. He felt as if he'd had a rotten trick played on him.

"If I had known you were such a babe, I would have given you that raise you asked for," Harry said, knowing he was antagonizing her and not caring.

"What was that?" Sharon asked, a look of disbelief on her face.

Harry shrugged. "I'm sexually harassing my employee. It's what I do."

Jaimie clenched her jaw and said, "Very funny, Harry."

Ted starting laughing, even though he looked as confused as Sharon. "What the hell are you two talking about?"

"Nothing."

Harry smiled and Jaimie wanted to stamp on his foot. "McLane had Kath Kopf call the *Times* to find out why I'd left. My buddy answered and he thought it'd be a great joke to tell her I'd been fired for sexual harassment."

Ted laughed so hard, tears appeared at the corners of his eyes, and Sharon gave him an elbow, but she was laughing too. Jaimie was not quite as amused.

"So," Ted said, wiping his eyes, "she told you about the pool."

Panic, hard and fast, ripped through Jaimie's body. "Of course he knows about the pool," she said quickly. "He's standing in front of it." *Nice try, dumb head.*

"What pool?" Harry asked Ted, apparently knowing Jaimie wasn't about to come clean.

Ted starting laughing again. "She didn't tell you?"

"Ted." A warning shot over his head that wasn't about to stop his assault, so Jaimie decided she'd come clean and tell Harry the truth.

"We had a pool . . ."

"We?" Ted interrupted.

"Okay, *I* had a pool where everyone put in five bucks with a reason you'd left the *Times.*"

"You bet on me?" Uh-oh. He sounded—and looked—mad.

Jaimie took a small sip of her Heineken and looked back at the empty pool. "You guys going for a swim anytime soon?" she asked in an obvious attempt to change the subject.

"I am," Sharon said quickly, pulling off her dry T-shirt. "It's so hot. Coming in, Ted?" She grabbed his arms and hauled him toward the pool. Ted, with the guilelessness of a ten-year-old, dove into the pool. "How about you, Harry. Hot enough yet?"

"Not yet." With that, Sharon did a cannon ball into the water, letting out a whoop, and landing about a foot from her husband. Harry smiled, but Jaimie could tell he was still fuming about the Harry Pool.

"Listen, it was harmless fun. And I gave everyone their money back."

"When?"

Jaimie chewed her lip. She did not want to remind

Harry of that phone call to the *Times* again, but it seemed she had no choice. "After you caught us calling the *Times*," she said in a low voice. "I know the whole thing seems shitty."

"As a matter of fact, it does."

"You weren't everyone's favorite person, you know, Harry. You'd fired three people and everyone was afraid for their job." She could hear Kath's voice in her head. *We think you should make friends.* At this rate, the entire newsroom would get fired. "But I know that's no excuse. It was insensitive." Jaimie knew she didn't sound all that sincere, but she was doing her best.

His response was a grunty sound.

Silence stretched between them. *Make friends. Make friends.* "I didn't know you did the social thing with your employees," Jaimie said, trying to sound chipper. Friendly.

"I don't. Usually. Ted assured me it would only be the sports guys." Harry knew he sounded irritable and didn't care. Hell, he was irritable. Not only was Jaimie standing in front of him looking like a man's fantasy, but he felt inordinately bothered that she'd been the one to organize the Harry Pool. And what if she had talked to the wrong person at the *Times*. He told himself he didn't care what anyone thought, but for some reason he did care what Jaimie thought.

"Sorry." She flipped her red-gold hair over her shoulder and twisted a bit to watch Ted and Sharon fooling around in the pool. He couldn't help it; he drank her in with eyes that still didn't believe what they were seeing. How could a woman be lush and taut, sexy but with girl-next-door appeal all at once?

"I didn't mean that I wouldn't have come if I'd known you'd be here," he said. He could hardly swallow, never mind carry on a normal conversation with her standing there in a tank-whatever glued to her perfect body. It didn't matter that the other women standing around the pool were also wearing bathing suits.

She looked up at him, her eyes sparkling as if she knew what was bothering him. "Then how did you mean it?"

He grinned. "I guess I did mean it like that. As publisher slash managing editor I don't really think it's a good idea to get too chummy with anyone on the editorial staff."

"Except the sports guys."

"You know it's different. Sports is a different animal, and frankly, Ted's doing an incredible job with the staffing he has." Her eyes flashed. *Uh-oh. Wrong thing to say.*

"Say again?" Two words could not have come out more cold.

"I didn't mean to imply you are not doing a good job. And you know it." He let out an impatient breath. He shook his near-empty ice water. "I need a refill," he said and started to leave.

"Harry."

He turned and saw she was smiling, and in that moment, with the afternoon sun shining brilliantly down on her reddish-gold hair, she looked amazing. He half expected an orchestra to begin playing in tribute to her beauty.

"I'm a little sensitive to your criticism. Maybe you've noticed that."

"I've noticed." And damn if his eyes swung down to her breasts. It was as if they had a mind of their own—a dirty mind. When he finally dragged his eyes back to hers, she looked slightly pissed but mostly amused. He felt his cheeks flush, something that hadn't happened to him in front of a woman since college.

"Harry, Harry, Harry," she said sadly, shaking her head.

He gave her a good-natured shrug. "Just don't walk around the newsroom like that and all will be well."

"This is an extremely conservative swimsuit."

Harry looked across the pool to see the young sportswriters still ogling her. "Still, maybe you should put on one of your sweaters," he suggested with a pointed look to the drooling masses.

"What makes you think that bothers me? Or does it bother you, Harry?"

"It bothers me as a liberal-minded male who believes women should not be treated as objects."

Jaimie let out a snort.

"You don't believe me?" he asked, pretending offense.

"I have two older brothers. I know how men's minds think. And I also know that once they stop thinking about body parts for a millisecond, most guys are pretty nice and actually can carry on a conversation with a woman in a bathing suit without staring at her breasts every two seconds."

He felt the horrible urge to glance again, just quickly, at those aforementioned breasts.

"Congratulations, Harry, you almost made it to four seconds." She laughed and walked off, leaving Harry feeling as if he'd been completely out-maneuvered and out-classed.

"Hey."

She turned around looking sexier than a city editor had a right to, raising one eyebrow in question.

"What the hell have you done with Jaimie?" He made a valiant effort not to sound as sulky as he felt. "Clearly, you're her evil twin."

Her smile broadened and something very strange

happened to his gut. God, could that woman smile. "That's Work Jaimie. I'm Weekend Jaimie." She turned and walked around the pool back toward the house, waving behind her shoulder as she did.

He watched her walk away, completely unapologetically taking in her very nice behind. He watched her, because he had the distinct feeling she knew he was watching her. He jiggled his glass and drained the last bit of water from it. Jaimie kept surprising him. Just when he thought he'd had her pigeonholed into that area of frustrated and shy women who had only their careers and their cats, she turned out to be something completely different. Weekend Jaimie. The only thing was, he was pretty certain he liked Work Jaimie better. He knew what to expect from her at work.

He didn't know who the hell that woman was he was just talking to.

Jaimie tugged on her tankini and frowned at her reflection in the Buckners' huge guest bathroom. "You," she said, staring into her blue-green eyes, "are an idiot."

It had been a long time since she'd flirted with a man—and, of course, she had to pick her new boss. Great job. She wasn't certain what had come over her. Okay, she did know. In the newsroom, Harry hadn't looked at her with more interest than a man looking at a new Bic pen. Well, she'd seen an entirely different look out there by the pool, and it was heady, powerful stuff. But it was still stupid. She should not be honing her flirting skills with Harry. He was off-limits, which was really too bad because he was sneaking into her thoughts way too much.

She hadn't really decided whether she even liked him

and she'd begun wondering what it would be like to kiss him. Just kiss. She had not allowed her mind to move beyond that, because it was so impossible, so very ill considered, Jaimie refused to think about him naked and sweating and shaking over her, his mouth tugging on her nipple as she reached down and gasped in surprise at how large his . . .

"You pig!" she said, purely disgusted with herself and that glazed look in her eye. She took a deep, cleansing breath and shook her head, rattling those inappropriate images of Harry out of her addled brain.

She studied her body, and smiled. Those big, baggy sweaters and pants had no other purpose than to make her comfortable and warm, because she was one of those unfortunate and admittedly annoying women who were always cold. She'd been blessed with a hootchy-kootchy body and that was the reason she'd selected a semi-modest tankini and not a bikini—she was proud of her body but she didn't like flaunting it.

It started in high school when a teacher old enough to be her grandfather came on to her. He'd been one of her favorite teachers, probably because he was always so nice to her. She'd been too naïve to understand the sub-tleties of flirting, but one day he'd actually asked her on a "date" to his house. "No one will be home," and he'd stared directly at her breasts to make certain she got the message. Jaimie had been crushed and mortified. When she complained to her usually conservative mother, she didn't get entirely the response she was looking for.

"Jaimie," she said, "you've been blessed and cursed with a beautiful body. It's up to you how you see it. Either cover up or show it off, but other than that, there's nothing you can do."

So, she turned a bit schizophrenic—covering it up, showing it off, depending on the situation.

She'd hated her body as a teenager. Over the years, though, Jaimie had developed a healthy appreciation of her own assets. She worked out four times a week and, unknown to most people, had honed a body that would make most men weep. Not that any man had seen her body up close in a pathetic amount of time.

"What good is that body if you're always hiding it? When was the last time you had a good fuck?" Kath's words of wisdom just last week when she showed her the new bathing suit. Kath was so *precious*. She resolved to only talk to her mother about dating and men from now on. Her mother still thought she was a virgin and was waiting for Mr. Right.

She splashed cold water on her face and left the bathroom, telling herself she should stay an hour and make an excuse to Ted and Sharon and leave. She might be attracted to Harry Crandall physically, but the guy intimidated her and Jaimie didn't like that. She just didn't get the warm and fuzzies from him. She didn't get anything but . . . bothered. He was too good-looking, too smart, and too much of a mystery. And now there was this sexual thing that she was probably imagining but was there nonetheless. She had to stop it in its tracks, that's what she had to do. Because how could she work with a man she was attracted to? What if it developed into a crush, or worse? She'd seen too many newsroom romances bloom, then wilt and die an ugly death. It always ended with one of them leaving the paper.

Now, that's a sure way of forcing myself to make a move, she mused as she walked toward the kitchen. She could hear Sharon's laugh, a snorting contagious explosion of sound, coming from that direction.

Before she made it down the hall, Harry was there, looking like he'd just eaten something bitter, looking at her.

"I'm going now. I'll see you Monday." Hard Harry was back, icicles dripping from his words.

"Oh. Okay. Bye. I'm leaving soon too."

"Why?" he asked, though truthfully, he didn't seem to care.

"I thought I'd start working on a story, a follow-up to the Tate murder. We haven't done a follow-up in months."

"Assign it to Ryan. He's starting Monday and it will be a good way to get him familiar with the story."

Jaimie fought from showing the surge of anger his brusque suggestion produced. "I want to do this one. I've got some good ideas and plenty for him to do."

"Fine. But I want to see it before Nate does." And then he left, walking out the front door as if he couldn't get out of the house fast enough.

"What was that all about? Harry looked mad about something," Sharon said, handing Jaimie another beer.

"No thanks. I'm going, too, in a couple," she said, pulling her shirt and shorts out of her bag.

Sharon shrugged and took a sip from it herself. "So, what's he all mad about?"

"From what I've seen of Harry, he's got two emotions: pissed and way pissed." She bit the side of her mouth. "Okay. I did actually see him smile once or twice."

"Come on, Harry's not that bad. I think he's shy."

Jaimie thought of the way he'd leaned over her, about the dirty things he'd said in that sexy down-low voice that only a man who was not shy would have discovered. "No. Shy he is not. I'm beginning to think I bring out his bad side. I think there's something about me that bugs him."

Sharon's eyes widened. "He's attracted to you and fighting it. And now that he's seen you in a bathing suit, he's a goner."

"Oh, yes, I forgot. My lethal body," she said, mimicking a bad actress. "Oh, what am I going to do when I get back in the office and Harry begins drooling on me?" She tugged on her shorts.

"Harry likes you," she sang.

Jaimie narrowed her eyes. "Now I know why you and Ted make such a great couple. You're both children."

Sharon grinned. "And you like Harry." More singing.

"As much as an internal exam," she said, deadpan. "Listen. I do have to go. Thanks for the beer."

"Jaimie, you have to stay. Ted's entire sports staff will riot if you leave."

Jaimie waved a hand at her as she grabbed her purse from their gray granite countertop. "They'll find another, younger woman to harass as soon as I'm gone."

Sharon followed her to the door. "I know why you're really leaving. Harry's not here and all the excitement is gone."

"Honestly, Sharon. If I knew Harry was going to be here at all, I probably wouldn't have come."

"Liar. You would have worn your yellow bikini." She pushed her out the door with that parting shot.

"No, my electric pink thong." Jaimie laughed and waved again as she got into her car, watching as Sharon closed the door. She didn't have an electric pink thong, but for the first time in her life she wondered if she had the courage to wear one.

Chapter 5

Cedar Heights wasn't much more than a massive grid of quarter acre lots connected by roads paved twenty years ago and neglected ever since. It was the type of neighborhood with toys in the front yard and broken-down junk cars in the back. The houses came in three styles—capes, ranches, and colonials. Joshua Tate had lived in a ranch with his mother and new puppy, and he died with his puppy near a stream behind a colonial.

His murder—and that of his puppy—had shocked Nortown, for though the depressed city saw its share of crime, no one had been murdered in the city in ten years. A kid murder was even more shocking. He was a cute kid, too. The *Nortown Journal,* as well as every other paper and network in the country, had published his fourth grade picture. He had blond hair, cut short and spiked up in front, bright blue eyes, and a smile that made your heart ache to think he was dead.

But even a cute kid was no match for a dead puppy. That aspect of the case had people scratching their heads. *Yeah, kill the kid, but why'd ya have to go and kill the poor little puppy.* A puppy murder brought out all the animal activists, generating even more stories. A reward had been set up, $50,000 for information leading to the conviction of Joshua's murder, and animal lovers everywhere amassed a $150,000 reward for information leading to the same for the puppy killer. Go figure.

Joshua's murder had been a huge story, and initially Jaimie had assigned three reporters to cover it, mostly because a story of that magnitude required big coverage, and partly because the lead reporter, Maxine, was incompetent. Jaimie had helped the now-fired Maxine, walking her through the story step by step, until they'd done a decent job covering it. The *Journal* had done a story about the initial murder, talked to the neighbors, the schoolteacher, the priest. They'd gotten the facts from the cops. Then they'd done a couple of follow-ups about how the murder of a child affects other kids, and of course, the follow-ups about how the police had no suspects and few leads. Maxine had folded under the stress of the stories a few times. She couldn't bring herself to interview the mother, sobbing in the newsroom bathroom for twenty minutes before Jaimie agreed to do it. Jaimie should have fired Maxine then and there, but hadn't. She'd felt sorry for her—and understood that Maxine had no business being the cop reporter. Instead of firing her, she'd given her another beat.

Joshua's murder, for a while, had put the spotlight on Nortown and the *Nortown Journal*. They'd gotten details about the murder that the *New London Day* hadn't, mostly thanks to Jaimie's sources. But no one had been caught, and no one ever could figure out why someone would murder a kid and his dog. Joshua had not been sexually abused. He'd been found fully clothed, a large stick in his hand. The police hypothesized he'd used it to try to defend himself. At least that's what they'd said officially. It wasn't until four months later over a beer with the case's lead detective that Jaimie had heard anything different.

Jerry Brandt had been one grade ahead of Jaimie at Nortown High. They went to Junior Prom together and remained friends. Jaimie had even been in Jerry's wedding party because he'd married one of her old high school friends. After his shift ended at eleven, he'd go to Duffy's once in a while for a couple before heading home. Jaimie would see him the nights they'd put the paper to bed early. It was during one of those meetings he'd offered up a theory that he hadn't even told his lieutenant.

"I think the kid killed his own dog," he'd said softly, leaning his elbows heavily on the bar.

"Why?"

"Because he had a screw loose. The kid used to get in trouble all the time. He was seeing some sort of psychiatrist twice a week. Hell, he was ten years old and his mother was scared to death of him."

"Did she say?"

"No," he admitted. "But we got called to their house one night. I wasn't there, but I talked to one of the guys who was there, and man this kid was warped. He told his mother he was going to wait until she was asleep then cut her throat."

"But he looked like an angel. And everyone we talked to acted like the kid was perfect. Happy, friendly."

Jerry shook his head and laughed. "C'mon, Jaimie. You know people never say anything bad about dead people. Especially dead kids."

"So, he bashed his puppy. He didn't bash himself."

"No. He sure as fuck didn't." Jerry took a last swallow of beer, looking tired and worn out. "I feel like a shit just saying it out loud. This case has sucked from day one. He was just a kid. Kids don't kill their own puppies." He scrubbed his face with his hands. "Forget I said anything. Okay?" And he'd looked at her, long and hard, as if just realizing he'd been talking to a news-paper editor.

"Jerry, you don't have to worry. Okay? I'd get strung up by half of Nortown if I even hinted that Joshua was anything other than a victim. I'm sure you're wrong about this."

"I wish I was as sure as you are."

Jaimie, of course, hadn't done anything with the in-formation, and chalked it up to two beers and a tired cop. But she hadn't forgotten it, either. It stayed in her head, nagging at her. Even now as she pulled into Joshua's driveway, she could hear Jerry's voice in her head. *I think the kid killed his own dog.*

Jaimie didn't know much about Liz Tate, Joshua's mom. She had interviewed her at the time of the mur-der, but it had been a brief and emotionally draining interview. The woman had been a wreck, with eyes so old they'd have fit better in the eyes of an eighty-year-old woman—and one who'd had a hard life. She looked ten years older than her forty-one, with limp gray hair to go with her overall limp and sagging appearance. It was as if life had dragged her down so hard, her body showed the wear. What else would you expect, Jaimie had thought after leaving the poor woman, she'd just lost her baby in the most brutal way.

Liz Tate was a single mom, now just single, living in a ranch that needed a paint job. The yard was a brown, brit-tle mess of sun-baked grass and weeds. It looked like the sort of house where you'd find a mother of a dead son.

She saw a curtain move in the front window, then sec-onds later, the front door opened, revealing Mrs. Tate, a woman who Jaimie hardly recognized from their last meeting. The woman standing at the door looked like someone who could be Liz's younger, better-looking sister. Liz smiled and stood back, letting Jaimie in.

"Thank you so much for talking with me," Jaimie said, pulling out her small tape recorder and note pad, and pulling on her ever-present sweater. She rarely listened to the tapes she made, using them only if she knew she'd missed a quote. She'd also pulled out her recorder when angry sources claimed they'd been misquoted.

"Oh, is it too cold?"

"No. My internal thermostat is broken," Jaimie said, smiling an apology. "As I told you on the phone, we're doing a follow-up story to Joshua's murder. Many times stories such as these put a case back in the spotlight and hopefully the police respond."

Liz smiled. She'd dyed her hair, Jaimie noticed. And she was wearing make-up. And nice clothes that fit her filled-out body quite nicely. Jaimie looked at the older woman's hands, folded serenely in her lap, remembering clearly that they'd been bitten and torn during the last interview. She remembered because she'd noted that detail in her story. Now, her nails were clearly professionally manicured, perfectly oval without a chip or cuticle in sight.

"I have to tell you that you look much better than the last time we met."

"That was a horrible time for me," Liz said, and Jaimie felt like an insensitive jerk for saying such a thing even if Liz had perked up at the compliment.

They talked about the past several months, about the investigation, about any suspect she might have in mind. Was she frustrated about the lack of progress? Had she joined any victim activists groups? Was she afraid the killer would strike again?

Liz Tate answered calmly, never once losing control

of the emotions that had been so fragile during Jaimie's last visit. Jaimie looked around the living room, curious. The room was small, the carpet spotless, the furniture neat and covered with pillows. On the mantel were a vase and a few knickknacks, including a small statue of a mother holding a child. The walls held nondescript landscapes, nicely framed, like the ones you'd find in a good hotel.

"I was wondering if I could see Joshua's room, just to get a better sense of what he was like."

For the first time, Liz became slightly flustered. "His room?"

"I'm sorry, is that too personal?"

"Oh. No." Her face flushed. "I'm afraid I redid his bedroom into a sewing room. It's been almost eight months."

Jaimie felt like an idiot. Of course she wouldn't keep his room exactly the same. "I'm sorry. It has been quite a while." Jaimie looked down self-consciously at her notepad. "I was wondering if you had any other pictures of Joshua. We keep running the same one over and over and so does every other newspaper. I was wondering if you had something else, maybe something you took."

"Hmmm. Now where did I put those?" She drummed her manicured fingers against her lips. "There's a box in the attic full of stuff. Why don't we look?"

Jaimie smiled her encouragement, but was thinking, *You don't know where pictures of your dead son might be?* She followed her into a hall and watched as Liz pulled down the attic door, then yanked on the ladder. "I haven't been up here in months." She must have realized how that sounded, and added, "I was just tortured every time I walked by his room. I couldn't stand to see all his things. You know, and have him be gone."

"You must miss Joshua," Jaimie said, and Liz turned and gave her the oddest look.

"Of course I do." She chuckled. "He was a handful."

Here was the opening. Jaimie closed her eyes briefly and decided to gently approach the subject of Joshua's behavior. "I understand he was seeing a psychiatrist." Jaimie expected one of two reactions: anger and insult, or embarrassment and admission.

"No. He wasn't. Where did you hear that?"

Shit. "We get calls all the time."

"He was seeing a *therapist.* Just little boy problems. Mostly because of the divorce," she said, walking up the ladder. Jaimie felt an almost sickening wave of heat when she followed her up. She took off her sweater and draped it over her arm.

"How old was he when you and your husband separated?"

"Five."

"Where is your ex-husband now?"

Liz stood in the tiny attic, her head hunched over to avoid hitting the nails sticking through the rafters. "Is that important?"

Maybe. "Not really."

"He's in prison." Liz let out a sigh and sat down on a box that sagged slightly beneath her weight. "He was a monster. He was a monster to Joshua. And I think that's why . . ."

Jaimie held her breath.

"I think that's why he was so sad all the time. He was such a sad little boy. And I was so wrapped up in my own pain, I didn't notice what was happening."

"It was an abusive relationship?"

Liz looked up at her. "You're not going to print this, are you? About his father?"

God, she hated this stuff, when a person finally opened up and forgot you were a reporter, and then remembered and looked at you as if you'd tricked them into saying something. "It would make Joshua an even more sympathetic person. It would make people care even more," Jaimie said, trying to be nice when she knew, technically, she could print anything that had been said. But Jaimie knew most people were not savvy about the press, unsure what to say and what would end up in print.

"I don't know." She shook her head. "I suppose it's all right. It's not really that big a secret, anyway. It was in all the papers back then."

"Where was that?" Jaimie was positive she would have remembered a local man getting prison time for domestic violence involving a child.

"We were in Indiana at the time. I hated it there, all those endless fields. You could drive for miles and see nothing except cornfields. I'm from Groton."

"Not too many cornfields there," Jaimie said, chuckling.

After that, Liz immediately found some pictures, and Jaimie picked out one of him sitting at a picnic table with a mound of ice cream in front of him.

"That was his ninth birthday," Liz said, staring at the picture. She blinked, then handed it over.

"He was such a cute kid," Jaimie said, and she was almost sure Liz, standing in the middle of the sweltering attic, shivered.

Two miles away, Harry was in his apartment and staring at his message machine, a cold sweat breaking out.

"Hey, Harry. Just calling to say, um, hey. Oh, it's me, Anne. Ha ha. Call me sometime. Bye."

He took a deep breath, hating his physical reaction just to hearing her voice again. Why the hell had she called? Just to say hey? That wasn't like Anne at all. Anne cut things clean, she always had, to the point Harry used to call her heartless. That was not an insult to her; she'd always smile and purr, "That's why I'm the best journalist in this city."

She might be the best, Harry acknowledged, but he'd bet she wasn't all that heartless. She was just good at freezing off her heart when it came to him. To be honest, he'd gotten pretty good at that trick himself. Maybe he'd gotten too good at shutting down his heart. The only one he let inside was Anne, and now she was gone. It hurt like hell, even after all these weeks. One more betrayal, one more stab in his back.

Harry stared at the little "one" on his message machine, no longer blinking, but letting him know that if he wanted to, he could listen to the message again. He stared at that number for a good long time before finally giving into it and listening again. *Hey, Harry.*

That's what she'd say after making love, after he'd made her come, after she was lying on top of him, a grin on her beautiful lips. "Hey, Harry." As if she hadn't known it was him. It always made him smile, and he'd say, "Hey." And he'd kiss her and she'd get up and wash up and by the time she'd come back, he'd be asleep. Anne had not been a cuddler, and Harry, surprisingly he'd discovered, was. He liked to pull her close, to feel her warm body curled against his. But Anne would roll away after a few minutes, kissing him, and tell him she was suffocating. Harry should have known then and there they were doomed. The entire relationship was suffocating to Anne. Every time he'd bring up marriage—okay, the two times he'd brought up marriage, she'd just laughed. "What do we want to get married for? We're fine."

Harry had agreed, but thought maybe it was time for kids, a house instead of a tiny Manhattan apartment, and a wife. Anne could not visualize herself as anyone's wife and every time she saw a baby thanked God for modern medicine and birth control. Harry thought she'd get over all that; most women did. But in that last year before things started falling apart, he'd started to realize that Anne meant it: She didn't want kids. And that was fine, except, Harry did.

Just as well they hadn't gotten married; they'd probably be divorced already.

He gave that "one" another hard look before pressing the delete button.

Message deleted.

Chapter 6

Harry was discovering that the *Nortown Journal* was in deep financial shit, when Jaimie knocked on his door wearing yet another big sweater, this one yellow. Good. He didn't need the distraction of her body right now. He had to focus on how the heck Paul managed to keep this paper afloat all these years because these numbers just weren't adding up. Either the paper had to generate more revenue, or he was going to have to lay someone off.

"Do you have a second?" Jaimie said when he hadn't acknowledged her. She looked frumpy again, but for some reason he couldn't help but think she looked sexy in overlarge sweaters. Damn. He didn't like redheads with straight hair. He didn't like freckles on pale skin, blooming all over her body. Maybe in unexpected places . . .

"Yeah. Come in," he said, keeping his eyes glued to the spreadsheet in front of him. No way he was going to let her guess what was going on inside his head.

"You know I'm working on that story about Joshua Tate." Jaimie got a blank look, and she wondered if he'd even been listening to her when she'd told him about the story on Saturday. "The little kid who was killed."

"Yeah, sure. Go on."

"His father is in prison for beating the wife and kid. Some real nasty stuff. It's interesting, but I'm not sure what to do with it." She handed him a fax. "Indiana State Police sent this to me this morning."

Harry focused on the document in front of him, scanning it quickly. "Jesus, this guy was one sick bastard."

"So, I don't know what to do with it," she said again.

"Yes, you do."

Jaimie took a deep breath, and said slowly, "No, that's why I came in here, to get your opinion."

"Run with it," he said, then turned back to whatever he'd been staring at when she'd walked in.

"I don't think so," she said slowly, vaguely surprised by his quick decision. She'd expected at least some sort of discussion. "It's not really pertinent to the story right now. It's old news. It doesn't have an angle. We'd be printing it for sensation only. It doesn't have any real newsworthiness. At least not now."

"It's part of the story. Poor murdered kid, turns out his life sucked right from the beginning. Write it, then give it to me. We'll put it on the front page."

Jaimie couldn't believe what she was hearing. "I disagree."

And then he gave her a look of exasperation and impatience, holding his hands palm up in an insulting display of supplication—as if he were asking God to save him from her presence. "Okay. Don't go with it. It's little more than gossip and bad journalism."

He was clearly placating her, and that made her even more confused. "Yeah, but it *is* interesting. It's a great story and you may have a point about it . . ."

"You're kidding me, right?" he asked.

"What?"

"You're arguing both sides."

"So are you."

He almost smiled and Jaimie's heart sort of slowed,

pumping out molasses instead of blood. "There's a difference between what you are doing and what I am doing. See, I don't really care one way or the other. I'm putting you through an exercise to prove that you do know what to do. But you know what I found out?"

"What?" Jaimie said, glaring at him.

"You really don't know what to do with this information. Come on, Jaimie. You *know.* Tell me."

"My gut tells me to hold off," she said slowly.

"Why?"

"Because I think there's something bigger here. Something else that no one knows about."

Harry leaned back in his chair and folded his arms over his chest and Jaimie tried really hard not to look at those biceps of his. "Bingo."

"But if the *New London Day* gets this, they'll go with it and we'll get beat," she said, tapping her pen against her lips.

"That's true." He stared at the pen in irritation so she stopped her tapping.

"And I hate getting beat by the *Day* on something I have. It really sucks."

He leaned back in his chair and gave her a level look. "So what are you going to do?"

Jaimie closed her eyes briefly, then said reluctantly, "I'm holding it. For now." She scrunched up her face. "Right? Hold it?"

"How did you get through the past twelve years?"

She grinned. "I'm only decisive about other people's stories. For some reason when it comes to my stuff, I'm clueless."

"Do you think there is something more to the story?"

She nodded. "Yeah, I do."

"Then hold it. But if the *Day* gets it first, you're fired," he said.

"You're kidding."

"You tell me."

Jaimie narrowed her eyes, scanning his face, his stern, I'm-giving-it-straight expression, his set jaw, his . . . twinkling gray eyes. Twinkling gray eyes? On Harry?

"Yes, you're kidding," she said definitively. "And by the way, Harry."

He lifted his chin in question.

"I just figured you out."

Great, Harry thought, now if only she'd let him in on the secret. The phone rang just as Jaimie was leaving and he jabbed the speaker button. "Harry Crandall."

"Hey, Harry."

He felt the blood rush to his head and he grabbed the phone before Anne could say another word, his eyes on Jaimie to determine if she'd heard the intimacy of that *Hey, Harry.*

"How are you?" he said, sounding not happy to hear her, lying to himself.

"Great. You didn't return my call." Anne sounded funny, softer somehow, when he knew Anne was the toughest woman he'd ever met. Even when she'd finally given in and told him she loved him, it had been a grudgingly given confession, as if making such a statement weakened her position in their relationship.

"I didn't see the point."

"I thought we were still friends."

"This is how I talk to my friends. Get laid lately?"

She sighed. "You're mad at me."

"No."

"I don't blame you."

Who the hell was this woman, all soft and breathy and acting as if she were a girly-girl and not the hard-as-nails reporter he knew her to be? It was why they'd done so well together, two tough, in-your-face journalists competing in and out of bed to see who was the best. Except Harry found out that as soon as he got knocked down a bit, as soon as he showed he was just a bit more human than they'd both thought, she'd left him.

"Anne, why are you calling?" He could picture her face, black and white, her pale skin against her shockingly black hair and dark brown eyes. She kept her hair short and precise, as precise and sharp as the rest of her. Anne didn't have a soft part on her entire body. Even her small breasts were firm. She wore brown, gray, and black. That was Anne and he'd loved her because of that. She never would have come to him like Jaimie had, asking his opinion, flip-flopping, unsure of herself, questioning her motives.

"I don't know." *She didn't know?* Then: "I miss you." It was a rush of words, staccato and clipped.

"What's wrong?"

There was a long pause. "Nothing. I just wanted to hear your voice. Bye." And she hung up before he could say something really stupid like, "I miss you too."

Harry placed the receiver down slowly and stared at the phone a long time. What the hell was that all about? He hadn't heard from her in weeks, and now she calls to tell him she misses him? Maybe she did. But he couldn't imagine the Anne he knew making that phone call, saying those words. *I miss you.* For some reason, he looked out into the newsroom and watched Jaimie work. Jaimie, bright, soft, sexy, smart. Other than the smarts, Jaimie didn't have a thing in common with Anne. And yet, here he was, looking at her when he shouldn't, looking at her when Anne's "I miss you" was still ringing in his ears.

Paul Mayer had the grace to look embarrassed when Harry brought up the matter of the newspaper's finances. "I've been subsidizing the paper for three years, but that's got to stop." He leaned forward, his voice low, so no one else in Duffy's would overhear him. Harry looked around the bar, wondering just who Paul was trying to keep things from because the place was damn near empty at four p.m.

"Why?"

The older man gave him a look of surprise. "Well, I'd like to go to law school, and that costs money."

Harry narrowed his eyes, refusing to believe Paul's good ol' boy manner was genuine. "No," he said with forced patience. "Why does the paper need subsidizing?"

"Oh, gotcha," and he flashed a smile that reminded him of Jack Lemmon in *Glengarry Glenn Ross,* a sort of hunted look masked by a nervous grin. "Well, circulation's down. Ad revenue, too. The *Day's* been kicking our butt and next year it plans to open up a bureau in our back yard and, well, it's killing us." Paul waved a hand at him to stave off his next question. "This paper needs you and . . ."

"And you didn't think I'd take the position if I knew the *Journal* was in trouble."

"There's that. Plus my brother was getting impatient about the lack of revenue."

"You have a brother?"

"Down in Florida. Martin's been living on my hard work for about ten years now. It's a family-run paper. You knew that. I've been putting him off for a while

now, and hiring you placated him. He gets the *Times*."
Paul said the last as if he thought Martin was a bit full
of himself.

Harry nodded, trying not to lose his temper. "I didn't
know there was more family than you. You have a sister
I don't know about?"

Paul chuckled and shook his head, still trying
valiantly to keep the conversation light. "The thing is,
Harry, he owns fifty-one percent of the paper. My father
thought that it was only fair because he was the older
brother. Fair," he spat. "He hasn't set a foot inside the
building since he was thirty-five, but he's real good at
going over the financial report. That's why I've been
covering the paper's losses."

"Jesus, Paul, you've been falsifying income reports?"

"Only to Marty. The IRS gets the real deal, don't
worry about that. The thing is, I don't have any more
money to cover the losses. And when that happens,
Marty's going to want to sell."

Harry closed his eyes as the full impact of what Paul
was saying hit him. "He's got a buyer already, doesn't
he?"

"Penworth."

Harry shook his head, feeling defeat cover him like
soot. "Tell me Penworth doesn't want to turn the *Journal* into a shopper."

"That's how they make their money. All ads, a little
bit of canned copy, little or no staff. Marty doesn't care,
he doesn't know the paper, he has no emotional ties to
it. He doesn't care about the people who have worked
here nearly their entire lives. Look at Cloris. She started
here twenty years ago in production. In those days, we
had to put everything on the page by hand. The paper
looked like crap, but it was the best little daily in the re-

gion. When we started paginating on the computer five years ago, she went to class and learned how to do it rather than lose her job. She's fifty years old, for God's sakes, and she learned how to use a computer."

"Jaimie."

"Yeah. Jaimie. Her entire adult life has been spent at the *Journal.* I still remember her walking in. She looked twelve, but she was a sophomore at UCONN. She worked for free for two years, learning the ropes."

He smiled fondly at the memory and Harry wondered if Paul had somehow had all his sense deleted when he quit the *Journal.* Jaimie would be devastated if she knew the *Journal* was so close to going under. Right or wrong, Harry knew she lived and breathed this paper. "Does Jaimie know about all this?"

The poor guy looked so depressed Harry almost felt sorry for him and would have if the urge to strangle him hadn't been greater. "No. But I was thinking it's time for her to move on anyway. I'm not worried about Jaimie. She'll be fine. She's tough."

Harry was taken aback. "You think so? Jaimie?"

Paul grinned. "Tough as they come."

"Then why didn't you tell her about your brother's threats."

"Because she'd try to fix it and she already works too hard as it is. That's your job. To fix it."

"It would have been nice if you had told me about the financial problems first. I've lost more than two months already." Harry pressed the heel of his right hand against his forehead, feeling the pain from his neck edging up.

"To be honest, I was surprised how long it did take. I was giving you another week before I told you."

Harry wanted to scream. He wanted to quit. Hell, he'd

taken the job because he'd thought it would be easy. The paper runs itself, Paul had told him. You've got a city editor who needs little or no supervision. Heck, I only worked four hours a day, and that was a long day for me. Ha ha.

If Harry thought Paul was malicious instead of naïve, he would strangle him. But the guy honestly thought the best way to save the paper was to hire him and the only way to hire him was to lie about the financial solvency of the paper. This job was giving him more stress than he'd bargained on, and he was sorely tempted to quit. Here and now.

Paul pressed his hands flat on the marred pine table in front of him, moving them back and forth lightly. "Harry, I didn't know what else to do," he said, losing his forced cheerfulness. "I couldn't tell Jaimie. I couldn't tell anyone. By the time I realized what was happening, it was too late. The thing is, I really do care about this paper. I just don't have the energy or desire to fix it. I was hoping you did."

"You screwed me over, Paul."

"Yeah, that's what I do," he said, staring down at his hands. "You going to stay?"

"Until the Penworth sale. Sure."

Paul winced. "There are things you could do to make up some revenue."

"The fiscal year is over in four months." Harry shook his head, gritting his teeth against the pain that caused. His head felt as if it might explode and fall off his shoulders. "You need a specialist in here. I am not the guy for this. You needed to hire a business guy, not a journalist." *Crap.*

"You have a business manager," Paul said weakly, and Harry tried hard not to laugh, mostly because it would have hurt his head. The *Nortown Journal's* business manager was Irene, a seventy-five-year-old woman who, while a brilliant accountant, didn't have a necessary vision or expertise to dig the *Journal* out of the mess it was in. Harry's head was beginning to hurt so much, it was getting more and more difficult to think. He'd have to set up a meeting with advertising, circulation, and Irene, who must have known about the paper's financial difficulties but had remained quiet out of loyalty to Paul. Maybe a circulation drive, a couple of ad specials, an insert or two. Circulation. That was twenty percent, right? Boost that . . . His thoughts were getting more and more jumbled as the pain in his head overtook everything else. Shit, that's all he needed now was one of his infrequent but monster migraines.

"I'll call a meeting and let you know," he said, and escaped out of the bar, which had suddenly become too bright and too smoke-filled. Outside, the late August heat hit him hard and he could taste bile in his throat as he swallowed and tried not to vomit. He headed to his office, closed the door, pulled the blinds, and shut the lights off, wishing he had his migraine pills with him.

Jaimie gave Harry's office a worried glance. He'd been in there, lights off, for two hours. Nate noted her concern and motioned an imaginary bottle to his lips: drunk.

"No way," Jaimie said, but she wasn't all that certain. She's never smelled a hint of alcohol on his breath. Not even at Ted's party. Jaimie's college roommates had accused her of having a nose like a bloodhound when it came to that. Still, when he'd walked into his office he'd had the strangest look about him. Something wasn't quite right but Jaimie couldn't put her finger on it. And now it was nearly ten o'clock and he was still in there. She pushed back her chair.

"I'm going to check on him. He could be dead for all we know."

"God forbid." Nate, apparently, was still scared he was going to lose his job.

Jaimie knocked softly, tilting her head to one side to hear the smallest noise. Nothing. "Harry?" Nothing. She eased the door open and peeked inside. He was lying sprawled out on Paul's battered old couch, his breathing audible and not quite a snore. Sleeping. Or passed out? She tiptoed over to his side and smiled. Harry asleep was so damned appealing. One arm was slung over his head, the other rested on his flat stomach. His hair, always perfectly combed, was mussed up and falling over his forehead and poking up in odd places all over his head. As if he'd pulled at it, roughly, leaving behind finger-tunnels. Maybe his meeting with Paul hadn't gone well. His jaw was darkened by his beard, and for some reason, that made him appear even more vulnerable.

Jaimie gently touched his shoulder. "Harry. Hey, Harry."

He opened his eyes and the look on his face was so startlingly happy, Jaimie's breath caught. And then he blinked at her and frowned. "I fell asleep. What time is it?"

"After ten."

"Shit." He swung his legs over the side of the couch and briefly rested his head in his hands, his fingers digging into his hair. "Okay. I'm awake," he said, sounding half asleep and rather grumpy.

Jaimie stood there uncertainly. "I wasn't sure if I should wake you up."

"No. You should have. It's okay. I'm just a little groggy. I had one hell of a headache."

"Looks like we're going to make last call at Duffy's tonight. You want to hang around and go with Nate and me?"

"It's too late to start drinking."

"Well, you could have a coke. They sell soda at bars, too, you know."

He gave her what had to be the most forced smile she'd ever seen. "I think I'll pass. But thanks."

"Okay. No biggie." But it was and Jaimie didn't know why. She felt foolish inviting him and ridiculously disappointed that he'd declined—almost as if he'd rejected her, as if she'd been asking him out on a date and he'd said no.

No. You bore me. And I don't date my employees. You must be some sort of slut.

Jaimie walked back to her desk, her cheeks burning slightly, her mind reeling with the disgusting knowledge that she had the hots for her boss.

Chapter 7

Every time Harry slipped on his old baseball glove, he felt it, that blood-singing thrill he'd had as a kid stepping out onto the field for the first time each season. It was the smell of the leather, the fine, heavy feel of the glove on his hand, the way his battered hat hugged his head, the way his cleats dug into the soft, fine dirt. He shouldn't feel that same emotion today, pulling on his glove for a company softball game, but he did. It was great to do something normal, to feel the hot sun baking his head, to smell the freshly mowed grass. So far, today was a good day. If every day had been like this, he'd still be in New York, still be at the *Times,* and still be living with Anne.

Harry grinned when he heard the pop of a ball hitting a glove. He couldn't help it. Taking a deep breath, he stepped toward the field, glove tucked negligently under his right arm.

"Harry," Ted boomed. "Heard you're a ringer."

"I would have been a ringer ten years ago, not now." He was looking around the field when a flash of bright yellow caught his eye. Jaimie.

He would never get used to seeing her without a sweater on. She wore a lemon-yellow tank top over khaki cargo shorts but somehow managed to look so sexy, he almost forgot not to stare. No woman he'd ever known could fill out clothes the way Jaimie did. She was sweetly rounded in all the right places, and those places drew his eyes no matter how hard he tried not to. On her shoulder she easily carried a worn bat bag, dumping it on the ground like an old pro.

If she can play ball I just might fall in love.

"Harry. You made it. Thank God," she said, with an obvious nod to Kath.

"I saw that," Kath said, giving Jaimie a soft jab in the upper arm.

Kath, with frizzy, wild hair and nondescript features, looked like a russet potato standing next to Jaimie's brilliance. She wore a brown T-shirt and jean shorts, and blended into the background until she disappeared. Maybe that's why she was such a good reporter, Harry thought idly.

Harry had expected Ted to take charge of the team, but it was Jaimie who made the batting list and assigned each player a position, an old ragged baseball cap shoved into her shorts. "Harry, you think you can handle shortstop?"

"I played third, so . . ."

Jaimie looked to Ted. "What do you think, Ted? You play short and Harry play third?"

"You're kidding," Ted said, looking down at his left knee, which had a large brace on it. "Put Harry on short."

"You're right," Jaimie said, scribbling frantically at what appeared to be an actual line-up sheet.

"You guys take this kind of seriously, don't you," Harry said, as he watched Jaimie pencil in his name at the shortstop position.

"Not we, *her*," Kath said, rolling her eyes good-naturedly. "Jaimie is rabidly competitive. She played in college."

"I am not rabid and I only played my freshman year."

Harry stared at her with new eyes. This sexy woman played college ball? He'd thought Jaimie was the ultimate girly-girl. She sure didn't look the part of a square-bodied jock with short-cropped hair and more testosterone than he had.

"Why didn't you play sophomore year?" he asked.

"That's when I started working at the *Journal*. Anyway, other than the fact that I liked to play, what was the point? It wasn't like I was going to go pro. Besides, I wasn't that good. I think I played four innings all season."

"Still. College. That's great."

Jaimie smiled, inordinately pleased he was impressed by her short-lived softball career. But her smile faded when she saw Carly Strickland, an assistant editor from the *Day,* walking toward them, a predator's look in her eyes as she took in Harry with a long up-and-down assessing look. And suddenly Jaimie found herself looking at Harry, at his body.

Oh my. Jaimie swallowed, wondering why she'd never noticed how nice he was from the neck down. He wore a T-shirt only a guy would think of as wearable: It looked like one of those shirts that you can see through if you hold it up to the light, the shirt was pulling away from the neckline leaving tiny holes, and one sleeve had a small rip. Jaimie smiled. Somehow she'd thought Harry would have gone out and bought something baseball-y. He looked so good in a suit, it was startling to see him so dressed down, so normal. So sexy.

Apparently Carly thought so too with that look, that feline smile. Carly made a show of saying hello to Jaimie before turning and acting surprised to find a new face among the old. "You must be Harry Crandall. I'm a big fan."

Jaimie thought her stomach just might turn seeing the pleased look on Harry's face. "You are?"

"Carly Strickland. I'm an editor with the *Day*."

"Assistant editor, right Carly?" Jaimie asked.

"Right," she said, dismissively. "It's so nice to meet you, Mr. Crandall."

"Harry," he said, and smiled.

Jaimie couldn't believe her eyes. She'd never seen Harry smile like that before, like a guy in a bar smiles at that night's target. Quickly, she gave Carly an assessing look. She'd never thought about it, but now looking at Carly, Jaimie realized she was rather attractive. In an ice-queen way. Carly had cold blue eyes, dark hair, and pale skin stretched tightly over her too-thin body. And Harry seemed, well, captivated. And she was wearing clothes—a royal blue silk T and black linen shorts—that were completely inappropriate for playing softball. Even though she knew she was being an idiot, Jaimie felt suddenly frumpy in her loose-fitting tank and baggy cargo shorts.

"You play softball?" Harry said, apparently so enthralled with Carly he couldn't see what was so obvious. *Of course* Carly couldn't play softball.

"Me?" And Carly gave him the most seductive laugh Jaimie had ever heard. She'd have to try that one when she got alone. Ha ha-ha ha-ha. Jaimie snorted when she laughed. "I don't play," and her blue eyes dipped down to his mouth, "softball."

"Oh, good God," Jaimie said under her breath, but maybe Carly heard her and maybe Jaimie was glad, because Carly's head jerked in her direction. "Do you have your team's roster?"

Carly handed her a slip of paper, then said out of the side of her mouth, which actually had lipstick on it, "She takes this all so seriously. Really, Jaimie, this is just for fun."

Jaimie didn't say anything because she'd have sounded catty no matter what she said. She felt catty. She felt like scratching Carly's pretty blue eyes of her head. Then maybe she wouldn't be staring at Harry with such a proprietary manner. Bitch.

Hello. Where did that *come from?*

Jaimie spun around only to see Kath trying to stifle her laughter. "What's so funny?"

"You are. Why do you let her get to you?"

Jaimie heaved out a sigh. "I don't know." Kath looked past her to where Harry was still standing talking to Carly. "I think it's because she's so convinced the *Day* is a better paper and she's a better editor. And maybe because she's right and I can't stand it."

"Yeah. Maybe," Kath said on a laugh. "They make a nice-looking couple. I think a romance is blooming. Don't you? Jaimie?"

Jaimie spared the couple a dark look. "She's too skinny."

"They have very similar coloring. Same dark hair, same blue eyes. They're both tall."

"Harry's eyes are gray," Jaimie said. *With green around the pupil, and tiny darts of black near the edge.* She'd noticed that, she just hadn't noticed the rest of the package, the finely-muscled, tall, piece of man-meat he was. She began taking the baseball bats out of the bag. "You could help me."

Ten minutes later, Jaimie was on the mound, lobbing the softball to the *Day* players, who pounded it time after time past the infield and toward poor Kath in right field who either ducked or hopped out of the way, then bounded after the ball like a puppy, completely oblivious to her ineptitude. After the fourth hit, Harry carried the ball over to Jaimie and plopped it into her glove.

"Hey, coach, maybe you should take Kath out of right."

Jaimie gave him a withering look. "They'd just hit it to her wherever she is."

"Put her at third."

Jaimie furrowed her brow then smiled. "You know, Harry, you're not as dumb as you look."

He grinned and trotted off to tell Ted to head to right field. Kath, thrilled to be within talking distance to another player, sprinted to third, looking eager and ready. The *Day* players tried in vain to smash it to Kath, but time after time, Harry scooped up the ball and threw it to first. After the second out, Jaimie actually sighed after watching him flow toward the ball, backhand it, and flick it with precision to first base. Poetry in motion. If she were starring in a musical, she'd flutter her eyelashes, sigh, and wither in a faint to the ground. Of course, a quick look to the *Day* bench told her that while she was on the ground eating dust, Carly would be stalking her man.

That's when Jaimie's heart really started to pound. Harry could never be her man. Never mind she didn't like the strong silent type. Never mind she was beginning to like him as much as she liked him. He was her boss and that should be enough to halt any more *my-man* thoughts. It would have to be enough. It would never work.

"You're a ball hog," Kath said good-naturedly to Harry when they were sitting on the bench preparing to bat. "Thank God."

Harry flashed Jaimie a grin and damn it if her heart didn't jump out of her chest and onto her sleeve. The cream on the top was the *Journal* was actually ahead at the top of the sixth. She knew it shouldn't matter, that it was just a fun game, but she really, really wanted to win. She just didn't want anyone on either team to know how much. So when the *Day* had two men on with two out and their best hitter at the plate, her nerves were thrumming.

"Hit it to me," Kath shouted, and the rest of the team snickered.

The guy hit it to right center, between Ted and Ryan. Ted got to the ball first and flung it hard toward home just as the runner rounded third. Jaimie watched the ball sail high, sensed a body hurling toward home, turned to see the runner go into a slide. And then heard the most sickening crack she'd ever had the misfortune of hearing. Almost as sick as the scream of pain that came out of Harry's mouth.

Not a person on the field had to ask what had happened; it was all too grotesquely apparent. Harry's leg was broken below the knee, bending in a spot that no leg would want to bend.

"Lay back, man, don't look at it," Ted said, pushing Harry's shoulders back into the soft dirt. The guy that had run into him kept saying how sorry he was as he dialed 911 for an ambulance.

Harry lay there silently, gritting his teeth against the pain, somehow making it more difficult to watch as he dug a trench in the dirt with his good leg. He was breathing in and out harshly, his eyes squeezed shut, making Jaimie feel so helpless she couldn't stand it. Making her way through the onlookers up to his ear, she hunkered down and lay a hand on his arm.

"Harry."

He turned to look at her.

"I think it's just a sprain."

He stared at her, then laughed. "Shit," he said, laughing and grunting in pain. "Don't make me laugh."

"I'll go with you to the hospital, okay?" she said, then propped up his head and slid her glove beneath it.

"I could go," Carly said, but her eyes kept darting to his twisted leg.

"It's okay, Carly. I live right next to the medical center. It makes more sense for me to go. Besides, I feel responsible since I made him play."

"Yeah," Ted said. "It's all Jaimie's fault."

Harry laughed, then grimaced again. A fine sheen of sweat covered his face and his shirt clung wetly to his body. She would have appreciated the view if it hadn't been so obvious to Jaimie he was in terrible pain.

"I take full responsibility." In the distance, she could hear the sound of the rescue on its way. Thank God. That leg looked like it hurt like hell and Jaimie knew if it had been her, she'd be screaming and crying and begging for someone to make it all go away. Maybe Harry would have carried on a bit more if he hadn't had such a big audience. "You all don't have to stick around. Ted, you still having a party?"

"Yes, he is," Harry said firmly.

"Sure," Ted said, sounding reluctant. "Everyone's still invited back to the house for a swim," Ted called as he helped gather up the bats. "Even you *Day* people. And Harry, you can come on over so we can sign your cast," Ted said, looking guilty about having a Labor Day party when his friend was on his way to the hospital.

By the time the rescue arrived, most of the people had drifted away, leaving only her, Ted, and Harry. "You holding up okay, Harry?" Jaimie asked.

"I'm just dandy."

"'Cause almost everyone's gone and if you wanted to

cry like a baby, I swear I won't tell anyone. Ted won't either, right Ted?"

"Oh, I'd tell," Ted said, grinning.

Harry chuckled. "Guys, I really appreciate you trying to make me feel better, but if either one of you makes me laugh again, I'm going to take my crutch and hit you over the head with it the first opportunity I get."

Jaimie sighed. "Okay. I'll try."

"And I'm going," Ted said, as the rescue pulled up behind the backstop. "Apparently I have to give a party I don't want to go to. You think you'll make it, Jaimie?"

"I'll try."

"Good luck, man. Don't let 'em cut it off."

"Ted," Jaimie said, exasperated.

Harry's jaw hardened as he tried not to chuckle. "You just won yourself a crutch upside the head."

"I don't know, Harry," Jaimie said. "I didn't hear you laugh. I don't think that counts."

Harry looked up at the sky. "I'm going to kill them both."

"You can't kill Ted, he's already gone," Jaimie said. "Here they come with the stretcher."

"You go. I can get a taxi home."

Jaimie gave him a look. "This is Nortown, not New York. Where do you think you're going to get a taxi."

"I know for a fact Nortown has three taxis. Go."

Jaimie hesitated. She didn't want to breach the employer-employee thing, but she also didn't think it was right to leave a guy with a broken leg lying in the dirt.

Jaimie stepped back to let the emergency crew help Harry. When they moved him onto the stretcher, he let out a moan of agony that ripped into Jaimie. There was no way she was going to let him go to that hospital by himself.

Chapter 8

"Harry?"

If there was a God, he would not lift his head up and see Jaimie standing there next to him in the emergency room, concern in her eyes. He looked up. Apparently there was no God. Guys didn't like women to see them use the toilet, spank the monkey, or scream like a girl, and he was perilously close to doing the latter. Man, his leg hurt like hell, and here was little miss chatter box to try to make him smile.

"Go away," he said, closing his eyes and not even trying to sound pleasant.

"I won't talk. I'll just . . . hold your hand."

He was about to tell her again to go away when he felt her cool small hand wrap around his and, damn if it didn't seem kind of nice. It took his mind off his throbbing leg and the fact that in a few short minutes some twenty-five-year-old intern was going to set his leg and he had a feeling it was going to hurt just as much as when he broke it despite the painkiller they'd given him.

"See? I'm not talking," she said softly near his ear. He smiled and gave her hand a little squeeze.

"Excuse me, miss, we have to take your boyfriend to get that leg x-rayed," a nurse said.

Jaimie dropped his hand in a flash.

"See you later. Honey," Harry said, craning his neck to see her reaction. Her cheeks were flaming.

"I'll be in the waiting room. Waiting." Jaimie turned and hurried toward a row of plastic chairs. Why had she held his hand? Now he was thinking that she was thinking she wanted something from him she definitely didn't. Sort of didn't. Okay, she did, but that didn't mean she ever would make a move toward making Harry more than a boss. If he hadn't been her boss Harry would be on the top of her list of guys she'd go out with. Actually, he'd be the only one on her list. Jaimie wasn't sure if that was sad or scary.

Jaimie drove silently, trying valiantly to avoid hitting the potholes that made up a major part of the roads in Nortown. Getting Harry into the car had been fairly easy with a nurse there to help. He grimaced slightly but settled in nicely. But as they drove out of the hospital parking lot she hit a curb and found out Harry's vocabulary could be on the colorful side.

"Sorry. I thought they gave you painkiller," she said, giving his leg a worried look.

"I think it's safe to say it's wearing off," Harry said, his voice strained.

Every time she hit a pothole, Harry would breathe in sharply and clench his fists and her grip on the wheel got so tight, her hands started to hurt. "Sorry."

"Stop saying you're sorry and just stop hitting the fucking things," he said.

"I'm trying," she said a bit desperately, just as her front tire dipped into one. "Sorry."

He swore under his breath.

"You know, I'm not hitting them on purpose."

"You could have fooled me."

Jaimie took her eyes off the road just long enough to give him a look of disbelief, grabbed the wheel tighter and scrunched up her face in determination. Not twenty minutes ago he'd been showing off in front of the nurse—the very attractive nurse—how good he was with his crutches and now he was yelping every time she drove over a pit in the road. Apparently, whatever they'd given him for the pain started to wear off big time. Or he was giving her a hard time.

Harry gave a small and audible prayer of thanks when Jaimie pulled carefully in front of his building, an old mill that had been converted to upscale apartments. She could tell his leg hurt like hell and he was staring up at the stairs leading to his building as if they were the Great Pyramid. Jaimie shut off the engine and let out a huge sigh of relief.

"What do I need to do?"

"I'm okay now," he lied through teeth clenched so tightly the words were barely audible.

Jaimie laughed. "Yeah. I can see that. Okay, idiot man, what do I need to do?"

She didn't know how many fires and car accidents she'd been to, but she'd learned pretty early on to divorce herself from the human tragedy and concentrate on details. Facts were never as unsettling as what was really going on, the pain and tears, the loss. She'd seen a lot worse than Harry's leg, but for some reason, it bothered her. A lot.

"I think I can make it up those stairs, but maybe you should spot me until I get in the door," he said. He opened his car door, awkwardly swung his legs out, and let out a curse when he banged his broken right leg against the curb. He'd broken out in a cold sweat and so the hair on the back of his head was damp and still spiky from playing softball.

At his sound of pain, Jaimie winced and hurled herself to his side of the car, hovering helplessly as he heaved himself into a standing position. "I'll get the door," she said, nearly closing it on his good leg.

Harry made his way to the steps, then started navigating them with remarkable ease.

"You sure this is your first time on crutches?"

He stood on the landing a good long time, moving his hands this way and that, finally giving up and looking back at Jaimie who was at the ready should he topple backward.

"My keys."

"What about them?"

He shook his head. "They're in my pocket and I can't get them, not without falling back on my ass."

"Oh. Well." Jaimie let her gaze drift down to his pocket. He was wearing cargo pants and the keys were buttoned up safely, warmly, against his upper thigh. Lucky keys. Jaimie shot a look at Harry. "I suppose I could get them for you?"

He put on a wicked smile and, if he wasn't her boss, she would have made him suffer for that smile. Jaimie crossed her arms and gave him a withering look. "Are you sure you weren't fired for sexual harassment?"

"Just get the keys. Please."

Jaime climbed the stairs, cheeks burning, hands reaching for his pocket. The button slipped easily and she smiled. "Okay, Mr. Crandall, I'm going in."

"Be gentle."

Biting her lips, she reached her hand in, deeper, deeper. "Hell, Harry, how far down does this thing go?" Then, "Aha."

"Careful what you . . ."

"Don't say it. Do not." And she produced the keys with a flourish.

"I have some money in that pocket and I didn't want it going all over the place. What did you think I was going to say?" He looked like the devil smiling down at her.

"I ought to let you fend for yourself, but I have a big heart," she said, handing his keys over to him.

She followed him into his condo, casting a quick look around to see a cozy living room, sparsely furnished and devoid of personal effects other than a bookshelf crammed with books. She went immediately to the kitchen and opened the refrigerator door. A half gallon of whole milk, four beers, a dozen eggs. And ketchup.

"Listen," she said, going back into the living room where he was sprawled on the couch. "I'm going to get us something to eat."

"I'm not hungry."

"You will be. Right?"

He nodded and Jaimie wondered if he was just too exhausted to answer.

"I'll be back in fifteen. Italian sub okay for you?"

Another nod. "I think I'm okay. I am okay. Thanks, but . . ." He sighed. "Why don't you get those sandwiches."

When Jaimie returned, Harry seemed better. Colder, but better, as if he'd realized, as she had, that they'd been crossing that imaginary line between employee and employer too much. It was dangerous territory and Jaimie was not going to enter into it. Her hand still burned from putting in down Harry's pocket. She could tell herself a hundred times she was just doing him a favor, but she shouldn't have enjoyed it so much. And Harry could have gotten his keys by himself, she was certain of that.

He was still on the couch when she returned, looking as if he'd dozed off for a while. "Why don't you eat that then go to the party."

"I wasn't planning to go anyway," she said, shrugging as she unwrapped the grinders. "I was hoping to get more work done on that Joshua Tate story."

"How's that going, anyway?"

"Good. I guess. The mother sure seemed better than the last time I interviewed her. Weirdly better."

"What do you mean?"

"I know it's been eight months and that's a long time. But she almost seemed happy. Too happy. She wasn't even sure where she'd put the kid's pictures and she's already turned his room into something else."

Harry shrugged. "Single mom enjoying her freedom?"

"Maybe."

"What? You think she killed the kid and the puppy?"

"No," Jaimie said, drawing out the word. "I just got the feeling something wasn't quite right. I've interviewed a lot of people who've lost their kids to disease or accidents, and she seemed disinterested in the investigation. I don't know, everyone handles grief differently I guess."

Jaimie sat down next to Harry and plopped his grinder into his lap. He stared at it. "I'm really not that hungry."

"Well, I'm starved. I hope you don't mind if I eat mine," she said, then took a huge bite. "I'll put yours in the fridge if you want."

"Jaimie."

She was about to take another bite, but lowered the sandwich.

"You really don't have to stay."

"I know. I just want to eat my sandwich." She grinned

at him. "Donnie's Subs. God, they're good." She delicately took some mayonnaise from the corner of her mouth with her pinky, then licked it off, oblivious to his warm gaze following the gesture. "Should have gotten napkins," she said, laughing. "I'm such a slob when I eat. I'll never forget in high school after the prom, we went to get pizza and I think I made my date literally ill."

"I doubt that," he said, and looked away.

"See? I'm making you sick, too." She laughed, and snorted, then laughed because she snorted, and snorted again. And then Harry was laughing, and damn if he didn't look good with his face all crinkled and happy.

Harry shook his head and looked at her with such heat, Jaimie thought she had to be imagining it. "I can't figure you out."

"I'm a tough one."

He got all serious and Jaimie wished he wouldn't. "Thank you."

She shook her head. "No thanks necessary. Just promise me you won't go out and break another leg."

"I've had worse things happen than a broken leg," he said.

"I'm all ears." She turned toward him in mock excitement.

He gave her an assessing look, as if trying to determine if he could trust her. "You remember the scandal at the *Times* a couple years back?"

"Yeah. A bunch of editors got fired. A reporter was caught making stuff up, right?"

"They got real paranoid after that. And someone decided it was time for me to go down. I had things showing up in my stories that I didn't write. You know, you don't read your own stuff after you write it. I don't have the time for that. I just assume the editors do their jobs and if there's ever a question, then I go back over it. Well, there were some problems with my stories. Misquotes, factual errors."

Jaimie shook her head. "But when you went back to your file, the story was accurate there, right?"

"No. The first time it happened, I went ballistic. I checked my notes, I couldn't believe what my file said, because I knew what I wrote. I knew. Then I started to doubt myself, thinking, maybe I did fuck up. My editor wanted to fire me then and there, but didn't. It happened again and I was gone. Nothing official, just an 'I think it would be in your best interest to find another position, Harry.' It was bullshit. After all the mess a couple years ago, my boss wanted it all hush-hush."

Jaimie didn't get it. Why wouldn't a Pulitzer Prize-winner reporter fight for his job? "Why didn't you go public?"

"The high road, huh? It's a hell of a lot easier to take the high road when it's not your life. Anyway, I didn't— and still don't—have any proof that I'm right. Look at it from management's position. A reporter not once, but twice, makes major mistakes in two very sensitive stories. What would you have done as editor? Probably the same thing they did. They pulled me in, made me aware of the mistakes, gave me another chance. From their perspective, I screwed up again. Maybe I did screw up. I'd swear on a bible I didn't, but maybe I did. And then I'd end up looking like an idiot. The worse thing is, I can't prove myself right even though I know I am."

Jaimie chewed thoughtfully. "Your boss either hung you out to dry or he's the one who did it."

"He's a great editor, but I think he didn't want to be the latest executive sent to the chopping block. Who knows? All I know is he's still working at the *Times* and I'm here."

"So you're giving up?"

Harry swore beneath his breath. "I know I could have eventually proven my innocence but I didn't have time. I was out the door before my computer was cool. Someone wanted me out and to this day I don't know who."

"Why Nortown?" Jaimie asked, clearly baffled.

Harry laughed. "Believe me, it wasn't my first choice. I tried L.A., the *Tribune,* the *Globe.* But they all wanted to know why I was leaving the *Times.* Guess what? They didn't believe me any more than my editor at the *Times.*"

"Someone sabotaged your stories," she said. She was getting that feeling, that surge of excitement a journalist gets when they're dancing on the edge of a great story.

"I thought of that, but they don't have access to our computers. We all have passwords and it would have looked suspicious for an editor to be hanging around my desk. It's possible but not likely."

"Someone did it."

"Either that or I'm losing my mind."

"You're a lot of things, Harry, but you're not crazy. And I didn't think you were a quitter." Apparently that was not the best thing to say, because in an instant his face went hard, his eyes flat and angry.

"What I don't need right now is little girl idealism."

Now it was Jaimie's turn to feel a surge of anger. "You walked away without a fight. You quit."

"You don't know anything about me or the situation I was in." Jaimie had a feeling that if he hadn't been completely immobilized because of his broken leg, he would have launched himself at her and shaken her. She wanted to stay angry, but damned if he wasn't right.

Even if he was being slightly jerky about the whole thing.

"I'm sorry Harry. I don't have the right to judge you. Even though it was sort of a compliment, you know, the 'I don't think you're a quitter' thing. See? A compliment."

He let out a small sigh. "Yeah. You've got a real way with words. Listen, thanks for the help. I'll see you Monday."

Translation: I'm still majorly pissed but I'm managing to control my temper because I'm such a generous guy.

"I'll see you tomorrow," Jaimie said. "Whether you like it or not, you need help. You have no food and guess what? You can't drive with that thing." He looked down at his right leg as if he forgot it was there and she thought she heard him swear. "I promise I won't call you a coward or any other derogatory term. I'll deliver lunch and dinner and leave you alone. Like Meals on Wheels."

He looked like he wanted to say no, but Harry was a smart guy and knew Jaimie was right. "Yeah. Okay. Thanks."

"See you tomorrow," she said. "You need anything else tonight?"

He gave her a look that made her face heat up, first with lust, then with mortification that she'd completely misinterpreted that heated look. It was anger, not lust on that gorgeous face of his, she was certain of it. Jaimie gave him a wave and practically ran out of his apartment.

Harry stared at the door a while, wondering whether he should have let her get under his skin so easily. Man, she could push his buttons. Every single one of them, good and bad. He wanted to tell her that he needed help getting undressed, taking a shower, and there was this other little nagging problem he had that she could take care of. Harry sighed and closed his eyes and wondered if anything could happen to make his life worse. What the hell was he doing in this town, completely alone with a shitty job and a lousy apartment, trapped by his own decisions and now by a broken leg. He glanced at the phone and wondered if he should call his mother, then decided against it. Mom was still in mourning from him losing his *Times* job. Jaimie had been kind compared to his mother, who nearly went to the *Washington Post* with his story.

"Pulitzer Prize-winning reporters don't get fired on bullshit evidence," she'd said. It was only after a heated argument that she'd finally relented.

Anyway, his mother had helped him all his life, this time he had to figure things out on his own.

Chapter 9

Jaimie had become his girl Friday, but without all the snazzy dialogue and hidden affection. Harry took her help reluctantly and rather grumpily. It wasn't as if Jaimie wanted a thank-you, though that would have been nice. He treated her like an errand girl, a nothing. Which, apparently, was what she was to him.

It wasn't her fault that a helpless sexy man was an aphrodisiac to her. She hated that her heart beat faster when she got to his house. She hated that butterflies-in-the-stomach thing that happened every time he opened the door and gave her a brief smile. Harry stayed out of work until Wednesday, meeting her at the door with a brief hello before crutching it over to the couch and putting his nose into a stack of papers he'd pulled out of his briefcase. She'd bring over the paper and he'd read it, a frown on his face, making little or no comment unless it was to point out something he didn't like.

And she was beginning to suspect Harry wasn't as helpless as he seemed. After a week of shopping for him, driving him to work and back, making certain he had everything within easy reach when she left, Jaimie was about at the end of her altruistic feelings. She had her own life and didn't have time for his. Okay, she did. And she really didn't mind all that much. What she did mind was the way her mind worked when he hobbled to the door and let her in and gave her a smile as if he was happy to see her. Then he'd asked what she got at the grocery store, dashing those silly thoughts. The guy was hungry not horny. At least not for her.

Which was good. Good, good, good. Because Jaimie really didn't need the complication of a relationship with Harry.

At the end of the day, Harry was wiped out, an idiot could see that. He worked long hours, bringing files home with him almost every day. Friday night, six days after he broke his leg, Harry invited Jaimie in for a beer. It was one in the morning and Jaimie was dog-tired, but it was the first friendly thing Harry had said to her all week, so she went in.

"You want a glass?" she asked from the kitchen. He didn't, so she popped the caps off two Heinekens and brought them into the living room. When she got there, Harry was half lying on the couch, his head back, his eyes closed, exposing his very nice throat. She never really looked at a guy's throat or neck, but Harry's was nice. Not too thick, not skinny, no big jutting Adam's apple bobbing up and down. Sexy. She cleared her throat. "Tired?"

"Beat to hell."

"I bet you thought this would be a cake job," she said, moving his good leg out of the way so she could sit on the couch.

"That's about right. Paul sure made it sound like one."

Jaimie chugged some beer and sat back, slumping on the couch. "Well, his job was cake. He really didn't do his job. But the paper went out every day. We got paid." Jaimie shrugged.

"Unfortunately, there's a lot more to this job than I was originally told. I like to be busy." He opened his eyes to look at her. "Keeps my mind off things."

Jaimie could feel her face flush again as if he'd said, "I want to see you naked" instead of what he had. She took a breath. "Nice," she said, patting the soft leather to get her mind off his sexy throat. She looked around the room, taking in the television and chair with ottoman, also leather. "But you need pictures or something on the wall."

"That's girl stuff."

Jaimie rolled her eyes. "Carly could help you."

"Carly?" He asked, sitting up.

And Jaimie was happy at the sound of disbelief in his voice. "You know, the woman at the softball game who was stalking you. The ugly one."

"She wasn't exactly *ugly.*"

Jaimie frowned. "Actually, she's pretty. I just don't like her. Professional jealousy, I guess."

"Too skinny. Even for an assistant editor."

Jaimie turned her head and stared straight into his face, a very nice smiling face. And then her eyes drifted up to his and saw that heat again, and this time she was pretty certain she wasn't mistaken. It had been a long time since a man had looked at her with that kind of heat, but she recognized it. She watched, heart pounding, lips tingling, as his beautiful eyes swept down her face and rested on her lips that were practically panting out short little breaths. Puff, puff, puff. Her ears started buzzing. Heck, her entire body was buzzing like a swarm of bees eager to get to a big ol' pot of honey.

"Tell me kissing you would be a mistake," he said, his voice low and sexy as hell.

Oh god, oh god. She swallowed. "Okay. If that's what you want."

A smiled teased his lips. "What do you want?"

"You don't want to know." *I want you to strip me naked and then I'll strip you and I'll kiss away the sweat*

and we'll make some more. Slippery, wonderful, intox-
icating sweat, glistening and sweet. And then I want you
to come inside me because if you don't I think I just
might die.

That heat flared again as if he were reading her dirty
mind. "I really think I do want to know." And he brought
his mouth against hers and she let out a sound he cut off
with his lips, firm and soft and very, very nice. No
tongue, not yet, just his mouth, pressing hers, moving
against her lips, and oh, those swarming bees were definitely headed for the honey. Jaimie let out a little laugh
and he raised his head in question.

"Private joke," she mumbled then pulled him to her
again and kissed the living daylights out of him. No talking, no wondering whether what they were doing was
right, no thinking about Monday at work when she'd see
him and want him and know that this probably had been
a mistake. Just mouths and tongues and his hard steady
hands on her shoulders pulling her closer and closer. God,
his hands were strong and wonderfully warm against her.
With a little grunt, he yanked her sweater off her, revealing a tank top. Oh. He'd moved the straps of her tank
down. He kissed her on her shoulder and made a low
sound from deep inside, rumbling so that she could feel
the vibration against her breasts.

"Nice shoulders, McLane," he said, brushing his lips
against one and moving his hand across the other.

"You like shoulders, huh? Never heard of that one."

He laughed. "Actually, I think I like a lot of you. This
part especially." He touched one breast and closed his
eyes briefly.

"Breast and shoulder man?"

"Not until now." With that, he grabbed the hem of her
shirt and in one fluid motion, took it off, revealing her

utilitarian sports bra beneath. He was being amazingly agile for a guy with a big cast on his leg.

"I think I like jocks," he said, then moved a thumb over one of her nipples, making her breath catch.

It had been so long since a man had touched her breasts, she'd almost forgotten how exquisite the sensation was. Jaimie lifted the bra up and over her head and watched his eyes get all loopy.

"You sure hide it well," he said.

"I'm not hiding it. I'm cold all the time."

He smiled. "I can tell."

Jaimie looked down at her nipples. She was the kind of woman, who if she wanted to, could rest a coat hanger on them. "I'm not cold now."

"Jesus," he whispered.

"No. Jaimie." She rolled her eyes. "Why doesn't anyone get that right?"

He looked at her as if she were insane, then let out a sharp bark of laughter. "You're amazing," he said, smiling widely. "Really, really amazing." And he bent his head and took one of her nipples in his mouth and sucked and sucked, until Jaimie thought she'd come just from that.

"I think we need to shed more clothes," she panted out. "Are you up for it? I mean," she said, laughing, "with the cast and all maybe this isn't a great idea."

"I think we can figure things out."

He was as gorgeous out of his clothes as he was in them, no doubt about it.

"I haven't been able to work out as much as I used to," he said, and his self-consciousness stunned her.

"You're kidding right? You're beautiful, Harry. I was just thinking it wasn't fair for you to have that face, this body *and* a Pulitzer Prize." He laughed, as she hoped he would. He wasn't rock hard by any means, but his abs were there, not carved out, but certainly visible. He had a lovely chest, brawny and sculpted with just enough hair to make him sexy as hell. "Let's see the rest."

She tugged down his sweat-shorts, giving a little peek inside. "I think we can carry on," she said, and pulled his pants over his erection. She bent to kiss his penis, loving the sound he made, all male, low and growly. He pulled her up, and kissed her, moving his hands into her jeans, cupping her bum and pressing her against him. She loved the way he smelled, sweaty but nice, clean somehow. It had been so long since she'd felt a man's skin against her breasts, since a man had held her and made her feel beautiful. "You feel so good," she said, pulling away and looking down at him.

"You feel pretty damn good yourself." He grinned and looked at her as if he were the luckiest man alive, and her heart skipped a beat, the beat that should have warned her this was a huge mistake. Instead, she kissed him until her mouth hurt, until her cheeks were pink from beard-burn, until she was slipping out of her jeans and panties, slipping on a condom, and slipping onto him.

"Your leg okay?"

"What leg?"

He moved his hand between them, pressing against her as she moved and completely went wild—four years of doing without was apparently culminating in this one moment. She'd never been a screamer, never uttered a sound when making love, but this time she forgot all that and let out a scream that was worthy of an X-rated movie.

She was still on him, still catching her breath, still not quite certain who that woman was who had been bopping up and down and screaming, when the phone rang.

"I don't have to get that," he said, which clearly meant

that he wanted to. Still, she gave him credit for waiting until the answering machine clicked on.

"Hey, Harry. I know it's late. If you're home . . ." A woman's voice, soft and clear.

He moved faster than she'd ever seen a man move, certainly faster than she'd seen him move since he broke his leg, abandoning her in a heap. "Hi." He looked at her quickly then looked away. "Actually, I was just making love to a beautiful redhead."

Jaimie heard the tinkling laughter of a woman. Disbelieving laughter, she guessed. He listened for a while, then said, "I'm okay. Job's okay." He took a breath. "How are you doing?"

That's when Jaimie started gathering up her clothes, feeling a bit like some hussy getting caught screwing a married man because it was embarrassingly obvious that Harry wasn't talking to a girl friend, he was talking to a girlfriend.

"I don't know. I suppose you could. I . . ." Then he shot Jaimie a look of apology and turned away from her even further, talking so low she could barely make out what he was saying. Clearly, he didn't want her to know, but Jaimie had no compunction eavesdropping on a man with whom she'd just made love and who was now talking to his girlfriend.

"Why do you want to come up?"

I miss you. That's what she must have said, because Harry said, "I miss you, too. All right. I'll see you Wednesday."

Harry hung up the phone, grabbed his sweats and pulled them up, struggling only slightly to pull them up over his cast. "My ex."

Somehow, that didn't make Jaimie feel any better. "How ex is she?"

Harry looked down at the floor. "I don't know. We lived together for two years. Things had started to go stale. Then I had to quit the *Times* and things went from bad to worse."

Jaimie didn't know what to say. She felt stupid all of a sudden to have made love to a guy whose heart clearly belonged to someone else. She was the unwanted one. The substitute. The quick bang.

"I've got to go."

"You don't have to," he said, but Jaimie knew she did. Staying would make her pathetic.

"I think," she said slowly, "that despite our best intentions, this was a mistake." She stood, fully dressed now, and faced him. The answering machine blinked that it had a message, the first part of Anne's call. *Hey, Harry. I know it's late. If you're home . . .*

She rallied and gave him a smile. "Off the record, you're a great kisser."

"What's the headline to your story?"

"Woman breaks four-year drought."

"Four years?" he asked, clearly flabbergasted.

"Don't get too flattered. I just haven't been presented with too many opportunities."

He gave her a smile she thought might be filled with a least a little regret. "The men around here must be idiots."

It was a nice compliment, but didn't make her feel much better at the moment.

"I'll see you Monday. Um, you can fend for yourself until then, right?" she said, trying to get out the door as quickly as possible.

"Sure," he said quickly. "We're okay, right? No weird stuff."

"We're fine." She always wanted to cry after having the best sex of her life.

Chapter 10

Monday morning. Ugh!

Jaimie stared at the clock and felt sick. Maybe she was too sick to work? She buried her head in her pillow and let out a scream and would have stayed there until she suffocated, but her cat jumped up on top of her and started kneading her with his razor claws. She turned over and Max jumped to the floor, giving her a dirty look.

"Blah blah blah," she said to Max, who eyed her indifferently before padding off to the kitchen to wait beside his bowl. "I don't know why I got you. I hate cats." Actually, at this moment, Jaimie hated herself. She wished she could go to work and pretend all was well, that she hadn't been bouncing naked on her boss's lap two days before, but she couldn't. It was only lust, on both of their parts. She knew that, especially now that the girlfriend was about to come on the scene. The problem was, she liked Harry entirely too much and now she was stuck desiring him too. Lusting. Leering. Drooling.

Jaimie put on her slipper-socks and shuffled to the kitchen feeling depressed and stressed. And alone. A single woman in a tiny house with a cat. It hadn't bothered her a month ago. Before Harry. Before Paul put all those you're-letting-your-life-slip-away-from-you ideas in her head. She'd loved her life, her little house that was completely hers—well, at least the $30,000 of it the bank didn't own. She'd almost liked her cat. Stupid thing.

Max chose that moment to rub up against her legs and purr and even though Jaimie knew it was just because the greedy little thing was hungry, her heart melted and she picked him up and gave him a hug. Cats are not huggable and Max was extreme cat. He suffered her embrace for three seconds before digging in his claws and squirming out of her arms.

"Brat." But when he rubbed up against her legs again, she smiled and got his breakfast out to the sound of ecstatic purrs.

"Okay, Max, pretend you're Harry. Here goes. 'Hi Harry.'" No, no. "Good morning, Harry." She clenched her teeth. "Wanna see more breast, Harry? Well why don't you just ask your girlfriend when she comes on Wednesday. And I do mean *comes,* you unfeeling two-timer. Yeah, that's right, I called you a two-timer. One phone call and—bam—that's the end of Jaimie. Well, let me tell you something. Talk about mistakes. The mistake was feeling sorry for you, for thinking you were a decent guy, for thinking that . . ."

She stared at the top of Max's head while he chowed down.

"So, what do you think? Too much bitterness?" She answered her own questions. "Yeah. Way too much. It's not Harry's fault that he's still in love with her. She is his ex-girlfriend. And I'm not even a friend." She raised her eyebrows in surprised self-discovery. "Apparently, I'm a slut."

No, she wasn't. She was a woman who was wildly attracted to a man who was, apparently, wildly attracted to her. No bad guys. Just victims. "Poor us," she said, realizing Harry probably felt as bad or worse than she did. He'd better.

Harry was as jumpy as a rabbit in a snake hole. Every time someone walked by his office, he tensed. What the hell was he going to say to Jaimie? This is why he never, ever should have kissed her, never mind stripped naked and pulled her onto his dick and . . . God what the hell had he been thinking of? Because there was always a morning after and that almost always sucked.

If only Anne hadn't called. If only she'd just leave him alone and let him forget her. He'd been fine—or at least could see a day when he would be fine—when she'd started calling. *I miss you.*

And he'd said he'd missed her. But he hadn't. Not really. Sure, in the beginning he'd felt betrayed, as if her sharp little claws had ripped his heart out, but he knew even in the beginning he was being unfair. One of the things he'd loved about Anne was her ability to know her limits. When he suggested they get married, Anne was truly perplexed by the idea. Why get married? Why ruin a perfectly wonderful thing? People get married to have children, she'd said, and God knew better than to allow her to be a mother.

"I don't have a maternal bone in my body, Harry, and you know it. I never played with dolls and when my dog died, I really didn't care. I cried because I think my mother expected me to. I'm missing that particular gene, Harry."

That had been fine, for a while. Harry had known, deep in his gut, he wanted a home and family. Someday. He was holding out hope the biological clock women were always talking about would go off in Anne one day and she'd wake up and want to be a mother. Whenever he'd gotten depressed, Anne couldn't take it. "I'm not a nurturer, Harry. You know that. I can't give you what you need." She forgot to tell him she was already thinking about having an affair with Bob Porter.

No, Harry hadn't missed Anne, he'd missed their life together, their long, heated but intelligent talks about New York politics. The sex was good and fairly frequent. She was as low maintenance a woman as a guy could want. They both worked long and irregular hours and neither felt the need to give an accounting of where they'd been. They saw each other in the newsroom more than they did at home. It was a neat, satisfying life, and would have continued for God knew how long until Harry's world crashed in around him.

Now, for some reason, she was calling sounding all girly and breathy and telling him she missed him. Something was terribly wrong with that.

Harry picked up that day's edition in an attempt to refocus his thoughts. He knew the instant she walked in, her hair back in its ponytail, wearing an ugly brown sweater she seemed particularly fond of that covered her down to below her lovely behind. She walked straight to her desk and flicked on her computer without glancing in his direction.

So that's how she was going to play this. He waited for ten minutes, hardly taking his eyes off her even when he got a call from the president of the Chamber of Commerce inviting him to the next Business Breakfast. She studied the story in front of her, her fingers flying over the keys when she changed something, her movements quick and efficient. She sat straight, her back never touching the chair, perfect posture that seemed at odds with her frumpy attire. She didn't look at all like that woman who sat on his leather couch all loose and languid and naked and luscious. He was giving himself a hard-on thinking about it, and he grimaced. He was going to have to do something about her, he just wished to hell he knew what.

"McLane."

Jaimie took a deep breath. "Here goes nothing," she said to herself, shooting Nathan a look to see if he was watching. No one knew what had happened between her and Harry and no one ever would. Nathan glanced up then went back to editing the local section. He didn't suspect. Of course he didn't. Why would he or anyone else? For all they knew, she still didn't like him, was still "making friends" for the sake of the staff.

She walked in the door, surprised to see Harry staring at a map of Nortown tacked to the back wall that Paul had framed years ago. "What's up?"

"I'd like for you to show me something," he said, his back toward her as he seemingly stared at the map. His crutches were tucked beneath his arms and his hip was cocked to one side.

"That's not all that accurate anymore," she said, walking up to him.

In one fluid motion, he took her by the shoulders, pressed her up against the wall, and kissed her, deep and long. Amazing how well he could maneuver with those crutches, she thought, before getting lost in his kiss.

"Uh-oh," he said against her lips. "I made another mistake." His office door was open, but they were against the wall next to it, completely hidden from view should anyone walk by. Now, if anyone happened to walk into his office, that was a different story. But it was early, the newsroom practically empty, and Jaimie couldn't help but be happy. She smiled and so did he, so when he went to kiss her again, their teeth met instead of their lips. "I keep making the same mistake, over and over."

"And over," she said, pulling him closer, opening her mouth, loving the feel of his tongue against hers. It was wet, noisy, and wonderful.

"You taste good," he said, and Jaimie couldn't believe what he was doing.

"Harry." He must have sensed the slight bit of question in that word.

"I thought this would smooth things over. You know, make this less awkward."

"Mmmm," she said, kissing him. "I think it worked."

Someone walked by and he eased away from her. He reached out and touched her lower lip, the oddest smile on his face. "You have a nice face, McLane," he said, and she grinned.

"You're not so bad yourself."

"How about dinner Saturday?"

Jaimie's eyes widened. "A real date? No clandestine meeting in the morgue?" she said, referring to the dank room where the newspaper's old clippings were still kept.

He waggled his eyebrows. "That actually sounds intriguing."

"I bet." She watched him as he made his way to his desk and sat down, looking all boss-like and definitely cooling her ardor. What the hell was she doing kissing her boss behind his office door?

Getting all goofy, that's what.

His extension rang and he held a finger up, a gesture she found slightly unnerving: *Just wait a minute, honey, while I take this call. You go on now and make yourself pretty for me, hmmm?*

Maybe it wasn't fair, but that's what Jaimie felt like, standing there with beard burn on her cheeks waiting for him to get off the phone. Which reminded her immediately of another phone call, another interruption—another woman. A few kisses and she'd forgotten all about that faceless woman, the one he'd said he missed, too.

When he hung up, she said, "On second thought, maybe dating wouldn't be a great idea."

He stiffened slightly and Jaimie wasn't sure if it was because of her question or because he'd just felt a stab of pain in his leg. "Why?"

"There's the whole boss thing. And the ex-girlfriend thing. I don't know." She searched his face to gauge his feelings, but saw nothing to tell her what he was thinking. She took a deep breath, slightly surprised to realize what she was about to say. "Friday was a situation born of circumstances. Right? It wasn't a mistake, per se, but something that just happened. But if we date, and make it a conscious thing, a planned thing, then don't you think it will all get a little messy?"

"If you don't want to go out with me, just say so."

"It's not that. You know this isn't cut-and-dry. You have issues."

"Issues," he said softly.

"You know. Ex-girlfriend issues. She is coming to visit you, is she not?"

He relaxed slightly. "That's over."

"It didn't sound over. It didn't sound close to being over." She tilted her head to see if he was getting what she was saying. "I like you. You're good looking, you can play ball. You're a decent kisser."

"But?"

"I think your heart is somewhere else right now." She wanted him to deny it, but she watched as he sagged imperceptibly back into his chair. Damn, she'd been hoping she was wrong.

"It was just a date, McLane. Not a marriage proposal."

Jaimie narrowed her eyes. "No shit, Sherlock. I *hate* when men assume women have commitment on their minds even before the first date. I just wanted to be certain, before I *commit* to going out with you *one* time, that you're not sitting there wishing I was someone else. I'm going back to work now."

"Fine."

"Fine," she shot back, just to get the last word in. She was steaming as she sat down at her desk.

"What happened in there?" Nathan asked, a worried look in his eyes.

"Don't worry, we weren't talking about anything important. Just suffice it to say that I'm done "making friends" with Mr. Crandall."

That night, the anger Jaimie had felt was long gone, replaced by an uncharacteristic melancholy. Harry had left the office hours ago without a word of good-bye. He'd taken a taxi and part of her wondered why he hadn't thought of that days ago. It would have avoided this entire mess. His silent departure wasn't any different from any other night before, but for some reason this night it hurt. And because of that, she knew for certain she'd made the right decision to not go out with him. What if they had gone out and what if she'd fallen in love with him and what if he really didn't care about her and then what? She'd be pining after him in some sort of pathetic, unrequited-love scenario. She'd be feeling like she was now, sad and unaccountably lonely.

"I loved a man once, a long time ago. Oh, the

laughter we shared. But that was a long time ago."
Little girl: "Is he the reason you never married, Auntie?" Close-up on old hag: "He's the reason I never looked at another man."

The paper was wrapped up and all Jaimie had to do was straighten out her desk and leave. And go home to her cat. A cat that never even acknowledged her presence unless she had a pouch of Meow Mix in her hand.

With a sigh, she decided to get last call at Duffy's before heading home. Nathan and a handful of reporters were already down there, probably bitching about work. Maybe about her. She'd been in a foul mood and even yelled at the new cop reporter for spelling a sergeant's name wrong. The kid was an arrogant little prick anyway, so Jaimie didn't feel all that bad about it. She disliked the two new reporters Harry hired, both kids who should be thanking their lucky stars to have a job at a daily instead of walking around with their noses up in the air. Columbia snobs. They could write, but they didn't know diddly about being a reporter, about building relationships with their sources.

When she walked out of the air-conditioned building, Jaimie was buffeted by warm, humid air. She pulled off her sweater and dumped it in her car before heading to Duffy's, which was only two doors down from the paper's main entrance. It was crowded, with nearly every bar stool and booth filled. To the right, the young cops hung out wearing their off-duty uniform of cargo pants and T-shirts. To the right, the *Nortown Journal* staff sat in three booths yammering away. She spotted Lt. Jerry Brandt sitting by himself in the cops' section looking miserable so she decided to say hello. He was a friend and one of the best sources she had on the police department, and so she knew when he had that look on his face something wasn't going well.

"Jerry," she said, sliding onto the bar stool next to him. He gave her a scowl that would have made the young cops next to her quake, but she just laughed. "Nice try," she said, and motioned for Roger to get her a Heineken. Someday she ought to, just for fun, order a glass of white wine just to see Roger's expression. "So, what are you all gloomy about?"

"Fuckin' chief getting' on my case," he muttered low so no one else could hear.

"He's an egotistical jerk who's retiring in a year. Keep saying that, over and over, just one year, just one year."

"I guess." Jerry stared into his beer.

"What's he riding you about now?"

"The Tate case, what else. Eight months nearly gone and we don't have squat and he's blaming me. Saying the investigation was shoddy. I don't know where else to look. For all we know it could have been some creep passing through town. No one saw anyone. And there's other stuff, too."

Jaimie was only half listening, because across the bar a burst of laughter came up from the Nortown reporters, and in the middle, entertaining the troops, were Harry and Ted. Harry must have gone home to change because he was dressed in a black golf shirt and jeans, and his hair, always perfectly combed, was slightly mussed. And then, her stomach clenched because she realized just why his hair was messy and who'd been doing the messing. Carly Strickland sat next to him, a snake in the middle of oblivious mice. Jaimie's face flushed with humiliation. Just that morning he'd been kissing her, and tonight, ten hours later, another woman was tousling his hair, his silky, thick hair. Sure, she'd told him they shouldn't go out but that didn't mean he had to go out that day and get a replacement. Maybe he'd just wanted sex.

"So, I don't know what's up," she heard Jerry say.

"I'm sorry, what Jer?"

"The kid. I was talking about the kid and the puppy. That something's weird about the whole thing but I just can't put my finger on it."

Jaimie forced herself to focus on Jerry even though her face was still burning. "I'm working on a follow-up and . . . What the fuck." She was kissing him. Right in the middle of Duffy's. Right in front of her and he was smiling. The bastard.

"What?"

"Oh. Nothing." Bastard. "I interviewed the mom again. She's a strange bird."

"Why do you say that?"

Jaimie shrugged. "I don't know, she seemed distracted and vague when we talked about Joshua. She wasn't even sure where she'd put his stuff. Isn't that kind of weird?"

"Maybe she was on something."

"I don't think so. I just got this feeling she wasn't all that broken up about him being gone. Maybe I'm wrong."

Jerry chuckled. "You think the mom killed him and the puppy?"

"No."

"She has a rock-solid alibi."

"I don't think she did it. I thought it was strange that she didn't have a single picture of the kid except for in the attic. You have to admit that's strange."

"Yup and nope."

Jaimie rolled her eyes.

"Okay. You already know the kid wasn't the angel that everyone said he was. He'd had some rough early years."

"I know about the father."

Jerry nodded. "Well, I think the father fucked him up real good. Screwed him up, you know what I mean? The kid wasn't entirely normal."

"You have a motive?" she asked.

Jerry withdrew a little as if realizing he was not talking to an old friend but a reporter. "This is off the record, right?"

"Deep background."

And then he gave her nothing because Jaimie believed he had nothing to give. "Could be. But anytime a kid gets killed, you're not dealing with a normal motive."

"He wasn't sexually assaulted. He wasn't, was he?" And suddenly Jaimie thought maybe he had been and for whatever reason, the police hadn't released that information.

"No. He wasn't." Seeing Jaimie's skepticism, he stressed, "He wasn't. And that's the thing that makes this case so difficult. Someone killed this kid because they wanted him dead. They knocked him in the head, killed his puppy, and left. That stuff just doesn't happen to little kids."

"Maybe mom hired a hit man."

"Believe it or not, I checked that out. Couldn't find a damn thing. Which is why my prick of a boss is giving me a hard time. I was working on another lead, but the chief said I was nuts. Sorry, Jaimie, but he laid into me right before the shift ended. I'm lousy company tonight."

"We all have boss problems," Jaimie said, finally allowing herself to look over to where Harry sat with Carly. "I'll talk to you later, Jer. And don't worry, nothing we said will go anywhere." She grinned. "Unless I find the killer before you do."

"Then I don't have a worry in the world."

* * *

Harry didn't see her coming. If he had, he would have disengaged Carly's hand from his thigh. No one, ever, had come on to him as strongly as the *Day's* assistant editor was. He could get laid tonight, and maybe every night this week, if he wanted to. Of course, he wanted to, but just not with the human tentacle sitting next to him. He didn't want to embarrass the woman, but if she messed up his hair one more time, he just might tell her to go away.

"Hi, guys."

He looked up and there she was, the lights from the bar putting her head in backlight, making that red hair of hers glow. She was smiling, but he saw her eyes dart to his thigh, to that hand on his thigh, and her smile became brittle. Ted and Sharon sat at the same table, and they looked as uncomfortable as he felt.

"Hello, Jaimie. Just getting out now?" Carly asked, raising a delicate wrist so she could look at her watch.

"Actually, I was sitting across the bar talking to an old friend. I've been here for quite a while," she said, then gave Harry a pointed look that said: *I saw everything, you piece of shit.* "I've never seen you here before. Don't you usually hang out in New London?"

"Usually," she said, with a mysterious smile. At least Harry thought she was trying to be mysterious.

"Sit down. I'll scootch over," Sharon said, jerking over toward Ted who gallantly tried to press his large body even closer to the wall. "There's room, see?" Sharon patted the ten inches of booth she'd managed to expose.

Jaimie stared at the sliver of seat, then surprised him by sitting down, he figured just to torment him.

"So," she said with false cheerfulness. "Is this a date?"

Harry felt his cheeks heat, and Jaimie's smile grew, as

if she were enjoying his discomfort. He did not want to be sitting next to this woman when he was across from the woman he really wanted. Jaimie looked . . . lovely. Her cheeks were slightly flushed, her eyes burning with a heat Harry didn't want to interpret. She wore a sleeveless shirt, exposing her nice shoulders, the same ones he'd kissed just a few days ago. She'd piled her hair on top of her head, but a few slippery strands fell to her neck, her wonderfully sensitive, pale neck.

"Does Peter know about this Carly? I don't know if he'd like you fraternizing with the enemy."

"Honestly, Jaimie, Peter doesn't even think of the *Nortown Journal* as competition." She turned to Harry and patted him playfully on the arm. "No offense."

"Peter might be in for a surprise," Harry said, knowing he had nothing to back up his statement. The *Journal* was on the verge of bankruptcy, one of the owners was threatening to turn it into a shopper, he was wondering if he should quit the place, and here he was getting his feathers ruffled because the competition didn't take the *Journal* seriously.

"We've beaten you on every major story in the last six months," Jaimie said, and he wanted to give her a smile.

"Every *Nortown* story," Carly said with a deprecating laugh, as if Nortown weren't worthy of the ink it took to print the paper. "We only have one reporter covering Nortown. But I'll let you in on a little secret. Peter's opening a bureau here next year. He'll need an editor to run it. Maybe you should apply? I'll warn you, though, I've already got the inside track on the job." Carly laughed and Harry couldn't help but think she was a nasty little piece.

"Gee, Carly, I don't think Peter would have wanted us to have a year's heads-up on his plans. Or is that why you're here?" Jaimie said good-naturedly, but something about her eyes told Harry she was nervous about the *Day's* plans. Hell, she ought to be nervous. Even if he got the paper out of its jam this year, if the *Day* did open a bureau, that meant the advertising dollars would be split. He wouldn't blame the small businesses that supported the paper if they advertised in the *Day*. It was a bigger paper with wider circulation.

Carly's eyes glittered. "It's no secret. Harry already knew."

Harry pushed back slightly in the bench, a futile attempt to avoid the daggers shooting from Jaimie's eyes. "Paul told me. He didn't think it was something the rank and file should know about yet."

"Rank and file." Jaimie swallowed. "When were you planning to tell the rest of us serfs?"

"Uh-oh. Didn't mean to cause a rift in the happy family," Carly said, practically giddy.

"Guys, let's not talk about business, huh?" That from Sharon, who was looking extremely uncomfortable. "We have some news. Want to hear it?"

She gave Ted a look and Jaimie squealed. "You're pregnant."

"Jaimie," Sharon said with exasperation.

"I'm right, aren't I? You are?"

"Yes," she said begrudgingly, her announcement ruined by her friend.

And talk turned to babies and marriage and Ted going out to buy a shotgun if it was a girl to keep the teenage boys away. The entire conversation left Harry feeling slightly depressed. Hell, the entire night left him feeling majorly depressed. He felt rotten sitting across from Jaimie, wanted to be alone with her, wanted her naked in his bed, wanted her looking at him the way Sharon looked at Ted. No woman had ever looked at him like that, not even Anne.

"We should get going," Sharon said finally. Jaimie looked at her watch, a Timex with a frayed nylon band, and slid out of the bench.

"I think I'll call it a night too," Jaimie said, trying valiantly not to sound as bitchy as she felt.

"That just leaves us two," Carly said, snaking a hand up to rest on Harry's shoulder. Jaimie tried not to notice.

"Why don't you just put your hand on his crotch now and get it over with?" she muttered, and Sharon nearly choked. "God, did I say it that loud?"

"I don't think they heard it, but I did," Sharon said, trying hard not to dissolve into laughter.

"I've got to get going, too, Carly." Harry gave her a warm smile. "Sorry. Busy day tomorrow planning our method of defense."

Mr. Charming to the end, Jaimie thought, feeling sick again about not being part of the paper's inner circle. "See you guys later," she said, and moved to the exit as quickly as she could given that the way was blocked by oblivious people having fun.

"Jaimie, wait. I want to talk to you."

She stopped, let out a puff of air and spun around. "What?"

"Paul and I thought that if you knew what was happening that you wouldn't be able to not tell the others."

"I see."

"You do seem to have a problem distinguishing between employees and friends."

She actually saw red spots in front of her eyes. "You're kidding, right? Mr. Let's Go Out Saturday is criticizing me about crossing lines? Mr. Kiss Her in the Office? Mr. . . ."

He held his hand up. "Okay. Point made."

"I haven't even begun to make my point," she said angrily.

At that moment, Carly walked by. "Good night," she said, and Jaimie noticed that Harry's eyes followed her progress down the street. Harry firmly took her arm and tried to pull her along with him, failing clumsily because of the crutches and almost pushing both of them to the ground. "Just follow me," he growled, and led her around the corner of the building so they wouldn't be interrupted again. Jaimie went only because she wanted to yell at him some more.

"I practically ran this paper for five years and I did a pretty damn good job of it with the resources I had. Fine. Maybe I should have been tougher on some people, but . . ."

"Stop."

"I don't want to stop. I want to tell you how wrong you were to exclude me about something that's going to affect my staff. We should be planning how to deal with the competition, we should be developing a strategy."

"We are," he said softly and with a look that almost seemed pitying.

"Oh."

"For what it's worth, I think you've made a case for your input."

Jaimie knew her face was red, knew her eyes were betraying just how close she was to angry, hurt tears. "Don't throw me any bones."

"I'm not. I think Paul was worried that you'd want to solve all the paper's problems by yourself. That's my job. But you need to know what's going on editorially. I'll convince Paul to let you in on our meetings."

Jaimie looked at him uncertainly, trying to gauge whether he was being sincere or simply placating a nearly hysterical woman. She was angry about being left out of the meetings, but Jaimie wasn't blind to the fact she was also angry Harry had been sitting in a bar next to another woman. He was trying to be fair and the least she could do was meet him half way.

"All right. I'm sorry I got so angry. It's just that I feel as if I've been demoted."

"You were right to be angry."

"Stop being so understanding. It's irritating."

Harry let out a chuckle. "Now about Saturday night."

"Go out with Carly. Or better yet, your ex."

"I want to go out with you. Anne will be here one day. God knows why, but she's coming for a visit. When she's gone, she's gone. And I'm pretty sure I'll be free on Saturday."

Jaimie couldn't help herself. "What about Carly?"

He shrugged. "I don't like her. Too clingy." And he mimicked a shudder.

"I still don't think it's a good idea."

"Why?" he asked, moving slightly closer.

"You're my boss. The boss thing is a problem."

"Is it?" He moved closer still, his chest touching her right shoulder.

"Yes." But she didn't move away even though that voice of reason in her head was screaming for her to say goodnight.

"I know you're right. But you have such nice shoulders."

"I thought it was my breasts you were so entranced with," she said with a little smile.

"Nope. The shoulders." And he pressed his warm lips against her shoulder. For some reason, that made her head sort of flop over, exposing her neck to his mouth. "And the neck."

"Harry."

"No, no, you don't. Don't 'Harry' me. Please don't," he said, pretending to beg. "This jaw bone ain't so bad."

"Such language for a journalist."

"And the lips."

When he finally kissed her, Jaimie thought she just might melt. He didn't seem to kiss any differently from any other guy she'd ever dated. Lip to lip, tongue moving inside. But it was different. The subtlest movement of his mouth made her want to tear his clothes off and ravage him. With simple kisses, he had her panting, pressing closer, loving the feel of his erection, wishing they were in a bed, not standing on a sidewalk. She didn't know what it was, but Harry could arouse her with something as simple as a lip to a shoulder. Maybe they could separate work from this. Because this, this was wonderful.

He pulled away and shook his head, looking at her as if all this kissing was her doing. "Saturday?"

She put her hands over her face and looked through her fingers. "One date?"

"Maybe more if it works out."

"If I don't kill you."

"If *I* don't kill *you.*"

Jaimie smiled. "Have you ever dated someone at work before?"

He withdrew, and his eyes flickered. "Anne and I worked together."

"She was a staffer for the *Times?*" Jaimie asked, obviously impressed. Or was that jealousy. "How old is she?"

Be old, please be old.

"She's twenty-eight now, but she was twenty-four when she started. She's an incredible reporter."

Jaimie begrudgingly had to admit she was impressed. She was probably gorgeous, too. And funny. And coming back to get her man.

Chapter 11

Anne Levine pulled onto Concord Street and into a small parking lot marked with a dirty, chipped sign that said, "*Nortown Journal* visitor parking." The dirt lot held three cars, one of which looked abandoned. "What a piece of shit," she said, looking up at the old building.

She shut off the engine of her rental car, glad to be done with the three-hour drive. Driving through Connecticut was a nightmare, only made worse when the destination was so unappealing. She stretched, feeling her legs and arms quiver, and grimaced slightly at the sharp twinge in her side. It was morbidly hot and humid, so she moved quickly to the front of the building, grateful for the blast of cold air when she entered.

A sign that looked like it had been painted in the 1950s directed her to the newsroom, pointing to a long flight of stairs, straight up, no landings in sight. Along the wall were framed copies of the paper, all with glaring banner headlines: Pearl Harbor Bombed, Eisenhower Elected, Kennedy Shot. They ended with Nixon Resigns. "Guess nothing important happened in the past thirty years," she muttered. Or maybe that great headline writer croaked.

At the top of the stairs, she turned right into a huge room, an old-fashioned newsroom that still had the old production tables up at one end.

"Can I help you?" a youngish woman asked.

Anne looked around for Harry. "I'm here to see Harry Crandall. Anne Levine."

Jaimie felt the back of her neck prickle when she heard those words and she couldn't stop her heart from pounding about ten times faster. Here was the famous Anne Levine, the woman who had loved Harry, who had seen him completely naked, who had probably done all kinds of wonderfully nasty things with his body.

From the corner of her eye Jaimie watched her, a smart navy blue suit, elegant, casual, and an expensive-looking briefcase tucked under one arm. Jaimie never could master that casual elegance that some women found so easy. She looked down at her big sweater and gave a thought or two dozen thoughts about taking it off. But it was so cold in the newsroom, her nose felt like ice and her fingertips were numb. And what did she care anyway that she looked frumpy. Harry knew what she looked like underneath and had let her know he liked what he saw. But that was before *she* arrived, looking like an ad for Ann Taylor.

Anne knocked on the door and Jaimie, knowing her back would be to the girlfriend, looked over and got a quick snapshot of her profile. Her nose was too big for her face, she decided. Yup, too big. Big nose. Small breasts.

"Jaimie," Kath whispered. "Who's that?"

Jaimie glanced over to the office, noting with a small amount of disappointment the blinds were down blocking any view of what was happening in there. Would he greet her with a kiss, pull her close and tell her how much he'd missed her? Or would he stay behind his desk, give her a cold hello, cross his arms over his chest and stare at her until she cried. Jaimie knew he could do that; he'd almost done it to her. Or maybe he would strip her naked, throw her down on the couch, and make savage love to her.

"Jaimie," came Kath's impatient whisper. Jaimie went over to Kath's desk.

"It's his ex."

"Oh. Is she looking for a job?"

Jaimie rolled her eyes. "For God's sakes, Kath, your job is safe, okay?" Jaimie looked again toward the office and jerked back in surprise. From this vantage point, she could see through a crack in the blinds into Harry's office, could see them hugging, could see the ex dab at her eyes. She nodded toward the office so Kath would look. "He asked me out for Saturday. I don't think we'll be going. What do you think?"

"He asked you out?" she asked, completely affronted Jaimie hadn't told her.

"But clearly things have changed."

"When did this happen?"

Jaimie gritted her teeth. "It doesn't matter, we're not going."

"He asked you out and you didn't tell me?"

"I would have. I was going to wait to see what happened with the ex. I've got a feeling she's not an ex anymore."

The two women stared through that small crack and watched as Harry kissed the ex. "Oh. I see what you mean."

The two broke apart and Jaimie and Kath could no longer spy on the couple.

"Do you really like him?" Kath asked cautiously.

"I was doing it for the good of the paper," Jaimie said.

"You know it would have been a bad idea anyway.

Remember what happened to Brian and me? It got a little ugly."

"A little? That was World War Three."

Kath laughed. "I thought you said you didn't like Harry."

"He was kind of growing on me. I think I got blinded by his ability to play shortstop. Anyway, he's too alpha for me. You know I like big ol' puppy dogs."

Kath pulled a face. "You do not. You date puppy dogs, then you step on them."

Jaimie let out a small laugh, then sighed. "It could have been wonderful. He's a very good kisser."

"You kissed him. All this was happening and you didn't tell me?"

"It was awkward. You know, with him being our boss. I wasn't even sure it was a good idea to go out with him at all. Strike that. I thought it was a good idea, just not a smart one. He's got that zing thing, you know?"

"Oh, Jaimie," Kath said, completely commiserating with her friend. "The zing thing is so hard to find."

"Yep. Zing a ling a ling." She shrugged. "Oh well."

"Not oh well. That only happens maybe two or three times in a woman's lifetime. A guy touches and you practically orgasm. You can't give up the zing that easily."

"I can. Anyway, it's not up to me. He's got issues."

"And zing."

"Yeah," Jaimie said, sounding depressed. "He does have that."

"Maybe she'll just go away and that will be that and you can get your zing back."

Jaimie laughed and gave her friend a little hug. "You need a man," she said.

"No. I need some zing."

The two laughed, and Jaimie went back to her desk

and tried not to listen for the door to open, tried not to think about the one and only man who'd ever made her feel so incredibly sexy was being stolen right out from under her nose.

At the knock of the door, Harry steeled himself. She let herself in.

"Hey, Harry."

"Anne."

"It's a shitbox," she said, and sat down in front of his desk, holding her briefcase on her lap.

He laughed. If there was one thing he'd missed about Anne, it was her blunt honesty. "Yeah. I thought so too when I took the job, but it's kind of growing on me. It's got that *His Girl Friday* appeal."

"Looks like it got caught in a time warp, that's for sure."

Harry looked at Anne, surprised he didn't feel more. He was glad to see her, sure. Like seeing an old friend. He'd been worried about his reaction, that he might feel that sucker-punch-blow to his gut when he saw her. But he hadn't. He'd felt a tiny twinge of longing, that's all. She was beautiful and put-together, and she stuck out like a sore thumb here. Just like he did when he'd started. He'd lost most of his suits, and these days came to work in a jacket, khakis, and no tie. Her hair was cut short, her makeup perfect, her nails manicured, her face flawless. Except for those dark circles; they were new. "So, Harry. I bet you're wondering what the hell I'm doing here in the middle of the week when I should be working." She took a deep breath, and for an instant, looked so uncertain, so vulnerable, Harry felt a frisson of worry.

"Okay. So." She nodded a couple of times. "I'm pregnant." And Anne, who never cried, who showed about as much emotion as a rock in times of crisis, dropped the briefcase, exposing a small mound at her midriff, buried her head in her hands and started sobbing copiously.

Harry immediately stood, grabbed his crutches, made his way over to her, and pulled her up for a hug, startled by the obstruction there.

"Shit. Sorry. Shit," she said, viciously wiping away the tears. "I meant to come in here and just tell you and then go. But shit. It's the hormones. The freakin' things are driving me insane."

"I've heard that can be a problem. It's Bob Porter's?"

"I screwed up. Oh, what happened to your leg?" she asked, looking down at his cast, then immediately losing interest. "The bastard said he loved me and now that I'm pregnant, he won't leave his wife and I end up looking like some, some pathetic . . . girl. I mean, I'm an intelligent woman. Tough. I know better than to fall for some guy who's married, for God's sakes. And get pregnant. Can you believe it? I always thought only idiots got pregnant by mistake. I don't know what I was thinking." She was still in his arms, still crying a little, but now they were angry tears.

"What are you going to do?" Harry stepped back and she sat back down and blew her nose.

"I always thought that if something like this happened, I'd just get an abortion. Right?" She looked at him beseechingly. "But I can't," she said, incredulously. "I can't do it. It's the strangest thing, like some alien has invaded my body and is turning me into some kind of a, a . . ."

"Human?" Harry asked, humor in his voice.

"Yeah. And so I'm going to be this single woman, knocked up by her boss." She stopped and took a deep breath to regain her composure. "No one knows. Except for Bob, the bastard."

"What about your parents?"

She shook her head. "I just can't tell them yet. They have this image of me. Miss Perfect. And now. Harry, I fucked up so badly. I don't know what to do or where to go and so that's why I'm here."

"Why?"

"Because you're the only friend I have in the whole world. I realized that when it happened. I didn't have a soul I could tell. No one. I'm not friendly, I know that, but to realize that you don't have a single friend, no one to turn to except the one guy who was ever nice to you and who you screwed over. I wouldn't blame you if you threw me out."

"Anne. Stop being so self-deprecating. It's annoying and completely out of character."

She threw her hands out to her sides. "See what I mean. See what I've become?"

Harry chuckled. "I don't know what to tell you. I'll help you any way I can, but it'll be tough with you in New York and me here. And frankly, Anne, I'm not the good friend you seem to think I am. You left me, just like that old song says, just when I needed you most. Now you come in here and want me to help you. I don't think so."

Anne twisted the tissue in her hands. Harry knew if she'd done it in anger, he would have been able to throw her out then and there. Like he should, if he still had any balls. But she twisted that tissue hard and the look on her face was so devastated, so unlike Anne, he felt himself soften toward her.

"What do you expect from me?"

"I took a leave of absence from work as soon as I started to show. Everyone would have known whose baby it is and neither he nor I want to face that. Bob agreed it was best. I'm not running away, I'm preserving my career. And his, I suppose. I subletted our apartment."

"Your apartment."

Twist, twist. "Right. I thought I could stay with . . ."

"No. I can't do that right now."

She took a couple of shallow breaths. "Why not?"

He gave her a look of incredulity. "You're kidding, right? You want to move in with me, after what happened to us?"

"I'll pay half your rent. I'm already seven months pregnant. It'll only be for two months."

"No."

Don't look into her eyes, don't let her get to you, don't soften. Keep your balls intact.

"I don't have any other place to go." Her eyes—she always did have big beautiful brown eyes—filled with tears. Anne was not the kind of woman who used tears to manipulate a man. In fact, Anne was not the type of woman to ask for help. She must be scared out of her mind, he realized. She must be desperately afraid. And lonely. He knew what that felt like, knew exactly what she was feeling.

"I know I hurt you, Harry, and I know I don't deserve your friendship." She closed her eyes and he watched her gather strength from some place. "I'm sorry. I'll just go." When she stood, she looked more herself, but when he looked down at her hands, they were shaking, and then he saw that damned stomach of hers, and he felt miserable.

He didn't know what was worse, being mean enough to send her away or a big enough wimp to let her stay. She turned to leave and he heard her name come out of his mouth even before he'd fully decided what to do. "Anne."

"Yes?" No triumph in that word, nothing disingenuous.

"Okay. Sure. You can stay. But as a friend. I have a life here. I know you think it's shitty, but I'm starting to like it. And I have a date on Saturday and I'm planning to go out on it."

She gave him a tremulous smile. "Thanks, Harry."

"And I'm not going to be your birthing coach or whatever the hell it's called." *There, he still had one ball left, though it was dangling precariously.*

"Okay."

Harry walked out with Anne and he looked at Jaimie who stared at her computer screen as if she was reading the most fascinating story she'd ever read and he felt like an even bigger prick. He could just hear himself telling her his ex-girlfriend was moving back in with him but it was all innocent. Really. We're just friends. Yup, things were going to work out just dandy.

His life had just gotten a few degrees lousier.

Chapter 12

Harry never came back to work. Not that she was going to let it bother her. After all, what had they shared other than a couple of very nice kisses and some incredible sex? Okay, she liked him. A lot. And he was good looking.

And could play baseball.

And he was most likely naked in bed with his formerly ex-girlfriend.

Jaimie banged out some headlines and sent the story to pagination with hard snaps on her keyboard.

"Trying to kill it?" Natc asked.

She gave him a quick, insincere smile. "Just having an off day." She looked around the newsroom, then up at the clock. It was nearly ten o'clock and three reporters had yet to return from covering their meetings, exciting stuff about school budgets, zoning board decisions, and new sidewalks on Main Street. The front page sucked, the local section was worse.

Ryan Fletcher, the new cop reporter, walked in, sprawled into his chair and began flipping casually through his notebook.

"Hey, Fletcher, got anything I can put on the front page?"

He looked up and grinned. "Some guy rode his riding mower into a lake and drowned."

Jaimie burst out laughing. It wasn't funny, of course, but reporters laughed at horrible stuff all the time so it wouldn't be so horrible. "Interesting, but not page one, I'm afraid. Was he a politician?"

"Nope. Just some guy out mowing his lawn. Rescue thinks he had a heart attack first. I don't have anything else, just a couple small stories and the beat."

Damn. Was she really going to have to put the city's plans for new sidewalks on page one? One by one, the reporters returned, all with mediocre, space-filling crap. And meanwhile, Harry was screwing Anne. Maybe she should put that on page one.

"Ex Returns for Mind-Blowing Sex"

A New York Times reporter and ex-girlfriend of the Nortown Journal managing editor got together last night for a spark-filled reunion, leaving new love-interest Jaimie I-only-had-sex-once-in-four-years McLane in the lurch.

"I want to go home," she said, knowing she sounded pathetic.

"Why don't you? I can handle the rest," Nate said.

Jaimie narrowed her eyes. In all the years they'd worked together, Nate had never volunteered to put the paper to bed—not even when she'd been half-dead with the flu. "Why are you being so nice?" And Jaimie knew by the look in his face he was going to tell her something she wasn't going to like at all.

"I was going to wait until tomorrow, but I suppose I can tell you now. You're already in a bad mood." He smiled, uncharacteristically happy, and Jaimie felt dread start pounding in her stomach. "I got a new job. Communications Director for Connecticut College. They want me to start October one."

"You bum," she said, but she smiled because she was

happy for Nate. "That's great, Nate. Wow. Communications Director."

"Yeah." He was grinning from ear to ear unable to hold in his complete happiness. "Better money. Better hours. More stability. Charlotte's more excited than I am." As if realizing he was making Jaimie even more depressed, he stopped gushing. "You'll be able to find someone, right?"

"Sure. If worse comes to worse, Harry can help out for a while." Knowing Harry, he probably had a stack of resumes ready to fill the position, all eager young co-eds with their lips already pursed to kiss his ass. "It's no problem, really." She stood up and gave Nate a hug. "Congratulations. Wow."

"So, are you going to leave? I really don't mind finishing up here. It will help with the guilt factor and all."

"Nah. I'll stay. What am I going to do anyway? Go down to Duffy's? Go home and play with my cat?" Nate smiled and went back to work, but Jaimie's mood just got darker. He was moving on, up and out, and she was still here, editing zoning board meeting stories, going home to a cat, eating Healthy Choice meals for supper at her desk.

While Harry was screwing his ex.

Her phone rang and Jaimie scowled at it before picking up. Probably some Nortown resident calling to complain about paper delivery. It didn't matter how many times she told the receptionist not to forward those calls to her, sometimes the complainers insisted they talk to the editor and she'd have to listen to some crazy person yelling that they wanted her to deliver their paper in person.

"Jaimie McLane."

"Jaimie, it's me." Jaimie immediately recognized Lt. Jerry Brandt. "You didn't get this from me. Talk to a Geoffrey Fox. Ask him about Joshua." He hung up. And just like that, Jaimie's blood began to sing and the black cloud that had been hovering over her head since the casually elegant Anne Levine walked into the room began to dissipate.

On the phone the next day, Geoffrey Fox was exceedingly reluctant to talk to Jaimie. She hoped the guy would soften up when she met him in person. Mr. Fox lived four houses down from Joshua Tate in a small ranch kept meticulously. The lawn was lushly green with perfectly parallel mower marks still visible and not a footstep in sight, leaving Jaimie to wonder if the guy hovered above his lawnmower when he cut the grass. Bushes were precisely trimmed boxes and the flowers—six rows of six of them—were planted in straight little lines. The house and yard had a computer-generated look to it that was downright spooky. Even the dirt around the flowers was neatly patted down without a single weed in sight.

Jaimie pressed the doorbell and listened to the footsteps grow closer, hard, clipped, measured. This guy's scary, she thought.

Jaimie stifled a gasp when the door opened. Before her stood a tall, lean man, completely hairless—not from disease, but from a razor as she could see the tiniest bit of shadow. Even his eyebrows were gone. What the hell had Jerry sent her into? "Mr. Fox, I'm Jaimie McLane. I'm so glad you've agreed to talk to me."

"Hmmm." But he stepped back and let her into the house. "Would you mind removing your shoes?" He stared pointedly down at her beat-up driving shoes as if they were covered with something foul and he was too polite to say it out loud. With a grimace, Jaimie took off her shoes hoping her socks looked clean. A small plastic runner led down the hall to the rest of the house. Jaimie followed him to a small eat-in kitchen with gleaming appliances and a floor so clean it looked as if it had just been installed. Jaimie noticed these things because people who were neurotically neat always baffled her. She might be called neurotically messy, although she liked clean things. But this, this was weirdly neat.

Jaimie sat down at the table and placed her notepad in front of her. "I really don't know if you can help me. I'm writing a story about the Joshua Tate case. It's been nearly eight months and I'm doing a follow-up story to see where the case is, how people are coping, how the neighborhood is doing. I'm here because I got a call from a police officer friend who suggested you might be able to help me out."

"Is this a puff piece?" he asked, and if he'd had eyebrows, they would have been angrily furrowed.

Jaimie gave him a quick smile. "It's a balanced piece. And I've really just started conducting interviews so I don't know where this story might go. I can say with confidence, however, that it won't be a puff piece. It's about a murder."

He stared at her for a few seconds then slapped his hands on the tabletop, making her jump slightly. "It's just that no one believes me and I'll be damned if I'm made the butt of some joke. I don't want my name in the paper. I don't want my story in the paper. I just want justice."

"Justice?"

"That goddamn kid killed my cat," he said loudly.

Jaimie couldn't hide her surprise. "Joshua?"

"See? You don't believe me either."

"No, Mr. Fox, I do. I'm beginning to realize that there might be more to this case, this little boy, than has been reported. How did he kill your cat?"

"Well," he said, then stopped, glaring at her hand poised above her notebook. "Why're you taking notes if all this is off the record?"

Jaimie put her pencil down. "Let's set the ground rules so we both understand them and no one gets surprised. Off the record means I cannot use anything you say, but if I obtain the same information from another source, I can use it. For example, if you filed a police report about this, I could use the information in that report and print your name. Did you file a report?"

He frowned. "I called the cops and complained and they didn't do anything. I don't even think they questioned the kid. If that's filing a report, then I did."

"If there is anything on file about that incident, I can use it. And I may come back later and ask if you'd be willing to go on the record. Does that sound okay?"

"I don't want to read my name in the paper tomorrow," he said.

"You won't. And chances are, unless your story becomes relevant to the investigation or the story, you never will."

He still looked suspicious, but he nodded slowly, apparently satisfied she was telling the truth. "I was next to my garage trimming the grass along the side. Trixie, my cat, was in the front yard dozing in the sun. Trixie was thirteen years old and wouldn't chase a mouse if it sat on her tail. All the neighborhood kids loved her, so it wasn't unusual to have the kids trooping on my lawn to pet her. I didn't mind. Well, this kid, this Joshua kid, he was petting Trixie for a while and I stopped paying attention. Then the kid goes to get his bike and he rides right over her. Doesn't swerve, doesn't even pretend it's an accident, at least until I started yelling at him. He got off his bike and I thought he was trying to see if the cat was okay, then he ran off, pushing his bike. Killed her." He thrust his jaw out and Jaimie was afraid the old guy was going to cry.

"It could have been an accident. I'm sure it looked like he did it on purpose, but . . ."

"Miss. I found fishing line around her neck."

"Fishing line?"

He swallowed hard and his face contorted slightly, but the guy held it together. "Best I can figure out, he tied her down so she couldn't get out of the way. When he was checking on her, he cut the line and took the anchor. Sick little bastard. I told the police and they talked to the little brat, but they didn't do nothing. Said I couldn't prove it. Said the fishing line could have been on there from before. Sure, it could have but it wasn't."

"Why would he kill your cat?" Jaimie said, not disbelieving his story.

"Because he was sick. And you know what I think? I think the little bastard killed his own puppy. That's what I think. You ask the police about that. You ask them about that puppy and what kind of injuries it had."

"My God."

Mr. Fox nodded, satisfied to finally have an audience to tell his gruesome theory to. "And another thing. Trixie wasn't the first."

"What?"

"There were other things that happened. The kid was one of those psychos. If he had lived, he would have turned into one of those serial killers. I think someone was trying to stop him from growing up. I think someone knew about him and killed him."

Jaimie felt a shiver go up her spine and she wondered fleetingly if she were talking to that "someone."

"I've interviewed a lot of neighbors and no one's ever even hinted about something so horrible."

"That's right, call me crazy. But I'm right," he said, pointing a finger at her. "You'll see. You gonna use that? You gonna print that in your paper?"

That small shiver was turning into a frisson of fear. "Mr. Fox, you didn't kill him, did you?" Jaimie forced a laugh, trying desperately to make that question come out as a half-joke.

He didn't seem at all insulted by the question. "I don't believe in the death penalty, Miss. That's why I called the police."

Sick, but liberal. Jaimie wasn't certain he was telling the truth about any of it, but she knew Jerry had been curious enough about his story to tip her off. Clearly, Chief Girard hadn't thought it was worth following up and Jaimie wasn't so certain either. Joshua Tate, by all accounts, was a cute little kid with some minor emotional problems because he'd had a tough time early on. That didn't mean he went around torturing animals. Jaimie disliked news stories that castigated the victim, as if it were somehow the victim's fault they got murdered or raped.

"Thank you, Mr. Fox. You've helped me a great deal."

"You going to do anything with it?" he asked.

"I'm not certain. As I said, I've just started working on this story. Thank you again for talking with me. I can see myself out."

As she was walking out the door, she heard a spray bottle being used vigorously in the kitchen.

Chief Ronald Girard, his fat, piggy face looking pleased, shoved a pile of police reports about two inches thick in front of Jaimie. She had a sinking feeling she knew what it was, but she asked anyway.

"What's all this?"

"Geoffrey Fox is a nut. Twenty-three calls just last year complaining that the neighborhood kids were trespassing on his property," he said, pressing a plump, surprisingly well-manicured finger on top of the pile. "Fourteen calls to report his cat missing, stating the damn thing was kidnapped. Do you want to continue?" The chief was so arrogant, so sneeringly superior, Jaimie almost said yes, but she shook her head instead.

"You're obviously dismissing the cat-killing complaint. There's just one thing, chief. Someone put fishing line around the cat's neck. Someone killed it. Are you saying he did it himself?"

He looked at her as if she were an idiot. "I'm saying the guy's a nut. You met him, right? What do you think?"

"That he's a nut. But maybe he's a nut with a murdered cat."

"Give me an ef-ing break, McLane. And by the way, tell your friend to stop talking to reporters."

Jaimie stared directly into his piggy eyes. "I was following up a tip a former reporter got when she originally covered the story." It wasn't quite a lie. Maxine had made a note in one of her notebooks shortly after the murder. "Jeff Fox. Dead cat. Check." Obviously, Maxine never had checked, and if she had, she hadn't told anyone about it.

"Maxine? She had more sense than you, then. Leave the police work to police, hmmm McLane?"

She could picture him with ease in hog form rooting around the ground snuffling around for food. Donuts. Jaimie liked cops for the most part, though she'd noticed the profession attracted short men with big muscles and big attitude, à la Napoleon. Still, she knew enough good guys to make up for the jerks like the chief, the ones who fit the fat, overbearing *Dukes of Hazzard* stereotype.

"Thanks for the time, chief," Jaimie said, feeling angry and frustrated and slightly disappointed even though she'd thought Fox as crazy as the chief did.

"And McLane," the chief called, all cheerful. "You let me know when you find Tate's murderer. I want to give you a nice quote." He snorted out a laugh, and Jaimie gave him a fake chuckle wishing she had the guts to flip him off.

Chapter 13

Jaimie worked all morning that Saturday interviewing Joshua Tate's neighbors and learning nothing new. Everyone she'd talked to said the same things they'd said shortly after the murder. Joshua seemed like a polite, cute kid, but they didn't know him very well. No one had ever had a pet turn up mysteriously dead. Geoffrey Fox, Jaimie decided, was as crazy as he'd seemed and part of her wondered whether he really had killed the kid. He was the only one with a motive, the guy thought Joshua had killed his beloved cat. And he'd gone on his lawn, which, according to Chief Girard was nearly as grave an offense in Fox's eyes. But Jaimie couldn't imagine Fox walking out into the woods, picking up a stick, and beating a kid to death. It was all too messy.

So far, the story, even though it was about a murder, *was* a fluff piece. Things had calmed down in the past months, and the fear parents had immediately following the murder had eased. It was late summer and although some parents still wouldn't let their kids out of their yards without them, most had slipped back into their old life. Kids rode bikes and splashed in pools or sat in front of their TVs playing with their PlayStations. Many parents said they figured whoever had killed Joshua Tate was long gone—at least they hoped so.

Back at her apartment, Jaimie threw on her running shorts and shoes and went for a run she hoped would lift her out of her sour mood. She told herself she was disappointed with the story so far, but the truth was she was in a funk about Harry. She hadn't talked to him in two days, saw only glimpses of him as he went in and out of his office. He'd had the top half of his cast taken off and now he walked around without crutches. Before the ex showed up, Jaimie would have gone with him, would have cracked open a beer and celebrated. Now, they hardly exchanged a word.

He'd had a meeting with the circulation manager and the advertising manager but hadn't bothered to fill her in on what was going on. He was cutting her out in more ways than one and she was trying desperately not to let it bother her. But of course, it did. Every time she saw him, her heart would speed up and her stomach would feel as though she'd just eaten too many donuts. She had a major crush on him and she didn't know how to stop it. No amount of self-chastisement was working.

So, on an unusually hot mid-September afternoon, she ran four miles hoping to drive away thoughts of Harry. Instead, the run left her feeling even more foul, as well as slightly lightheaded. She peeled off her sweat-soaked tank, without showering, lay down and fell asleep, dragged out from too little sleep, too much work, and too many thoughts about Harry. A knock at her door woke her up from a deep, drugged-like sleep.

Trying to open her eyes wide enough to see, Jaimie stumbled out of bed and to the door just as another knock sounded. "One minute, please," she said, placing her foot so if it were an intruder, they couldn't force themselves in. She opened the door, looked through the crack, and scowled.

"What are you doing here, Harry?"

He grinned and Jaimie scowled even deeper. "Don't we have a date tonight?"

"No. We don't. Bye."

She tried to shut the door, but he stopped her progress with a hand. "Jaimie, come on, we at least have to talk. And I can see you got all ready for me, so you might as well let me in."

Jaimie looked down at her faded old sweat shorts, her grungy running shoes and her sweat-stained sports bra. She looked at him looking at her breasts and rolled her eyes. "Hold on." He let her shut the door and she ran to her room and tugged on a T-shirt, gave her mirror a quick look, saw the unfortunate results of running, no shower, and a nap, and grimaced.

"Okay," she said, swinging open the door. "I'm ready for our big date."

Harry laughed and walked in. "Jesus, you're a slob."

Jaimie looked around at her messy house and couldn't have agreed more. "Yup. An unshowered, smelly slob. So, what are you doing here, anyway."

"Maybe I like smelly slobs."

"Maybe you like stick women in Nicole Miller business suits." She let out a breath. "Sorry. I wake up grumpy. Make yourself comfortable," she said, gathering up clothes, books, old mail, and newspapers off her couch and tossing them onto a rocking chair, the room's only other piece of furniture. "I'll take a quick shower. As much as you like your women smelly, I'm afraid I'm going to have to insist."

Jaimie gave him a quick smile, then jogged off to the bathroom cursing her luck. What the heck was he doing here? He hadn't talked to her in three days after disappearing with his ex, and shows up to go out on a date.

She had to find out from Ted that Anne was living with him. Living with his ex-girlfriend and dating his city editor. Did he have absolutely no sense of ethics, never mind morals?

And, of course, he shows up looking like he stepped out of the pages of *Men's Health,* all fine and sexy and wearing clothes the way very few men can, the way they were meant to look, even with his cast. With her sweaty and smelly and half asleep. Did she deserve such punishment?

Jaimie showered and threw on a pair of tan capris and a white linen shirt, not bothering with her hair. She didn't wear makeup, but her hair was a daily ritual, a curse she hardly ever neglected. But since she figured they weren't actually going out on a date and she had herself convinced she didn't care what Harry thought of her, she walked out looking like Carrot Top, her hair curling and wild and flopping all over the place.

Harry blinked. "Did you get a perm?"

"No one gets a perm anymore. Unless you live in a trailer. This," she said, taking both hands and attacking her springing locks, "is natural."

"Wow."

"Harry, I really don't want to talk about hair fashion right now. I want to know what you think you're doing here while your girlfriend is waiting for you at home?"

He didn't even have the good grace to look embarrassed. "She's not my girlfriend."

"Neither am I."

He looked at her curiously. "Do you mean to tell me that you somehow straighten your hair every day?"

She was dumbfounded. "What?"

"Your hair."

"I know you're talking about my hair," she said with forced patience. "And as fascinating as that subject is,

I'd rather talk about what the hell you're doing here when you've moved your girlfriend back in."

He kept staring at her hair, but he did manage to focus on her words. "She's not my girlfriend. I told you that."

"Do I look stupid?"

He grinned. "No. But that hair sure makes you look sexy."

"Oh, for goodness sake. Get out of here."

He truly looked baffled.

"Harry. Get out." She pointed what she thought was a forceful finger toward the door. He didn't budge.

"Okay. You win. She's pregnant with her ex-lover's baby and I'm the only one she trusts. I'm her only friend. And that's all."

"Oh, please. You can't be that gullible."

"I'm not gullible. But I couldn't just throw her out on the street."

"So now she's facing homelessness. One minute a staff reporter on the *New York Times,* the next, a pregnant bag lady wearing designer business suits. Why would she come to you if not to get back together?"

He looked down at the floor, made a face when he saw it needed vacuuming, and let out a long sigh. "I'm her only friend."

"I don't know, Harry. I don't think I can go out with you. What if those old feelings come back? What if she begged you to try again?"

He clenched his jaw in a way that made Jaimie realize he'd wondered about those same things, and she knew there was no way they could begin anything as long as Anne was living with him.

"What if it was just sex, then?"

"What?"

"No, huh?" He smiled in a way that told Jaimie he was joking. Sort of.

"Nice try, Crandall." She put on a thoughtful face. "Though I bet it would be good."

"No strings," he said, a mock hopeful note in his voice.

"You'd just fall hopelessly in love with me. You know how men are. Give them free sex and the next thing you know they're throwing a ring at you." She shuddered. "I'm not ready for that."

He laughed and she was glad she could make him laugh, but sad that laughing together was as far as their relationship would ever get. Just friends. Friends who wanted to screw each other silly. It could work.

"Well. I guess I'll go."

The disappointment Jaimie felt in the pit of her stomach was almost frightening. But he was right. He should go.

"Hey, if we can't have sex, how about a good-bye kiss?" he asked, looking so completely charming that Jaimie couldn't not smile.

"I don't know, Harry, will you be able to stop after just one little kiss."

"Okay. You're right. How about a make-out session? On the couch."

She walked up to him, turned him around and shoved him toward the door. "See you Monday. Oh, and congratulations on the cast."

He stood at the open door smiling at her. "You're something else, McLane."

"So I hear."

Then he grabbed the back of her head and pulled her toward him so quickly she stumbled against his hard chest. "Just wanted to touch that hair of yours once," he said, his lips a mere inch away from hers as he squeezed her curls beneath his fingers. He kissed her, letting out a small, deep sound, before letting go and walking out the door leaving Jaimie standing there slightly off balance and very much alone.

"How was your date?" Anne asked, looking up from a book she was reading—"Politics and Religion in Ancient Rome." She was wearing leggings and a cropped T-shirt that accentuated her pregnancy.

"Shouldn't you be reading a book about parenting?" Harry asked, eyeing what he knew Anne would consider light reading.

She shrugged, closed the book and gave him her complete attention. "Why back so early?"

"She's not very understanding about my living with my ex-girlfriend."

"Screw her then."

"I wanted to, but she said no."

Anne narrowed her eyes, apparently not appreciating his dry wit. "Didn't you tell her we're just friends?"

He nodded slowly. "She wondered why you're here at all, whether or not this is just a ploy to get me back." She laughed and even though he didn't want her back, Harry was insulted and a little bit hurt.

She stopped laughing long enough to speak. "You don't think that, do you?"

"No," he said slowly.

"You do!"

"No, I don't."

"But? There's a but there, I hear it dangling out there."

"When you showed up here Wednesday begging me . . ."

"I didn't beg."

"You cried."

"It was hormones."

Harry gave up. Anne would argue for years the sky was purple, not blue, if she got the inclination. "Fine. You didn't beg. You asked whether you could move in with me and I caved and said yes. And here you are."

"What's your point?"

He didn't think she was being nearly meek enough for a woman who was in such a tenuous position. "My point is that you're not destitute. You must have savings. Why move out of New York? Why move in with me? I think we should have thought this through a bit more before jumping into this."

Anne gave him a level stare. "You're kidding, right? I barely was able to pay for that apartment never mind put anything in the bank. In case you weren't listening, I'm having a baby in two months. I need to save whatever money I have to pay for a nanny. And you know why I can't go to my mother. I don't even know where she is right now and apparently she's turned off her cell phone in some new-age no-tech thing she's going through. Do you think it was easy for me to call you, to ask to live here with you?"

Harry wasn't moved by her impassioned speech. "How much do you have in savings? I know you had a stock portfolio that was worth about ten times what I had."

To his horror, her eyes welled up. "It's all gone."

"Gone?"

"The stock market took a dive, remember? I was too involved. I got crazy 'cause Bob told me I was being too conservative and he was making so much more money.

Things had already been going down, but I took his advice and . . ." She clenched her fists together on her lap, just beneath the swell of her belly. "I lost almost everything. I didn't sublet the apartment. I got evicted."

"Oh, Anne."

"And Bob wouldn't help me. He got hit real hard, too. And his wife . . ." She swallowed hard. "His wife has money," she whispered.

"I knew he was a prick, I just didn't know how big a prick he was."

"Yeah," she said, her nose all stuffed. "I thought about staying at the *Times,* but he's my boss and everyone knew we'd been dating. Except his wife." She let out a bitter laugh. "I just couldn't face it. The humiliation of it all. Being dumped is bad enough." She brushed away a tear with a shaking hand. "I wasn't kidding when I said you're the only one who could help me."

"Why didn't you tell me all this Wednesday?"

She gave him a look like he was dense. "I was embarrassed. And I did beg, didn't I? Oh, God," she said, burying her head into her hands. "What the fuck am I going to do?"

"First you should clean up your language if you're going to have a kid."

"Fuck you."

Harry laughed. "Glad to see part of you has survived all this."

"Just my luck I finally fall in love with a guy and he turns about to be just like me. Not that I didn't love you," she added quickly. Then she added softly, "I didn't love you enough. I would have stayed if I'd loved you enough."

Harry figured that was Anne's attempt at an apology and he let it go at that. "Are you hungry? There's a pretty good Chinese place about a block from here. It's not as good as Chung's, but it's not bad."

Anne gave him a watery smile. "Okay. And sorry I messed up your date. I still say she should have gone out with you."

"You're just one more complication. It's probably best in the end. She works in the newsroom. I never should have asked her out in the first place." He was lying and he knew it, but he hoped saying it out loud might snap him out of his funk. He wished he'd never seen her all dewy fresh from her shower, her hair curling around her, making her look so incredibly desirable he'd wanted to throw her down on her messy floor and make love. Well, maybe he could have convinced her to vacuum first.

He'd just have to put Jaimie out of his head. Treat her like any other reporter with beautiful, curly, bed-me-now hair. He could do it. He'd have to.

Chapter 14

Paul gave Jaimie a guilty look as he shuffled a folder jammed with papers in front of him. He sat at his old desk looking strangely out of place and extremely uncomfortable. Jaimie sat between Howard Pollock, the circulation manager, and Laura Byrnes, the advertising director.

Harry sat in a chair, its back against the bank of windows that looked out onto the newsroom, one leg slung casually over the other knee, his hands folded across his stomach. He wore a gray lawyer suit, but without a tie. His thick brown hair was darker and slightly clumpy from sweat around the edges. He looked tired and strained, with deep lines on either side of his mouth and Jaimie had a sense he wasn't feeling well.

"The paper is failing to meets its financial commitments," Paul said, staring down at the folder in front of him.

Jaimie felt a tingling of unease as she watched Paul give Harry a quick glance. She'd never seen Paul look so unsure of himself, so old.

"For years I've been supplementing the paper with my own income, but it's come to the point where I can no longer make up for the losses. The paper is facing a major shortfall."

"How bad is it?" Laura asked, disbelief and anger in her voice.

Paul opened his mouth and closed it, and Jaimie knew it was going to be bad.

"We're $2 million off budget," Harry said without inflection. "I believe we can make up that amount with some quick fixes."

"No way can I generate that kind of revenue in three months," Laura said, folding her arms over her chest. "My staff is already having a tough time."

Harry ignored her. "With a combined circulation and advertising push, I believe we can make up this shortfall. Or at least most of it."

"Two million dollars? No way in hell," Laura said. Jaimie felt the tension of the room grow tenfold. Harry gave Laura a look she prayed would never be trained on her. Silently, Jaimie had to agree with Laura's assessment, but she was willing to give Harry and Paul the benefit of the doubt. She didn't know squat about the paper's finances; it was the one area of the paper she was pleasantly ignorant about. Part of her wished she still was.

"A bridal supplement can generate . . ."

Laura snorted.

"Do you have a problem, Laura?" His voice was like steel and his gaze was flat, cold.

"We had a bridal supplement in April," Laura said, only slightly subdued.

"How about a groom supplement?" It came out without much thought, but Jaimie said it anyway.

"Oh, please," Laura said with derision.

"Wait. Why not?" Harry asked. "We could tap into areas that the traditional bridal showcases don't."

"Like cars," Laura murmured. "Guys like cars." She smiled and Jaimie could almost see her eyes turn into dollar signs. "Okay, Harry. I think we can work with that. What else do you have in mind?"

Harry went on to outline his plan for eight special supplements, each of which should generate close to one hundred thousand dollars. In addition, special discounts would be given to auto dealerships and realtors for pages that would run daily. The circulation department would begin a telemarketing campaign to expand readership.

"And it's your job, McLane, to get this crap off the front page," he said, holding up that day's edition. The lead story was a tediously detailed account of Main Street's planned improvements.

Jaimie's face burned. "I agree I've seen better front pages, but in my defense, Monday is always a little slow. If you want, I could commit a murder for you," she said pleasantly and pointedly looking at him so he had no doubt who she would murder.

Harry gave her a grim smile. "Let's just work on getting something a bit more interesting above the fold, okay? It's going to be pretty tough to increase circulation with 'Main Street Improvements Slated'" he said, reading the less-than-thrilling headline.

Laura stifled a snort and Jaimie wondered how she'd ever thought Harry was a nice guy.

"I want more local angles to national stories. I want better pictures. This is pure crap," he said, pushing the paper away from him.

If he'd slapped her in the face, he would have done less damage. Was this the same guy who'd grabbed her and kissed her silly not two days before? Thank God they weren't dating because Jaimie decided she couldn't take being treated like shit one minute and like a goddess the next. Having a relationship with Harry would be too schizophrenic. He must have seen something in her face, because he softened a bit, adding, "I know you can do better."

Jaimie stared at him, too mad, too hurt, to speak. She could not separate her personal feelings for Harry from her professional ones. If she didn't like him, she'd be angry, not on the verge of tears.

"I've got a question for Paul," Laura said. Paul looked up, startled, almost as if he'd thought everyone in the room had forgotten him. "Why did you wait so long to tell us?"

"What's important now is that we dig ourselves out of this little hole," Harry said calmly.

"No, no, Harry. It's okay. You all have a right to know. You've all been loyal employees. The paper has been losing money for four years. Before that, it was barely making a profit. Part of the agreement I have with my brother is that we keep the paper as long as it's profitable, as long as he got his money. But it was never this bad."

Jaimie felt the blood drain from her face, instantly forgetting her problems with Harry. "Are you saying that unless the paper turns a profit, you and your brother are going to sell?"

Paul looked at her, his eyes filled with regret and sorrow. "That's right."

"Maybe that wouldn't be such a bad thing," Jaimie said slowly, and Laura nodded. "If you sold it to a big conglomerate who could push some money our way. We could improve our printing press, hire more staff." Her voice faded as she looked at Paul's face.

"I'm sorry, Jaimie."

Jaimie looked at Harry, but he was looking out the window. *Oh, this is bad.*

"My brother already has a buyer. Penworth."

"Penworth?" Jaimie furrowed her brow in confusion. "But that's a chain of . . ."

"Shoppers," Laura said, rather too cheerfully. Sure, the sale wouldn't impact her, so suddenly the picture was far rosier. "Oh. Editorial."

"You can't let that happen," Jaimie said, hearing the desperation in her voice. "Sell the paper. But not to Penworth."

"It's not my decision," Paul said sadly.

"Well, that sucks." Jaimie looked at Harry again, silent, still, hard as a rock.

"If we're through, I've got a lot of work to do," Laura said.

"Nothing of this leaves this room, right?" Harry said. Laura and Howard nodded as they went out the door, but Jaimie stayed behind.

"Don't you even care, Harry?"

He clenched his jaw before turning. "I'm busting my balls trying to save this piece of crap paper."

Jaimie's eyes filled. It wasn't a piece of crap and she was getting sick and tired of him referring to it that way. Sure, maybe the *Nortown Journal* wasn't the *New York Times.* Maybe sometimes the front page was a bit weak. But she never slacked, never stopped thinking of ways to make the paper better. The *Journal* was her world, the only world she'd known for twelve years. Without the *Nortown Journal,* she didn't have anything except a tiny house that was too messy and a cat that was too stupid. She swallowed hard, willing herself to calm down, to toughen up.

"What can my staff do to help?" she said, glad her voice didn't shake.

Harry let out a long sigh. "Just stress to them the importance of writing good, accurate stories. A lot of this falls on you and Nathan to come up with eye-catching headlines. I know you do your best, but work on your layout. Put more sports stories on page one. Come up with some interesting features. I think everyone has slipped into a complacency and that all has to change if we're going to pull this off."

Nathan. Jaimie felt sick. "Um, Nathan gave me his two-week notice last Friday," Jaimie said glumly. Then she added angrily, "For the record, he starting looking because he thought you were about to fire him."

"He was right."

Jaimie, aware Paul was still in the room, tried to keep her anger from showing. Harry had been planning to fire Nathan and hadn't even consulted with her? "I'm sure you have some other people in mind."

"As a matter of fact, I do."

"Nice of you to let me know, by the way."

"Jaimie," Paul warned.

"I was planning to tell you," Harry said, sounding tired and making Jaimie feel suddenly petty and mean.

"When?"

"Saturday." And he gave her a look that made her remember how charming he'd been, how sexy. The rat. Two minutes ago he was making her feel like she was inept, and now he was looking at her as if he was picturing her naked.

She narrowed her eyes. "Really?"

"Really." He held up his hand like a Boy Scout.

"I guess I'd better get going," Paul said, gathering up his folder.

Jaimie stepped in front of him. "Don't think I'm through with you, Mr. Mayer," she said with a mixture of anger and affection. "Why didn't you tell me. All those lunches."

"I couldn't. Hell, I could hardly admit it to myself. I thought we were down fifty grand, not two million. Can I tell you something? I think this paper being sold would be the best thing that ever happened to you. Isn't that right, Harry?"

Harry held up his hands. "Oh, no. I'm not getting involved in this conversation."

"Paul thinks I'm wasting my life here. He won't believe I actually like what I'm doing."

"And you'll be doing it when you're fifty, you keep it up. Fifty, fat, and alone."

Jaimie rolled her eyes. "He also thinks I'm a lesbian."

Paul's cheeks turned ruddy. "Your mouth is too smart for your own good," he said. "But I'm right. I don't want to lose the paper, but if we do, it *will* be the best thing that ever happened to you." With that, Paul left.

"I don't know whether to choke him or give him a hug," Jaimie said. "I can't believe he let this happen. How long have you known about this?"

"About two weeks."

Jaimie looked at him, took in the deep lines around his mouth, the circles under his eyes, and wondered if this whole financial mess was responsible. "You look beat."

He looked startled, then embarrassed, taking a hand and raking it through his short hair as he limped around to his chair and sat. He stared dully at the pile of papers in front of him. "This job was supposed to be a cakewalk, not a nightmare."

"Two million. Do you really think the paper can generate that kind of money in three months?"

"Honestly? No."

Jaimie felt her stomach drop to her toes. "Sometimes, Harry, it's okay to lie."

"Listen. I'm going to try my damnedest to save this place. This paper's supplements have never generated a hundred thousand a pop. We're going to be short, Paul's brother's going to sell, and we're all going to be looking for a job. Everyone but Laura. She's the key, and guess what? She has the least incentive to try."

"You're saying we're screwed."

"Unless Laura surprises me." He shrugged.

"We're screwed." Then a thought came to her. "Penworth doesn't always keep the advertising staff. I know for a fact they replaced the advertising director at the *Baxter Tribune* when they turned it into the *Baxter Shop-a-Day*." Jaimie put her head in her hands. "Oh, God, the *Nortown Shop-a-Day*."

"Does Laura know that?" Harry said, raising his eyebrows suggestively.

Jaimie smiled. "No. But I think it would be in everyone's best interest if she did know. What do you think?"

"I think you're a crafty woman."

"I don't think anyone's ever called me crafty before. By the way, do I have a say in who you hire as my assistant editor?"

"No."

Jaimie shook her head. "You're a hard man, Harry." He grinned. "More than you know."

She gave him a level look. "Are you being a pig?"

"God, no," he said, barking out a laugh. "You have a dirty mind, McLane."

"That's what I hear."

He got serious on her. "I know I don't have to remind you that the staff should not know the state of our finances."

"Okay," she said slowly. "But shouldn't you give everyone some sort of notice?"

"I've thought of that. If it looks as though we won't make our obligations, I'll have a staff meeting in December. It will be up to Paul and Martin to decide whether to keep the paper going while it's being sold. My thinking is that once Martin makes the final decision to sell, the paper should shut down. It's not fair to make people stay and lose out on possible jobs. Plus, the staff will get so thinned out, it will be impossible to keep things going."

"I hope that doesn't happen. This is going to impact so many people."

Harry's answer was a shrug.

"Don't you care?"

"Sure I care. I care that a paper I took over four months ago is going belly up and that's going to look just dandy on my resume. I care that one hundred people, give or take, are going to be out of a job. I care that a paper that was founded more than a hundred years ago is vanishing off the face of the earth. But I can only do so much. I can't create a miracle. And I resent the suggestion that I wouldn't care."

"Well, I resent being treated like shit one minute and given the once-over the next." Those words flew out of her mouth like black crows, flying crazily, and completely unstoppable.

He looked so mad at that moment, Jaimie actually backed up a step. "Are you suggesting that I have been treating you differently in this office simply because we almost went on a date?" he asked so quietly, Jaimie knew he was extremely angry.

In light of his near-rage, Jaimie decided to do a neat back-pedal. "Maybe."

"Get the hell out of here before I say something I'll regret." Jaimie almost felt the blast of cold air.

"Okay," she said in a small voice, and tiptoed out quietly closing the door behind her. She heard him slam something down and winced, then turned around and went right back into his office.

"Jesus," he said, staring at her like he wanted to throw her physically from his office.

"I wasn't suggesting . . . I just didn't like you criticizing me one minute then . . . You did give me a look. I know what that look means. I'm not stupid. So, one minute you're saying the paper sucks, which is really like saying I suck, and the next minute you're giving me that look, and I guess that made me mad. And glad that we never went out because I don't think I could take the boss-Harry after the nice-Harry. You're like two different people." All in one breath. *Not bad.*

He glared at her, one eye squinty, as if he were trying to keep his head from exploding off his shoulder. "Leave. Now."

"See? It never could have worked. You're irrational."

"Jaimie," he choked out, his hands gripping the arms of his chair so hard his entire body shook.

"Oh. Oh." The anger whooshed out of her, deflated her, leaving behind a small and petty person. He wasn't angry at all. He was in agony.

"Harry, what can I do?"

"Leave."

She looked at him sitting there, his hands clenched in front of him, and slowly shook her head. She walked back to the door and closed it, took a deep breath, and turned back to him. "What can I do," she repeated. "Do you have your migraine pills?"

He nodded. Jaimie watched as he let out a shaking breath. "I already took it before the meeting. They should kick in any time now."

"I'm sorry."

He managed a crooked smile. "For what?"

"For whining. Accusing. Going into hysterics."

"You weren't hysterical."

Jaimie bit her lip, feeling stupid and obtuse for not knowing he was in pain. For being so self-centered that she thought his bad mood and nastiness were all about her. "It bothered me. Too much. I took everything you said to heart, as if it were a personal attack, not a professional one. I'm sorry."

"Don't be sorry."

"It's just made me realize that I don't have the mentality to date my boss. So it's just as well your girlfriend moved in with you. Maybe you should try to get back together," she managed to choke out.

"She's still in love with the other guy. I'm just the doormat she's walking on at the moment. Besides, I don't even think I like her anymore."

"That's too bad." But inside she was smiling brightly.

"Not really. Hey, there is an upside to all this if the paper does fold."

"What's that?"

He gave her a smile that warmed her to her toes. "I won't be your boss anymore."

Chapter 15

An air of doom and gloom hung over the newsroom. Jaimie was fairly certain no one knew what was happening, but every time she was called into Harry's office, she felt twenty pairs of eyes on her. Kath asked her point-blank what was happening and Jaimie was forced to lie.

"It's all about the *Day* and their new bureau. We're coming up with strategies to keep up circulation and ad revenue." It was almost true, and would have been true if Paul hadn't gotten the paper into such a fix in the first place.

Harry had turned back into a man who rarely smiled and never talked to his staff. He came to work early and left late, looking worn and exhausted. Looking like a man who hated life. Jaimie watched silently, her heart aching, as he left the office each day without a word to anyone.

The eight-month anniversary of Joshua Tate's death came and went. Jaimie, who had little to show for her hours of interviews, assigned a basic follow-up to the new cop reporter. Ryan did an admirable job, using some of the stuff Jaimie had gleaned from neighbors, as well as a couple of interviews from the cops. In all, it was nothing spectacular, but it was a better, more thorough story than the *Day* and caused a short blip in sidewalk box sales. Jaimie wasn't giving up on her story, but for now it was on the back burner. She spent most of her time coming up with strategies to make the paper more appealing, the headlines more exciting, the stories more interesting.

On top of that, Nathan was gone and she'd had a week without an assistant. The new assistant editor, a woman from a suburban Boston weekly, was set to start today. Jaimie had been so busy she hadn't even met the woman yet. She was five minutes late, which rankled Jaimie to the extreme.

"Hello, Jaimie McLane?"

Jaimie turned to see a small, stout woman in a Wal-Mart business suit. Kathy Bates in pin curls. Probably someone from the senior center with some big scoop about a quilting bazaar. "That's me."

"I'm Jennifer Southwick. Your new assistant editor."

Jaimie stared for two beats before recovering. "Oh. Hi. Welcome aboard."

Jennifer held out her hand and chuckled. "I know. I was surprised to get the job, too."

"No, no. I'm glad you're here. I've been swamped."

"I'm fifty-seven, five-foot-two, been in the news business for thirty-five years, and want to be closer to my son."

Jaimie put up both hands. "Jennifer, please. You are a bit older than I was expecting, but I'm glad to have you. I'm a bit older than I expect, too, when I look in the mirror."

Jennifer laughed and Jaimie thanked God the woman had a sense of humor.

As the day went on, Jaimie realized that Harry was as smart as he was good-looking. She had to give him credit; he knew how to hire good people. Of all the young reporters, other than an occasional bad attitude, she had no complaints. And now they had Jennifer, who was so fast at editing, so witty with her headlines, so damn competent, Jaimie began to feel slightly inadequate. It also made her realize how bad Nathan had been.

So, Harry had been right about Nathan. She glanced at his darkened office and tried to remember whether she'd seen him leave for the day. It was nine o'clock and he probably was long gone. Though last week he had fallen asleep, emerging from his door sleep-rumpled and extremely grouchy. He no longer looked like *GQ* New York boy. He looked tired and shabby and Jaimie's heart had wrenched when she saw him. Not only did the cast make him look pathetic, she had a feeling his once-infrequent migraines were coming on more frequently.

"Jennifer. Did you see Harry leave?"

The older woman craned her neck over her 21-inch computer screen. "Nope."

He'd probably fallen asleep. He was in there sprawled out on the too-small couch or drooling on his desktop when he should be home. "I think he fell asleep. I wonder if I should go wake him up."

"Does he do that a lot?"

"Oh, no. He's just been working so hard lately. Really dogging it. He works harder than anyone." She eyed the door again, knowing if she went in there she'd have to touch him, have to talk gently near his ear, have to be closer to him than she'd been in a very long time. "I'll go wake him up."

Harry felt a soft touch on his arm and knew in an instant that Jaimie was in his office. Her fingers were like ice even through his oxford. "Harry. Wake up."

"I'm awake," he said, but didn't open his eyes.

"Open your eyes. You're going to fall back to sleep."

Maybe, but certainly not while she was kneeling next to him touching his arm and smelling so nice. He pictured her just showered, her curling red hair flowing all around her, and he smiled.

"What's so funny?"

"You smell nice," he said, and wished he hadn't because she took her arm away and stood up. He opened his eyes.

"Are you awake?" She looked about ready to bolt from the room.

He let his eyes drift closed and muttered "smells good."

"Harry."

He almost smiled at the impatience in her voice. He felt her shake him again and knew she was bending over him, so he opened his eyes to stare at her. God she was beautiful. No, intriguing. He loved the way she looked skeptical, a quirky little movement of her eyebrow, a subtle shift of her lips, her green-blue eyes filled with suspicion. No freckles on her, just smooth pale skin and two bright blotches of red on her cheeks. A few strands of hair had escaped her ponytail and drifted to hang about six inches above his chest. He lifted one hand and curled it around his finger. And pulled.

"Hey. That hurts," she said, pulling back.

"It won't hurt if you stop yanking," he said calmly, smiling when he saw her eyes narrow.

"Harry."

"Jaimie."

"I mean it. Let me go. This is a bad idea."

"So was taking this job, but here I am." He pulled a bit more until he'd wrapped a good portion around his finger and drew her head to within inches of his. "Don't you want to kiss me?"

"You don't listen, do you? Do you have any idea what you do to me when you pull this stuff?"

"Torture, I know. I'm a masochist."

A small furrow formed between her eyes. "A sadist."

"One kiss, Jaimie." He pulled her gently downward and watched as her eyes flickered to his mouth. "One kiss can't be a mistake."

"Harry, please."

"Happy to oblige, M'am." He swore he didn't pull her hair an inch, but somehow they were kissing rather desperately. He let go of her the instant their lips touched, giving her a choice, giving her a chance to push back, though God knew he didn't think he had the strength to stop from pulling her back to him. She tasted like bubble gum and he smiled.

"Don't smile," she said, giving him a little shake. "Stop making this so hard not to do."

"You chew bubble gum, McLane. You are a very cool chick." He kissed her again and heard her sigh. If they were anywhere else he would have been stripping off their clothes. That little sigh made him painfully erect, and made his heart feel like it was about to explode.

"Is this a perk I don't know anything about?"

Upon hearing Jennifer's bemused question, they froze on the couch, Jaimie half on Harry, her thigh pressed nicely against his hard-on, her hands on either side of his head. And Harry, when he froze, had both hands down her pants and curved around her sweet behind. Jaimie nearly broke his wrists in an effort to catapult herself from his grasp.

"We aren't . . . We don't . . ." Jaimie stopped when she heard Harry chuckling behind her. She turned just long enough to glare at him. "This doesn't happen. It won't happen again. He . . . he . . . was dreaming and thought I was someone else."

"Someone with curly hair," he said, and was gifted with another dagger-eyed look.

"We are not an item," Jaimie said firmly. "I have to get back to work." She marched out of the office, her cheeks flaming.

Harry sat up and pulled out his shirt as he did to hide the rather obvious bulge in his khakis.

"Great timing, Mom," Harry said.

"Screwing the help, honey? Not very smart." Harry's mother sat behind his desk and propped her feet up. "You did say this would be an interesting job."

"Very funny. Nothing has happened between us."

"Oh, and you shove your hands down the pants of everyone on the editorial staff." Her body shook as she silently laughed.

"No. Just Jaimie's. Do we really want to have this conversation right now?"

She shook her head, still chuckling. "If you want me to help save this little gem of yours, you've got to do your part. Sleeping on the job and having an affair with your city editor is just not my idea of using your brains." She leaned toward him, studying his face as only a mother can, making Harry wish he'd never decided hiring his mother was a good idea. "Getting involved with that woman is perhaps the dumbest thing you can do right now. You do know that, don't you?"

"We are not having an affair."

"You want to," she said, insightful as ever. It's what made her one of the best reporters he'd ever known. "You're going back to the *Times,* kiddo. Don't forget that." She picked up a copy of that day's *Nortown Journal* and unceremoniously plopped it down. "This is just a way station until you're back on your feet. What's the latest on the investigation?"

Harry sighed. "I told you, there is no investigation. Not officially, anyway. Rich just called to let me know something's going on and he thinks it might be about tampering with stories. You know Mitch Godfrey? He's about a hundred years old and from the old school. That guy checks everything. He's a lousy writer but I've never seen him get a fact wrong. Three stories in a row came up with factual errors. Big ones. Apparently the old guy was near tears when editorial called him in. So now they've got two respected reporters claiming that their stories somehow got tampered with. Rich thinks they've got to look into it. But I'm not expecting a call any time soon. Besides, I've got no guarantee I'd get re-instated even if they did find something."

Jennifer snorted. "They'd hire you back and you know it. You've got to set your mind in that direction. Not," and she jerked her head toward the newsroom, "in that direction. Listen, honey, I don't know Jaimie at all, but I do know one thing. She's not New York material. She doesn't have the drive, that fire you need to get out of places like this."

"You seemed happy at that weekly all those years."

"Honey, you can't raise three kids alone and work the hours on a daily. I did what I had to do." She walked to the door.

"Do you ever wish you'd gotten your chance at a big market? The *Globe* or the *Times?*" He asked his mother, but he was really thinking of Jaimie. And thinking of himself and the choices he'd been forced to make.

"Sure. I'm human. But sometimes you don't have a choice. You get dealt a hand and you go with it. Anne got dealt a lousy hand, but she's got newsprint running through her veins. Times have changed since I was a single mom. She'll be back in New York when all this is over. And so will you."

Harry loved his mother, but it was times like this when he wished he had a more conventional, muffins-in-the-oven type of mom. "Yeah, but look where Anne is now. Pregnant and mooching off her old boyfriend."

Jennifer conceded his point with a shrug. "But she's a tough one."

"She's not as tough as you think. And don't bother telling me how wonderful Anne is to get me away from Jaimie. It's over with Anne and I'm not involved with Jaimie."

"Good. Keep it that way. The last thing you need is a big teary scene when you go back home."

"I agree. By the way, did you come in here to harass me or do you have a reason."

"How often do you fall asleep here?"

Harry felt his cheeks turn ruddy. "Infrequently."

"I'm not being critical, you know that."

"You know I get killer migraines. Especially if I'm already tired."

Jennifer leaned against the door jamb. "Okay, kiddo. You go home."

Harry gave her a crooked smile. "Thanks for filling in, Mom."

She waved a hand at him. "No problem. I missed it. Maybe when this place goes under, I'll look for another job."

He traced a finger slowly across the front page. "We could save it, you know."

She smiled. "But by then, you'll be back in New York."

Then a thought sneaked up on him. *What if I don't go*

back? What if I stay here and make a go of this run-down, piece-of-crap paper. What if I stay?

Then he laughed. Right. Like any sane newsman would pass up a job working at the *New York Times*. Harry might be a lot of things, but he wasn't insane.

Anne thought she was going insane. She was not this woman who turned into jelly at the first sign of animosity. She was tough, dammit, she thought, blowing her nose into yet another tissue. When the door opened and Harry walked in looking tired, she felt petty and bitchy and didn't care.

"You're late."

"I fell asleep." He walked to the kitchen with barely a look in her direction.

Harry was so distant lately, she thought morosely. Talking was the one thing she and Harry had good, and now they didn't even have that. The sex had been good. At least she'd thought it was good until she had sex with Bob. That's when she realized that coming was not the same with every man. Bob and she had chemistry, that gotta-have-you-now stuff that she'd never had with Harry. And she doubted Harry had ever had it with her. Then again, women were much better at faking it than men were. Men didn't even think about faking it. Women did. Before, during and after. She'd never faked a thing with Bob.

"Harry. Come here and talk to me."

He leaned against the door. He was a gorgeous creature, but he just didn't do it for her. A pity. Who would have thought a balding, middle-aged man with muscles that had atrophied into something softer would. She was cursed.

"I'm tired, Anne."

"I thought you said you fell asleep."

He let out a sigh and dropped onto the couch, his eyebrows furrowing when he finally realized she'd been crying. "What's wrong?"

"I'm bored."

"Jesus. Go home then. I'm not your entertainment." He made to get up and Anne stilled him.

"He called."

"Oh."

"He said he just wanted to be sure I was okay. I don't know what's happening to me. I made such an ass of myself." Her eyes welled up again and she was so drained she didn't bother pushing them away. Her throat was constantly constricted, her stomach sick, her eyes burning. Crying had become a way of life for her.

"What'd you say?"

"I told him I missed him." Actually, she'd cut him a new one, called his wife a bitch and him a bastard and told him he'd ruined her life and she wished he'd burn in hell. Then she'd hung up and clutched the phone to her heart and told a dial tone how much she loved him. And wanted him back. And would do just about anything to get him back.

"And what'd he say?"

Had he even said anything? She hadn't waited to listen. She was so hurt, so angry. So much in love she didn't want to hear him say anything nice, anything that would rip her heart in two. She knew what he would say: I love you, babe, but it's tough right now. We've got the house and the kids and I know they're mostly grown but Kim's still in high school and I just can't blah blah blah you're fucked.

"I guess I didn't let him say anything. I hung up."

"Maybe you should talk to him," Harry said, closing

his eyes and leaning his head back against the couch. She wished she loved him, even a little.

"Maybe I should call him back. It's only ten thirty. Maybe he's still in his office."

"Maybe."

"He called me from there. That was only an hour ago." She bit her lip. "I should call him."

"Go ahead." He moved to get up again and she stopped him.

"Stay. If you're here, maybe I won't get stupid." He gave her a look, but he settled back into the couch, making her feel even guiltier. Harry truly looked tired and she was using him. Again.

She was using him, again, but damn if Harry could garner enough energy to even care. Two months ago, his gut would have churned with jealousy and resentment at the thought of being in the same room as Anne when she talked to her boyfriend. Now he wished she'd just make the phone call and let him go to sleep. Next to him, she picked up the phone and dialed.

"It's me."

Harry turned his head and watched Anne to better gauge the conversation, to know whether she was going to dissolve once again into tears or fly into a rage. Her angular face had been softened a bit by the small amount of weight she'd gained with the pregnancy, and her hair was longer, less harsh, making her look almost girly. Not at all like the woman he'd fallen for all those years ago. He'd never seen a person change so quickly—or perhaps she was finally revealing herself. The Anne he knew was the calmest, least ruffleable person he'd ever known. He didn't recognize the woman she'd become, the weepy, bitter, pissed off, bitchy thing with a huge belly sitting next to him. It couldn't all be the pregnancy.

"I'm sorry about those things I . . ." She clutched the phone in a white-knuckled grasp.

"I'm fine. Getting big." Harry's eyes traveled down to her belly. Tall, thin, with a basketball tucked under her T-shirt, which made her look even more vulnerable than she acted.

She looked over to Harry. "He's here. Right next to me." A small smile. Then her face crumpled. "Oh, Bob, don't." She shook her head back and forth. "I know you do. I know. But . . ."

And then the waterworks started in earnest. "You did? When?" She bit her lips and her hand started to shake and Harry wondered if he should grab the phone from her and tell Bob to go to hell. "Oh, God, Bob. Oh God."

"Oh God what?" Harry said, but Anne just shook her head.

"I don't have a car. I'll have to get a train so . . ." She let out a sob. "You will? I love you. I love you so much." Anne dissolved into what apparently were tears of joy and Harry relaxed. "Let me give you the address."

Harry sat there and wondered when he started rooting for Anne to get back together with that ass of a boyfriend of hers. Maybe the guy wasn't so bad. Naw. The jerk had cheated on his wife, knocked up his girlfriend, given her lousy investment advice, let her lose nearly everything she owned, then deserted her. And Anne wanted him back. Love really did stink.

Anne hung up after telling Bob his address. "He left his wife and got us an apartment. He's picking me up tomorrow." Through her tears, she beamed at him, too happy to even try to hide it.

"Why do you love this guy, Anne. He treated you like shit."

She looked down at her stomach and smiled gently. "I don't know. I just do." She looked up at him, an odd expression in her eyes. "I'm sorry about us, Harry. It just wasn't there for me."

"You know, I'm beginning to think it wasn't there for me either. I thought it was my heart that got trampled, but I really think now it was my ego. I couldn't believe you'd dump me. Otherwise I'd be real pissed off about now. But I'm not. I want you to be sure about Bob, though. He's got a lousy track record."

"I'm sure. I love him," she said, with a small shrug. "I tried not to. I know what he is, and I still love him. And I'm pretty sure he feels the same way about me." She gave him a hug and kissed his cheek. "You've been great, Harry. I don't know what I would have done without you. I really fell apart, didn't I?"

"You really did."

She let out a sad laugh. "It's this damn love thing. It gets you and turns you into an idiot. That and the hormones have done a number on me."

"You think?"

She tossed a pillow at him. "I'm going to bed." Anne heaved herself off his couch, belly first, and walked down the hall toward her room. Harry watched her with a small smile, feeling of all things, envy. He didn't recognize that woman who'd just waddled away. They'd lived together for nearly four years and never in that time had she dredged up for him nearly half the emotion he'd just witnessed. Anne, hard as nails Anne, was madly in love.

And he couldn't even get a decent kiss from a woman he was crazy about.

Chapter 16

Jaimie snapped her bubble gum and tried not to smile as she went through that day's obits. Harry thought she was a cool chick. No one, not even she, ever thought of herself as cool. Jaimie was serious, determined, nerdy. Never cool.

"I'm cool," she sang to herself. The obituaries were flawless, already edited by Jennifer and she figured she didn't have to check her work anymore. She'd almost always checked Nathan, and usually found a few small things he'd missed. But Jennifer was amazingly thorough. She also had amazingly bad timing. Jaimie's cheeks still burned when she thought of the older woman discovering her on the couch with Harry. And her protests were embarrassingly weak. She should apologize, explain she and Harry had once almost been an item, but now were nothing.

Nothing but two people who were wildly attracted to one another and were fighting it tooth and nail. Well, at least she was fighting it.

"You haven't made a mistake yet," Jaimie said, craning her neck over her computer.

"Just doing what I do," Jennifer said in her clipped manner.

"About last night . . ."

Jennifer looked around the side of her large screen. "Forget it. I already did."

"Okay, but I know how uncomfortable it can be when two people are involved and I want you to know that Harry and I are definitely not involved. We were. Briefly. But now we're not. At all."

"Glad to hear it," she said, sounding bored.

Jaimie frowned. "We did date. Almost, anyway."

Jennifer stood. "Look, hon, I really don't care. And if you keep talking, I'm going to tell you something that's really going to embarrass you."

"I just didn't want you to feel uncomfortable. That's all."

Jennifer rolled her eyes. "No. You wanted to talk about how you and Harry aren't really an item when it is obviously clear that you are."

"Harry doesn't . . ."

"I know Harry doesn't. But you do," Jennifer said.

Jaimie flushed. "What do you mean?" Oh, God, had they talked about her last night after she left the office? Had Harry said something to this stranger? If he had, she'd have to kill him. Slowly.

"Harry and I go way back, kiddo," she said, giving Jaimie a rather pitying look. "I know how he operates."

"How he operates?" Jaimie asked dumbly.

Just then Harry walked in and waved to them both. "Let's go," Jennifer said, walking directly to Harry's office.

Panic set in, making Jaimie's entire body break out into a horrible, painful sweat. "What are you doing?" she whispered harshly, but she followed Jennifer anyway.

"Harry, tell the girl who I am, please."

Harry looked from one woman to the other with a

rather sick expression. "Jaimie, I'd like you to meet my mother."

Jaimie whipped her head around and stared at the woman who bore absolutely no resemblance to Harry. She was short, stubby, with too-curly hair and brown eyes that looked way too amused at the moment. "Why didn't you tell me?"

"Because I didn't want your relationship strained. You have to work together. You're her superior. And I hired her because I wanted a temporary replacement. I didn't want to hire someone who would be out of a job in three months. I didn't think that was fair. And if I explained my reasons to you, you would have argued we are going to save this paper when the true chances of that are about as remote as me playing in the big leagues."

"If that's the way you really think, why don't we just fold now. Let's make an announcement today." Jaimie tried to stop her voice from shaking, but was only marginally successful.

"Because. I still think I have a chance to play for the Yankees some day. I'm just as delusional as you are when it comes to this paper."

She studied his face, trying to see if he meant what he said. "Harry, you're never going to play for the Yankees."

He shrugged. "That's not the point. The point is, somewhere in this thick skull of mine, I'm holding out hope. I'm not giving up on this paper, but I know the reality of the situation. We have got to make up an incredible shortfall or Paul's brother is going to sell. That's reality. And that's why I hired my mother." Then he grinned. "Plus, she came at a cheap price and she's damned good."

"If you two are finished lifting each other up, I'd like something else made clear." Harry and Jaimie turned toward the older woman, who turned and faced Jaimie.

"Harry is going back to the *Times* as soon as this mess there is all cleared up. Isn't that right, Harry."

"What's she talking about?"

"There's an internal investigation into possible tampering with stories. Apparently I wasn't the only victim."

Jaimie felt her stomach drop to her toes and a dull roaring sound began in her ears. She'd never thought Harry would go back to the *Times*. But of course he would if he could. And she'd still be here at the *Nortown Journal,* still living in her little house, still living with her stupid cat. Still alone.

"Do you really think you'll get your job back?" she asked, trying to ignore the fact her gut was ripping in two.

Harry gave his mother a look that Jaimie couldn't read, and suddenly she felt like the outsider. They'd talked about her, she realized, they'd talked about *them.* And Harry, apparently, had reassured his mother he'd felt nothing for her.

"I haven't heard anything specific."

"Oh."

"But it's only a matter of time before they clear his name," Jennifer said, her voice snapping.

"Then you'll be able to go back. That's great, Harry. Really," Jaimie said above the roar that was growing slightly louder.

Harry shifted in his seat slightly. "Sure. After everything is settled here."

"That's great. Really."

"Harry belongs in New York. Did you read any of his 9/11 pieces? Best goddamn bit of journalism I've ever seen," Jennifer said, pride and a subtle threat in every syllable.

"We always knew Harry didn't belong here. We even had a pool going trying to figure out why he took the job," Jaimie said, forcing a laugh, just to let his mother know she knew what was going on. Harry was going back. She was staying here.

"You listen, young lady, don't get any ideas about Harry, because he doesn't belong at this paper. And he doesn't belong with you. I know it hurts, kid, but that's just the way it's got to be. My son's a star and you're a little nobody from a nothing little town. You'll only tie him down, hold him back. So for his sake, go home, kid. Here's ten bucks for a bus." [Close-up of young woman] Tears slide down younger woman's face as she holds out her hand for the money.

"Have any more relatives out in the newsroom?" Jaimie asked, keeping things light, forcing herself to believe she didn't care he was leaving. After all, he wasn't leaving her. They weren't even an item. They were something that didn't happen.

"I'm sorry I didn't tell you about my mother. I debated about it, but decided everyone would be more comfortable not knowing."

Jaimie smiled as if it didn't bother her, but it did. "I suppose you don't want anyone else to know?"

"No. I don't want you to have to lie. Even by omission. I'll send out an e-mail. Fair enough?"

"Sure. At least now I know why she's so good. I was starting to get a complex, thinking you hired her to replace me."

"You never know, kiddo." And Jennifer laughed infectiously, ruining any chance Jaimie had of completely disliking her.

Joshua Tate's birthday was October twenty-third. He would have been eleven years old. Jaimie marked her calendar: Tate story run? And then chewed on her pen wondering whether there even was a Joshua Tate story. The only story left to tell were who killed him and why. The chances of her finding that out were as remote as—she frowned—Harry making the Yankees.

Jaimie sat at her kitchen table, pushed Max aside, and systematically marked off the houses she'd gone to on a map she'd drawn up of his neighborhood. In all, she'd interviewed thirty neighbors, including Geoffrey Fox. She knew there was a slim chance someone she'd talked to had killed the kid, and that the most likely suspect was neat-freak Geoffrey Fox. Jaimie looked at the map and frowned. Her heart was no longer in this story, it was no longer even with the fight to save the *Journal*. What was the point? So she could work here another twelve years pounding out stories no one read, writing headlines over city council stories no one cared about?

You could always leave.

Jaimie hated that voice of reason that popped into her head. Chances were she'd have to leave if the *Journal* didn't make budget. And then what would she do? Get a cushy job like Nate working PR for a hospital or college? Just the thought made her feel sick. The *Day* would probably hire her; its editor Peter Shelby had hinted it enough times for her to feel fairly comfortable about her future. She wouldn't be city editor, that was for certain, but maybe she could finagle the job of new bureau chief for Nortown. That would be okay. More than okay if it meant she beat Carly Strickland out of the job.

"It would almost be as if I didn't leave, huh, Max?" she said, rubbing the cat between his ears. Max closed his eyes for a brief moment of ecstasy before jumping off the table. She could drive by the *Nortown Shop-a-Day* everyday and say good riddance. And she'd be damned if she'd be haunted by memories of anything, particularly Harry. He'd back in New York, back being a star and respectable. Back where he belonged. Jaimie pressed the heels of her hands against her eyes trying to banish all thoughts of the future. No matter what happened, nothing would ever be the same again. Even if by some miracle they pulled it off and saved the paper, Harry would be gone. Her heart . . .

She pushed against her eyes harder but it was no good. "I'm not in love. I'm in lust. In like." And her heart would not break when he left. He'd go, she'd give him a hug, a nice sturdy backslapping good-luck buddy hug. *I'll miss your foul temper, your complete lack of sense of humor. Your beautiful eyes. Your sexy mouth. The way you have five o'clock shadow at two in the afternoon. The way you hold me.*

"Stop it," she said aloud, angry and disappointed with herself.

Jaimie forced her attention back to the map in front of her.

Behind the Tate neighborhood was a thin stretch of woods leading to a new development. It was possible someone there had seen something without realizing it. Maybe Joshua had befriended someone over there. Probably not. The kid didn't seem to have a single real friend, just kids in the neighborhood who knew him. She tapped her pen against the map leaving behind little dots. It was Saturday, her one day off, and she was obsessing about a story she'd probably never write. That was better than obsessing about Harry.

Despite her instincts, Jaimie grabbed her notebook and headed out to Cedar Heights, a rather grand name for a neighborhood built in what used to be a cornfield and had almost no trees, never mind cedars. The developers planted a cedar on either side of the Cedar Heights sign, one of which looked dead. The houses here came in three styles: Colonial box, Colonial ugly, and Colonial pseudo-pretentious.

Twenty times she knocked on the doors: "Hi, I'm Jaimie McLane from the *Journal*. I'm doing a story about the Tate murder. Yes, it was terrible. I'm wondering if you knew Joshua. Or someone in your house? Because I'm a loser with nothing to do on a Saturday, my only day off, and I like wasting my time talking to people who stare at me vacantly."

Jaimie stared at the last house she was knocking on that day, because she was about to rip her notebook to shreds. She rang the doorbell and listened to footsteps approach. An elderly man answered, looking at her suspiciously.

"Hi. I'm Jaimie McLane from the *Journal*. I'm doing a story about the Tate murder."

"I heard about the kid when I was in Florida."

"So, you weren't here when it happened?"

"Oh, no. My wife and I go to Florida every winter."

"You didn't know him?"

He actually put some thought into it before he said, "Oh, no. Not too many youngsters around here."

Feeling defeated and tired, Jaimie said, "Well, thank you. If you think of anything, let me know."

"I will."

Jaimie left, thinking he was the kind of man who would lose a night's sleep trying to remember if he'd ever even seen Joshua Tate.

Harry had just hung up the phone from leaving Jaimie a message when he saw her walk in. She wore light khakis and a red shirt that clung nicely to her body and made Harry forget for an instant that he'd just heard the best news of his life. Lust was a cruel, cruel thing.

"Hey, McLane," he yelled because no one, not even a janitor, was on this floor. He'd come in to organize his paperwork, filled with the kind of high a person normally only got by snorting something. But in Harry's case, the high was completely natural. He rolled his eyes when she stopped to grab her big brown sweater, pulling it on as she walked toward his office. She tucked her hands behind her neck and flung them up, freeing her trapped hair, giving him for just a millisecond, a heady vision of her tousling her hair around her head like she did that day in his apartment.

"What's up?" she asked as she flung herself down onto the couch.

He grinned, he couldn't help it.

"How would you like to be acting managing editor and publisher for about a week?" He watched as her expression went from confusion to disbelief and suspicion, to a dawning awareness of what he was saying and why he was standing there smiling like an idiot.

"The investigation is official," she said, acting bored for the count of two before jumping up and flying around to his side of the desk, practically tackling him with her enthusiasm. "Harry, that's so great. I'm so happy for you."

He looked down at her smiling face, her eyes glowing, her hands locked behind his neck like a guileless child, laughing up at him. And suddenly it was hard to breathe, hard to take having her look at him as if she couldn't tear her eyes away. Looking at him, he thought with gut-churning suspicion, as if she were in love with him. Something must have shown in his face because she pulled away quickly, muttering an apology, wiping her hands on her pants in a nervous gesture he'd seen before.

She couldn't love him. Couldn't. But he was pretty sure that's what he was seeing. Not just happiness. Because you only got that happy for someone you loved. She was looking down, up, sideways, anywhere but at his face. And he just stared at her, not quite believing it, afraid it was true and just as afraid he was a royal idiot and completely misreading her.

"So. The investigation is official. Why do you have to go?"

"Apparently they've brought in an outside firm to conduct the investigation. They still hope to keep it private, but I think that's a little naïve."

"Or wishful thinking."

He nodded. "I have to give a few interviews, tell my side of the story, give them any theories I might have. It may not take all week, but that's what they told me to block out. I'd say two weeks, tops. I can be back at work by mid-November."

And out of here by January, Jaimie thought. "November. Wow. Not great timing, Harry." She felt her eyes fill up with tears and saw the look of pure panic on Harry's face. "Might as well just hang it up and go looking for a job." Jaimie blinked, spilling tears down her cheek, feeling like the biggest fool God had ever created. She'd seen that look on Harry's face, that holy-shit-she-loves-me face. She'd seen that look in her own mirror, except with her it had always been some loser guy falling in love with her. And that's why she was crying, not because Harry's absence would truly hurt the paper's chances of surviving. She loved him and hadn't known it until she felt that unbelievable surge of unadulterated joy when he'd told her he was getting his investigation. Even though it meant he'd probably go back to New York for good. She was happy for him and a person didn't feel that kind of powerful emotion unless . . .

Unless they were ridiculously in love. So ridiculously in love she'd foolishly let it show. And Harry had seen because he was an observant guy, a reporter. He didn't miss a trick. He'd seen, and he hadn't liked it. Because Jaimie was a damned good reporter too, and she hadn't missed that look of dawning horror on his face when he'd looked down at her looking up at him.

He cleared his throat. "I've got everything in place. Just follow the plan. And my mother, you know how good she is. She can take over your spot until I come back."

"I know," Jaimie said, brushing away the tears. "I just had a bad day, that's all. This Joshua Tate story stinks. It's not even a story, which means I've wasted about forty hours of my life working on something that will never see the light of day."

"Sorry."

"Plus I am worried about the paper. Now I'm going to worry about you and whether they can come up with proof that your stories were tampered with," she said with a little laugh.

"I haven't been given any guarantees about getting my job back no matter the result of the investigation," Harry said, an unusual edge to his voice. "Maybe I'm making more of this than I should."

"No, you're not. I'm sure of it." She searched his face. "But what if, someone makes the insane decision to not hire you back? What then?"

His face tightened and her heart dropped. "I don't even want to think about that." He looked like a man facing the possibility of the death sentence.

"Geez, Harry." She swallowed hard, not wanting to cry. Because if she cried now, he'd know for sure she was in love with him.

Chapter 17

He'd been gone for four days. His office was dark, and depressingly empty. Jaimie kept looking at the darkened windows, feeling about as low as she ever had in her life. In three hours, Harry was going to be interviewed by someone who didn't care about the outcome, who didn't realize he held someone's very life in his hands. The truth was, she didn't know what she wanted the investigation to find. She knew Harry hadn't made the mistakes they claimed he made; he was too good a writer and reporter for that. But if they didn't hire him back, would she be relieved or devastated? Probably a little of both.

Every time she thought about it, it drove her nuts. She'd known all along what a huge mistake it would be to get involved with Harry. She'd done her best. She'd tried to stay away, to protect her heart. Of course, she'd failed as she always knew, in her heart of hearts, that she would. She couldn't stop thinking about him, hurting for him, missing him. To top it off, she had this fantasy of traveling to New York City and being there when he walked out of the *Times*.

"Darling, I knew you'd come." He grasps her hand, his eyes filling with unshed tears.

"I had to be here. I love you so."

"And I you, darling." He pulls her close, presses his firm lips against hers, letting her warm him.

That's what watching too many 1940s movies at two in the morning did to you. Reality would probably be much more painful.

"Jaimie? What the hell are you doing here? Who's running the paper?"

"Um."

"Listen, babe, we had a good time. Let's just leave it at that, hmmm? I'm New York-bound, baby-cakes."

"Um."

So what if she actually got in her car and drove to New York? What if she camped outside the *Times* building and waited for him to come out? She could drive like a madwoman and get there in time. That didn't mean she was a complete idiot. It only meant she was crazy, and crazy wasn't as bad as stupid. The interview would last at least an hour, so if she left right now, she could be there with a bottle of champagne and a smile when he was finished. Everyone was always telling her to take time off. So she would take time off, to take a nice little jaunt to the Big Apple.

Jaimie thought his mother should go, but Jennifer refused to. "I can do him more good here," she'd said when Jaimie suggested she could go with him. "He's a big boy. He'll handle it and come out of all this smelling like a rose." She was right. Harry didn't need her there, he needed her at the paper.

She looked up at the clock. She could make it. New York was only two to three hours away, depending on traffic. She tapped her fingers on the keyboard. *Rat-ta-tat.* But wouldn't he think it was kind of weird for her to drive to New York? All she had to do was call and ask him how everything went. *Rat-ta-tat.* And going in person would only prove how pathetically in love she was with him. *Rat-ta-*

"Will you knock it off, please?" Jennifer snapped. "Christ, I can hardly think."

"Sorry." Jaimie's cheeks burned unnaturally bright. "Jennifer?"

"Yeah, what."

"I think I'm sick." Jaimie watched as Jennifer peeked around her computer to give her a good look.

"You look like crap. Go home. I can handle the rest, right?"

"I hate to do that to you." Guilt made her cheeks burn brighter.

"Honestly, the more I have to do the better." Jennifer's phone rang and she jumped, then snatched it up. "Southwick." A long silence, then a short nod. "Okay. Good luck, kiddo." She hung up the phone with a grim look and Jaimie felt her heart nearly stop. Harry. Something happened to Harry.

Jaimie swallowed hard. "Was that Harry?" she asked, trying to sound merely curious and not as if she wanted to put her hands around Jennifer's throat and throttle the words out of her.

"He just wanted to let me know that everything's on schedule." Finally she smiled. "Well, back to work."

Back to work? How the hell could she keep working? "Jennifer. What if it goes badly? What if he still can't prove he was right? Don't you think someone should be there? You should go."

"He'll be fine," she said, and banged up another story. "But you look like you're on death's door. I'll need you one hundred percent tomorrow. All that weekend crap to edit. So go home, will ya?"

Jaimie hesitated another minute, feeling as if she

might throw up. She had to go. Had to. She shut down her computer, grabbed her bag and headed out the door before she could talk some sense into herself.

"Hey, where are you going?" Kath asked, nearly bumping into Jaimie as she went out the door. "I could use a sandwich if you're going to Sal's. Chicken parm."

Jaimie hesitated a second, then waved for her friend to follow her down the stairs. When she hit the blast of chilly air outside, she hugged her sweater close to her, not stopping until she got to her car.

"What's up?"

"I'm going to New York."

Kath, her bushy hair pressed back by too much gel and an ugly barrette, shook her head. "No you're not. You could save about six hours of your life if you just put a sign on your back: I'm in love with Harry Crandall."

Jaimie lowered her head, closed her eyes, and let out a puff of air. "You're right."

"Thanks. Anything else?"

"But I'm still going."

Kath put her hands on Jaimie's shoulders. "Look at me." She waited until Jaimie opened her eyes and stared mutely at her before continuing. "You are staying here. God, Jaimie, you're not even dating the guy."

"But he's alone and if the news is bad he won't have anyone to talk to."

"By choice. His mother didn't even go."

"She's internalizing her feelings by continuing to work even though she's very concerned. I could tell."

Kath rolled her eyes. "Bullcrap. She knows he'll be fine. Listen to me." She gave Jaimie a small shake. "Listen. Cruel to be kind. Ready? Here goes: He doesn't love you. I doubt he even thinks about you when you leave the building at night. Come on, Jaimie. You've created this fantasy in your head that has as much to do with reality as Santa Claus does."

Jaimie leaned her head on Kath's shoulder, knowing she was right. Harry didn't love her. "I know. *I know.* The thing is, Kath, I do love him. And I want to be there for him."

"What if everything goes fine and he wonders what the hell you're doing in New York instead of Nortown where you belong?"

Jaimie looked up and made a sick face. "I'm pretty sure he already knows I love him. This may come as a shock, but I'm not very good at hiding my feelings."

Kath laughed. "The curse of the Irish.

"My point is, he already knows, so the damage is already done."

Kath let out a long breath of air. "You want me to tell you to go. So go."

"Really?"

Kath looked up as if asking the gods for help. "No, you idiot."

Jaimie felt her entire body sag.

"Are you going?"

Yes yes yes. "No. Of course not. No."

But God, she wanted to.

Harry walked out of the *Times* building feeling relieved and battered. It was rush hour and the sounds of the city were loud and comforting, the sidewalks crowded and familiar. From the corner of his eye, he saw her, Jaimie. It was her, he recognized the red hair, the nice behind. She turned the corner out of sight and he ran after her, elated that she'd come to New York, too happy to wonder what the hell she was doing there. He ran after her, a big grin on his face. "Jaimie! Hey, Jaimie." Either she was ignoring him or couldn't hear him above the roar of the traffic. The sidewalk was crowded and he kept losing sight of her as he half ran after that bopping head of hers. And then she disappeared, but not before he caught a glimpse of her profile and realized it wasn't her. He stood on the wide sidewalk as people waded around him, looking like a kid who'd lost his parents.

Then he closed his eyes and shook his head. It wasn't Jaimie. Why the hell had he thought it was Jaimie? He'd run down the street like a fool chasing after a woman who had red hair.

He ought to be feeling ecstatic about the interview, about how well this week was going. Instead he was embarrassingly disappointed that the redhead hadn't been Jaimie.

"Shit," he whispered, turning slowly around.

He didn't love her. Lust, yes. Like, sure. But not love. He couldn't love her, not when his life was getting back on track, not when he was going back to New York. Jaimie was not a low-maintenance woman; she was nothing like Anne had been. Anne and he'd gone days without seeing one another, both single-mindedly pursuing their careers. He knew he couldn't have that sort of easy relationship with Jaimie. She was the kind of woman you wanted to be with, the kind you married and loved until death. That sort of woman. And Jaimie wouldn't want to leave Nortown. And he sure as hell didn't want to stay. Not that he would, because he didn't love her.

Jaime had heard that people who are about to die enter a zone, a calm, almost acceptance of what was about to happen. Well, she'd just figured out she wasn't one of those people. She was going to fight to the bitter end to prevent Harry from realizing she was completely and foolishly in love with him.

After blubbering in the parking lot with Kath, Jaimie had put her chin up and walked right back into the newsroom miraculously cured of whatever had ailed her. She just kept thinking of Kath's words, over and over: *He doesn't love you. I doubt he even thinks about you when you leave the building at night.* So when Harry called his mother to let her know how the investigation was going, she had Jennifer pass the call over to her.

"Harry. It's Jaimie. How *are* you doing?"

"Jaimie? Where are you?"

"I'm in the newsroom." *You silly, where else would I be? I sure as heck wouldn't be in New York because then you'd know I'm madly in love with you and neither of us want that, do we?*

"You're in the newsroom."

Jaimie screwed up her face at his tone. "Working hard. Listen, just wanted to let you know everything's okay here. How'd it go with you?" Casual. Friendly. Polite.

"It went fine." Cold. Bored. Not in love.

Ted walked by and Jaimie frantically waved him over because her throat was threatening to close up and she was desperately afraid she might say something stupid.

"What?" Ted mouthed.

"I'm talking to Harry," she said, moving the phone down a bit. "Harry, want to talk to Ted? He's right here."

"Yo, Harry. You still fired or what?"

Jaimie smacked Ted on the arm and grabbed the phone back.

"Why are guys so rotten to one another? Well, are you?" She held her breath.

"Technically, yes. But I have a feeling the investigation is going my way," he said, sounding slightly distracted. "You weren't in New York, were you? I saw this woman and I chased her half across Manhattan thinking it was you."

Her heart did a hard plummet. "Nope. I was here."

"Well, maybe you have a twin."

"I was this close to hopping in my car and driving to New York so I could hold your hand," she said, laughing so he'd know she was joking. Right. "That would have been crazy. Right?" Jaimie ignored how much importance her ridiculous heart was putting on his answer.

"I suppose." If Harry had been sitting across from her, he would have been the recipient of her best withering look. *I suppose.* What kind of answer was that?

"Glad to hear you're doing okay. Things are going fine here." Things were actually going pretty darn good. Ad sales were exceeding needed projections, much to the surprise of everybody, including the advertising manager. The circulation department had boasted a ten percent increase in subscriptions and a fifteen percent increase in store sales. Not bad, considering the editorial side of things was suffering a dearth of good stories. It was pretty tough coming up with stellar front pages when the most pressing issue at city hall was the type of street lights to put up in the city's dying retail section. Stop the presses.

And it was always wonderful to be reminded by Jennifer at least three times a day that Harry would be returning to New York the minute he was able to. Jaimie filled him in briefly, keeping everything on a businesslike level. Though she did wonder what he thought when he thought he saw her. Had he been bewildered? Happy? Scared that she'd turned into some kind of deranged stalker?

Or had he felt sorry for her?

Oh, God, it was better off not knowing if he'd felt sorry for her.

"Nice to talk to you, Harry. Everyone sends their best wishes."

"Ummm. Okay. Bye."

Jaimie squeezed the phone and closed her eyes. "Bye."

"So. How's Harry?" Kath said, inches away from her, unapologetically having eavesdropped on most of her conversation with Harry.

"Go away."

Kath dragged her friend up by the arm and pulled her into the morgue. "Someday you'll be glad you listened to me."

"I know." Despite her misery, the musty smell of the morgue was soothing. She couldn't count how many hours she'd spent looking up old stories, straining her eyes to read copy projected by the ancient microfiche machine.

Kath made Jaimie look right into her gray eyes. "You okay?"

Jaimie looked at her old friend, knowing she looked scared and desperate and exactly like a person who was losing it. "This has never, ever happened to me. I never fell for a guy like this. This isn't me. This is some alien who's invaded my body and is making me want to do insane things. Why can't I be normal?"

Kath laughed. "You are being normal. Sort of. People do very strange things when they're in love. Most of the time, though, it's a mutual thing. It's all, 'I love you' and 'I love you, too.' It's not this clandestine thing, this unrequited love thing you've got going. It's not healthy."

"So you don't think there's a chance he feels the same?"

"Oh, honey." And she gave Jaimie a hug, which only made her feel worse.

Harry hung up the phone and stared at it for a good long time. Part of him had wished she hadn't been there, that it *had* been her he'd seen. He let his gaze scan the New York skyline, feeling sad and lonely and stupidly disappointed. She hadn't been there. She hadn't come. Of course she hadn't.

Harry stopped himself in mid thought. "Holy shit," he breathed. He did wish she'd come to New York to see him. And that could only mean one thing.

He shook his head hard, trying to rid himself of that little train of thought. Damn this city. It was making him think all sorts of crazy things.

Chapter 18

Just when Jaimie thought things couldn't get worse, things got a lot worse.

Two days before Harry was set to return to work—before, of course, he went back to the *Times,* Barry De-Silva, the paper's business reporter for two years and one of the most solid staffers, came into the newsroom with a big grin on his face.

"I've got you your lead story," he announced, all happy, all full of himself, and Jaimie could feel that old familiar thrill in her stomach. When reporters came in that confident, even if they were new, chances were they had one hell of a story.

"What is it?"

"Hampton's is going out of business. Two hundred lay-offs expected within a month. It's closing the Nortown store immediately, no notice. Nice guys, huh? Then slowly phasing out its remaining stores over the next three months. Geez, you'd think with all the advertising they did that they had a load of cash."

Those last words echoed in Jaimie's head for a long time. All the advertising. All that money. Gone. Barry couldn't know the significance of his story, that it meant not only the end of Hampton's but could horribly hurt the chances of the *Nortown Journal* surviving. Two grand old businesses felled by a single swing. Still, it was a fantastic story, big news in this already depressed piece of Connecticut, so Jaimie forced a smile, praying the impact to the paper wouldn't be too bad. "Great story. How'd you find out?"

"Friend of mine's mother works in the management office. She was told to pack up her personal stuff and leave. I got some terrific quotes from a bunch of employees. Oh, and they haven't even filed yet. They do that today. I'm going to hang out by the courthouse and wait."

Despite what it meant for the paper's finances, Jaimie grinned. "You think the *Day* will find out?"

"Hope not. Hampton's wasn't planning to put out a press release until tomorrow. After the fact, after all the pissed off employees were gone. But who knows? I found out on a fluke. If the *Day* hasn't checked the court records yet, they could get it. But not as good." His face was shining as he left for the courthouse.

Two hours later Jaimie was staring glumly at the headline "Hampton's Closing, Hundreds Lose Jobs." It was a huge story; Barry had done a fantastic job getting quotes, court documents—they filed just minutes before the court closed—getting pictures of workers standing in front of the old building looking sad and bewildered. Hampton's was a small independent department store, one of those old-fashioned places that were dying out everywhere thanks to malls and Wal-Mart. They'd seemed to be doing well, advertising like mad.

After giving the story a quick edit, Jaimie walked down to the advertising department, not wanting to alert anyone in the newsroom that she was less than thrilled about one of the biggest stories since the Joshua Tate murder. The advertising department was like a different world from the newsroom. It was modern, clean and looked like a real office. Money begat money.

"Laura? Do you have a couple of minutes?"

Laura's office was almost as big as Harry's and held a wealth of personal items. It was comfortable and cozy, with an overstuffed floral love seat against one wall, and matching upholstered chairs positioned in front of her desk. One month ago, Laura would have been home already, but she, like nearly every other manager, was working longer and harder in a desperate attempt to save what was most certainly now unsalvageable. She was looking over some ads and looked up, smiling when she saw Jaimie. "Sure. What's up?"

"Have you had any indications that Hampton's was in trouble?" she asked, shutting the door to Laura's office.

Laura furrowed her brow. "Well, they have been late paying for the last six months. Nothing big. And they've always been better than most of our accounts. Why?"

"Because they filed for bankruptcy today."

Laura turned white, not needing more than a second to understand the full impact of Jaimie's announcement. "Oh, God."

"Oh God what?"

Laura eyes filled with tears. "That's it then. We lose."

Jaimie sat down because her legs couldn't hold her anymore.

"Hampton's was our biggest account. By far. More than two million a year. Ten percent of our revenue came from Hampton's."

"But some of it, most of it, they've paid. Right?"

Laura shook her head and Jaimie wanted to throw up. "Most of it, sure. They owed us about a hundred grand. I wasn't worried. Until now." She let out a humorless laugh. "And we had them budgeted for another half million.

That's six hundred thousand. We're back to square one." She leaned back in her chair and looked up at the ceiling. "That's it. Might as well pack it in. God," she sobbed, to Jaimie's disbelief and horror. She truly hadn't thought Laura gave a damn about the paper.

"Even if they can pay the hundred, we're still short," Jaimie said thinking aloud.

"We were going to do it," Laura said with unexpected fervor. "We were going to make that damned two million we needed. Not by a lot. We were going to sneak by, just barely. One month left to raise another half million." She shook her head.

Jaimie sat there in silence, stunned, empty. What could they do? Nothing. Just ride it out and let Paul and Harry make the decision when to tell the staff the paper was being turned into a shopper. Some of the employees would remain on board, the production staff, copyeditors, advertising. It was the editorial staff who would suffer the most, of course. The people who'd made the paper what it was.

"We have to pretend everything is okay," Jaimie said dully. "Otherwise, there's going to be a mass exodus and the paper will fold even faster. You know, you'll probably still have a job."

"Probably," Laura admitted. "I don't know, though. A shopper. After that meeting with Paul, it hit me. I walked down those stairs and looked at those papers on the wall. It was like going back in time, more than a hundred years. I know it sounds overly dramatic, but this paper has been the heart of this city for a long time. It covers Little League games, school lunches, fiftieth anniversaries. You can bet the *Day* isn't going to run the crap we run. And it was during our watch that it got killed."

"Gee, stop making me feel better."

Laura let out a laugh. "You've been here practically your whole life, haven't you?"

"I was nineteen when I started here. A sophomore in college." Jaimie shook her head, not quite believing she was having this conversation. "I never seriously thought about moving on. People expected me to, I know that. But the thought of leaving made me sick. This just might kill me," she said, laughing sadly.

"What are you going to do?"

"The first thing I have to do is tell Harry what's happened. He was supposed to get back in town today and come into work on Monday. I'll talk to you later, Laura. Who knows, maybe we'll stumble on a miracle."

"Like finding out where Jimmy Hoffa is buried? Now a story like that would sell some advertising."

Jaimie stood at the door. "You are one cynical lady. I thought I was bad."

Jaimie left her laughing. Anything was better than that hysterical crying Laura had given into—even if it was only for a few terrifying seconds.

First she called Paul, then Harry—whom she hadn't talked to in days. She took a few deep breaths, to prepare herself to hear his voice, to make herself not say anything that he might construe as her missing him. She did. Terribly. Agonizingly. She couldn't wait until all this was over and he was in New York. Because she had to stop herself a dozen times a day from calling him.

Jaimie took a deep breath and punched in his number. "Harry. It's Jaimie. I've got some bad news and I think you'd better come in. One of our biggest accounts just filed for bankruptcy and we're out about six hundred grand. Paul is on his way."

"I'll be right over."

Four words, about as impassive as could be uttered, and her heart was pounding madly.

Harry hung up the phone and wished it would all go away. He hadn't signed up for this, it was supposed to be a cakewalk, an easy job to do until he could get his old job back. The *Nortown Journal* ran itself, Paul had said. He wouldn't have to do a thing except run an occasional editorial meeting, make certain the finances were on track. It wasn't supposed to turn into a complicated mess that not only needed someone who cared, but someone who had one hundred percent to give. He did care, more than he wished he did. It was a matter of pride, mostly, but also one of emotion that made him want to save this rotten little paper. He wanted it for pride, and for her. Mostly for her.

That wasn't supposed to have happened either, he thought, angrily pulling on a clean shirt. He'd always been good at ignoring women, at focusing on his job and his duty. He didn't know when he started thinking about Jaimie more than he thought about anything else, but it had happened, incrementally, sneaking up on him and then knocking him over the head. He'd just gotten out of a relationship, he wasn't supposed to immediately get back into one, not before he was back on his feet and could date a dozen or so women before he settled on one. Not that he was settling on anyone yet. No, there was no "yet" about it. He was going back to New York. He was claiming his old life. If only he could shake this temporary life off his back.

The thought came to him, along with a wave of guilt, that the *Journal's* demise had just handed him his ticket back to New York unencumbered. Say they'd managed to save the paper. Then what? When he left, it would be much more difficult. He would have been forced to choose between his new life and his old one. Now, his hand was forced. Of course he had to go back to New York. They hadn't made the offer official, but they would. Where else was he supposed to go? What was he supposed to do? Date Jaimie for a while, propose, get married, buy a house, have kids and live in this lousy town for the rest of his life?

That scenario should have made him slightly sick. Instead, it made him smile. And *that* made him slightly sick.

"I'm going back to New York. To my real life," he said aloud. Maybe Jaimie would come to New York. She was a great reporter, he'd recommend her. They could work together, live together, who knew?

Yeah, and maybe they could have the same kind of sterile passionless life he'd had with Anne.

No. It was better to cut things clean, to walk away before either of them got in too deeply. He'd stayed away from the paper for two weeks, mostly to avoid Jaimie. She did strange things to him, made him feel like a kid with a fatal crush. Made him feel like he wasn't in control anymore. If he could just not touch her, avoid all contact until he made the official announcement to the newsroom that the paper was folding, then he'd be okay.

If only he hadn't thought she was in New York. That had started all this damned thinking about why he'd been so disappointed that it hadn't been her. His gut was hollow, chewed out by a monster he couldn't see or defeat. If Harry had been a soft kind of guy, he would have recognized that hollow feeling for what it was—loneliness and desperate need. But Harry wasn't a softhearted guy. He stayed away for weeks, he'd purged her from his mind—when he was awake, at least. Sure, sometimes he'd see a redhead from behind and think it looked like Jaimie and his heart would kick up a beat. That was it. That wasn't love. That was his brain working. If he saw an ice cream cone, he'd think of his childhood. See a redhead, think of Jaimie. Made sense.

He'd get over this. He would. He had to.

When Harry got to his office, Paul and Jaimie were already in there. From the looks on their faces, neither was especially happy. He opened his door and shut it quickly to block out the sound of Jaimie's voice from the rest of the newsroom.

"This is not the best thing that could have happened, Paul. I can't believe you just said that. This paper has been in your family for two generations. You practically lived here."

Paul gave her a look as if she'd just proven his point. "You're just afraid to move on."

Jaimie's eyes spit fire as she turned on Harry. He hated clichés, but he'd honestly never seen Jaimie look as beautiful as she did at that moment, her eyes alight with anger, her cheeks flushed, her stance combative. If only she were naked, he could die happy.

"I swear, I could kill him right now, Harry. If I do, I want you as a witness that he is completely responsible for his own death by instigating me."

Paul chuckled, and Harry thought that sound just might push Jaimie over the edge—or rather, pry off the fingertips that were clinging to the edge. "Screw you," she said viciously.

"Always the wordsmith," Paul said with an underlying meanness that surprised Harry. Jaimie looked a bit surprised herself because she closed her mouth and almost looked as if her anger had immediately turned to devastation.

"That's enough," Harry said, and they both had the decency to look guilty. "Jaimie, fill me in."

She gave him a mulish look, before crossing her arms and sitting down on the old sofa. "Hampton's is going out of business. It's our biggest account and they owe us approximately a hundred grand now and we had another five hundred grand budgeted. It was one of our most consistent accounts."

"I always thought it was a mistake to count on Hampton's for so much of our budget," Paul said.

"Paul, you ran this paper for thirty years. You're the one who established that precedent." Jaimie looked at Paul as if he'd grown another head.

"I always left that up to advertising," he said, sounding defensive.

Harry looked from Paul to Jaimie and knew at that moment Paul was probably relieved this was all happening. This way, he couldn't be blamed. Hell, the old guy likely jumped for joy when he'd heard Hampton's was taking a dive. He'd finally be free and clear of the millstone he'd worn around his neck for years—*and it wasn't his fault.*

"Are you both saying the paper has no way to make budget?" Harry asked, though he already knew the answer.

Jaimie shook her head, the picture of misery.

"No way in hell," Paul said with too much jocularity. Jaimie glared at him.

Behind Harry, rain started to beat against the windows that overlooked Concord Street and Duffy's Bar. It was cold outside, so the rain held some ice, making it sound even louder in the office. It was the kind of sound that made you long for home and a warm fire and a place where no one lost their jobs.

"It's supposed to turn to snow," Jaimie said, her voice oddly blank.

"Now there's a good omen," Paul said, standing and grinning before remembering he was supposed to be sad about the paper going out of business. He walked over to where she sat staring at the icy raindrops glittering in the window. "I'm sorry, Jaimie. I know you don't think so now, but this is the best thing that ever happened to you."

Jaimie tore her eyes away from the window, from the promise of a snowy night. "You're very wrong, Paul. I'm tired of feeling guilty for being happy here. I'm not afraid, Paul, I'm happy. At least I was."

"You'll see," he said, and patted her on the shoulder before leaving the office.

Harry walked over to the couch and sat down. "Wanna go stand in the snow?"

She smiled. "Nah. It's not really snowing yet. We'll just get wet. And it's too cold. Plus you'll get your cast wet."

He held up his castless foot. "Come on. It'll make you feel better."

"Wow, you got it off," she said, unable to dredge up any enthusiasm. "Harry, I'm not really in the mood for standing in the slush."

"You're going to make me go out in the slush by myself. A man who's just gotten his cast off? Who not two months ago wondered whether he'd ever walk again?"

She rolled her eyes at his exaggeration, let out a puff of air and looked at him. He tried, he really did, to not let the sight of those beautiful eyes make his heart go nuts. "Come on," he said, and held out his hand.

She pressed her lips together in indecision, looking out the window again where fluffy stuff was actually falling.

"Okay," she said, getting up and ignoring his outstretched hand. Thank God, because he was about to break his own promise to not touch her.

They walked out of the newsroom, ignoring the curious looks from the reporters, and down the stairs, past the old papers tacked along the wall, and into the street. It was still snowing, impossibly big flakes dropping from the sky, and the moon was shining, making the snow look like bits of fairy dust floating down to earth.

"Oh." That single syllable held such a mountain of sadness that Harry's heart clenched. "It's so beautiful."

They stood silently for a few minutes, watching the snow fall and the silvery clouds move away until the snow finally stopped.

"It's stopping," she said, sounding sad and so disappointed he wished he had the power to make it snow all night.

"What would happen to that hair of yours if it kept snowing?"

Jaimie gave Harry a suspicious look, narrowing her eyes. He was trying to cheer her up and it was working, if only a little. "It would get all straggly, like hundreds of worms stuck to my head." She let out a mock shudder.

He reached back and pulled the scrunchie down until her hair was loose. And he smiled.

Jaimie tried to look away before he did because, God it hurt to see him smile like that at her. But she couldn't because he was just too damn beautiful to look away. She hadn't been able to look away from the falling snow, either.

Until it had gone.

The snow in her hair started to melt, tickling her scalp, cool against her face, making her shiver.

"You can't be that cold," he said, laughter in his voice.

"I am. Look, you can see our breaths." She blew air out of her mouth for proof then pulled her sweater around her more tightly. They stood on the sidewalk watching the clouds, waiting to see if it would start snowing again, for about a minute. "I'm getting really cold, Harry, and I have to work tonight."

"I'm sorry, Jaimie," he said. His words held such an undercurrent, she wasn't quite sure what he was sorry for. Certainly not the snow stopping. Maybe the paper. Or maybe he knew she loved him and he was sorry he couldn't love her back. Or maybe it was a little of everything.

All she could say was, "Me too," with a heart so heavy she wished he'd go away so she could cry for an hour standing in the cold.

"Your hair."

She looked up, startled. "My hair?"

"It's all curly. I knew it would. I asked you out here on false pretenses."

"And that's what you're sorry about?" she asked, dumbstruck.

Harry studied her for a beat, and then quickly added, "Oh, and about the paper, too."

Jaimie rolled her eyes. "Between you and Paul, I don't know who's happier about the paper going under."

He started to protest but Jaimie interrupted. "You don't have to explain or rationalize. The timing is perfect for you, admit it. You're one hundred percent and can go back to New York just as the paper you were temporarily working at goes under. Paul's not to blame. You're not to blame. It was just something that happened. I'm not mad at you for being happy."

"You're wrong. I'm not happy the paper's folding. Sure, it makes my decision to go back to New York easier, but don't think for a minute I'm glad." He looked up at the old building, the ugly shiny yellow brick, the dented lettering proclaiming this site as the home of the *Nortown Journal*. "To be honest, the place was growing on me."

"Really?"

"Really." He studied her face for a long moment. "You look pretty standing there. Your hair."

"With the hair again." But she smiled as if he'd just proclaimed his undying love.

"I'm not going to kiss you."

"Good."

"Because, it can't go anywhere. I'm going back to New York," he said with more force than she thought necessary.

"I know."

Then he got that sly look, and grinned. "Of course, if we both recognize that it won't go anywhere . . ."

"You're always negotiating, Harry, you know that?" And Jaimie put both hands on his face and pulled him down and pressed her lips against his. He tasted like rain, cool and warm and achingly familiar. His arms went around her, pulling her close, his head slanting, his mouth open and hot. She wasn't certain who lost it first, maybe it was mutual combustion, all that pent-up sexual energy exploding at once, but she'd never felt heat the way she felt it just then. It was crazy. *They* were crazy, and neither seemed to care.

The street was dark and because of the snow, empty. But Jaimie wasn't thinking about people discovering them at the moment, she was too busy loving the way Harry's hand felt on her breast, the way his tongue moved against hers, how hard his ass was beneath her hand, how hard his dick was against her pelvis. Somehow, by mutually blind consent, they ended up crammed in the alley between Duffy's and the paper.

His hand was so hot on her breast, because she was so cold and she wondered how he could be so warm. And then his mouth was on her breast and she could only think how wonderful it felt, how damned aroused she was, and how much she liked the grunts and murmurs of pleasure he was making. She grabbed his hand and put it between her legs, pushing hard, silently telling him that she wanted him. Now. Because she was not going to allow him to come to his senses and hers were already long gone.

Harry wasn't stupid, Jaimie learned fast enough, because the next thing she knew, her panties were off, her skirt was up, and he was plunging in, frantic and hard and fast. Neither said a word. No "Oh Gods," no "you're beautifuls," no "I love yous." Just raw heat, raw sex.

Her back was to the yellow-brick wall, his hands clutching her bottom as he moved into her. He bent his head and grabbed a nipple with his mouth and teased and sucked until she threw back her head. She came, letting out a small sound she couldn't hope to keep inside, and he kissed her, devoured her, then arched his back.

"Oh, God. Wow." That from Harry, who rested his head against the cool brick as she nestled her forehead against his shoulder. "Shit. It stinks here."

"Here" was the alley, where countless people had spilled beer and urine, leaving behind pungent and horribly identifiable smells.

"Yuck. You know, Harry, you always take me to the nicest places."

Harry laughed and eased out of her and helped her to stand. A good thing, too, because her legs had gone all rubbery on her. She managed to pull up her panties and pull down her skirt in the narrow space.

"Well," she said, feeling self-conscious and slightly slutty. "That's a first for me. An alley. Screwing in an alley. Mom would be so proud."

Harry pulled up his pants then peeked out to see if the coast was clear, then grabbed her hand and pulled her out of the alley. The air was instantly sweeter. "For the record, I've never even had sex outside before."

"You're kidding. Does a car count?"

"No."

"Then that was a first for me, too." Jokes always worked to cover up awkward situations, and Jaimie had never felt so awkward before in her life. Strike that. She'd felt damned awkward when Harry's ex had called right after they'd made love the first time.

Jaimie was looking down, pretending to check her shoes, when she felt a hand on her cheek. "Hey. You okay?"

"Oh. Sure. Fine."

She looked into his face and smiled, and he looked stunned, as if he'd never seen her before. A man who'd found himself deeply and inexplicably in love. Key up the music.

"Great. Myself, I'm still recovering."

She forced a laugh. They could laugh, because both of them knew nothing was ever going to come of it. She'd just fucked in an alley. With a man she knew she had no future with. With a man who'd never said the slightest thing to make her think she was special with the exception that he liked her curly hair. Of course, she'd never said anything to him, either. Not that he knew, anyway. But guys were different. Guys would take sex where they could get it and not ask questions.

Nothing was ever going to come of it. No siree. Nope.

He'd go his way, she'd go hers and never the two ships would pass in the night. She was fine. He was fine.

She'd just had sex in an alley.

She was not fine. Not at all.

"Actually, Harry. I think . . ."

He put a large hand over her mouth. "Don't think. And don't ruin what was the best sex I've had in my life."

She mumbled something unintelligible from behind his hand.

"What?" he said, removing his hand.

"That was the best sex you've ever had?"

"By far."

Jaimie grinned, suddenly not feeling so cheap and used anymore. "Yeah, it was pretty good, wasn't it."

"Honey, it was fucking great."

Chapter 19

"You call Monty yet?" his mother asked over dinner the day before he officially returned to work at the *Journal*.

Monty was his former boss and quite possibly a god to his mother and he didn't want to talk to him or about him at the moment. He was still too busy thinking about Jaimie and that incredible experience they'd had in the alley. In-fucking-credible. "As a matter of fact, I haven't."

Jennifer's eyebrows raised slightly, but other than that, it was difficult to see just how upset that information made her. "Why not?"

Harry shrugged. He didn't know why he hadn't talked to Monty. That should have been one of the first phone calls he made when he got back from New York. "I want to wrap things up here first. And enjoy a little down time before I jump back into the snake pit." *Maybe check out a couple more alleys. Damn, Jaimie was one fine woman.*

Jennifer chewed slowly. "Don't buy it."

"Monty should be calling me."

His mother made a small grunt of agreement. "I hear Anne's back."

Now it was Harry's turn to raise his eyebrows. "You've been talking to Anne?"

"Never stopped. I like her."

"You wouldn't like her now. She's gone all soft. All in love. It's weird."

"She's back working," his mother said with a note of triumph. "You know they're getting married as soon as his divorce comes through. After the baby of course, but that can't be helped. Nearly nine months pregnant and covering the mayor."

"You're kidding." He'd talked to Anne a couple of times since she'd gone back to New York and she hadn't said a word about working.

"You're worried about her. I knew you still had feelings for her."

Harry calmly put down his fork. "Anne is my friend. We have a history. Of course I'd be concerned that she was working full time covering City Hall. What the hell is Bob thinking, never mind Monty?"

"It's only part-time. Features," Jennifer said begrudgingly.

"Why are we talking about Anne anyway?"

Jennifer let out an exasperated sigh. "Because you haven't called Monty, that's why."

"I'll call him right now if it would make you happy."

"And shut me up."

Harry grinned. "That too. Come on, Mom. Leave me alone for just one night. I'm going back to the *Times*. But right now I work for the *Nortown Journal*." He ignored his mother's snort. "And until we officially turn it over to Penworth, I'm the managing editor here. Whether you like it or not."

Jennifer sat back and looked at her son. "I want you to answer a question. Honestly."

Harry hesitated, then nodded.

"If the paper were fine, if it were going gangbusters, would you still go back to New York?"

"Yes." A single word said without pause and with total conviction.

"What about the redhead?"

Harry had been lifting his water glass and stopped. "What about her?"

Jennifer smiled as if she'd just won another point in a game that left Harry slightly bewildered. "So, you don't love her."

"Of course not." But he looked down at his plate, aware suddenly that he'd lied twice to his mother without a second thought. Frankly, he just wanted her to lay off but he didn't want to hurt her feelings. Or piss her off, which was much worse.

"You do like her."

Sometimes his mother was like a pit bull, its teeth burrowed deep into your pant leg and no matter how much you shook, it stayed hanging on.

"You want the truth. I do love her. At least I think I do. But I'm going back to New York anyway. I wouldn't be happy here and God knows she wouldn't be happy there. Okay?" Man, he felt like shit.

"Okay," she said softly, turning into a mother instead of an interrogator for the first time since they'd sat down together in his apartment. "I'm sorry, honey. You haven't told her you love her, have you?"

"No. I haven't. *I'm* not even sure."

"You'll be fine then. Take some advice?"

"You'll just give it anyway."

She smiled. "Try to stay away from her. For her sake and yours. You don't want this to be more difficult than it's already going to be."

"You're scared to death I'll stay here, aren't you?"

"Not at all. I know you belong in New York. Kiddo,

even if you did stay, it wouldn't be for long. You wouldn't be happy here. You do know that, don't you?"

"I know."

"Harry. I'm pregnant."

He was standing outside the main entrance to the New York Times, *and there was Jaimie, monstrously pregnant.* "I can see that."

"It's Paul's."

"What?"

"It's Paul's. And yours. It's your baby. You both fucked me. Get it? Get the joke?"

The phone woke him up, jarring him out of the dream that left him in a cold sweat. "Yeah. It's . . ." He looked at the clock. Three in the a.m. "It's three in the morning."

"Harry, it's Bob Porter. Anne just had the baby. She wanted me to call you."

Harry's brain was still foggy from sleep. "Anne's not due," he muttered before the impact hit him. "Is everything okay?"

"It was scary but we have a little girl. Five pounds. A little peanut. She's fine. They had her on oxygen for a little while but she's breathing fine now."

"How's Anne?"

"Oh, great. She's great. Um, Harry. I'm sorry about everything." He paused, obviously uncomfortable making this phone call. "And I wanted to thank you for taking care of Anne."

Harry lay back against his pillow keeping the phone against his ear. "That's okay. Anne's my friend."

"Great. Hey, she wants to talk to you."

Before Harry could protest the passing of the phone, he heard, "Hey, Harry."

He smiled, because her voice and those words didn't send his heart pounding out of his chest anymore. "How're you doing? I hear you're a mom now."

"She's beautiful. Jacey. Is that too trendy?"

"I never heard it before so it can't be a trend."

She laughed, sounding happy and soft and totally unlike the woman he knew. "You have to see her when you come back to New York."

"I will. After the first of the year."

"Your mother told me about the paper. Sucks."

"It does that. Hey, I'm glad you're okay. And Jacey."

"Good night, Harry. And thank you for all your help. I was such a basket case but I'm so happy now. It's amazing. Fall in love. You'll see."

"Yeah. Good night." Harry hung up the phone smiling. Good for her. Jacey. Weird name. But he liked it.

One of Jaimie's favorite movies was *A Trip to Bountiful,* a film about an older woman who is driven to visit her childhood home. It was slow-moving and sentimental and the last movie she'd seen at the Nortown Theater, which had been torn down the next day. The theater had been built for vaudeville and later converted to the new-fangled moving picture theater. For most of her life, Jaimie had thought she must have been born in the wrong decade, because she missed the old theater even now. Sometimes she'd catch a scent of that dusty, popcorny, moldy smell and be instantly transported back to the Nortown Theater, filled with nostalgia for a time she'd never truly been a part of.

Someday she knew she'd have that same overwhelming sense of loss when she walked into a dark, dusty room that smelled like old paper and metal furniture, and be instantly transported back into the *Journal's* newsroom. That could sum up her life. Mold and dust. Nobody would be able to save this newspaper any more than anyone had been able to save the theater.

Barring a miracle, it was going to all be gone no matter how much she wanted it to stay forever. It hurt so much, there were moments she thought she couldn't function. Every story she edited, every reporter in the room, made her want to cry.

Hot tears had been falling down her face on and off for about two days. She kept them at bay at work, for the most part. She and Harry had decided to let everyone know about the imminent change about a month before Penworth took over. That gave them a week. Harry had wanted to at least tell Ted, but Jaimie nixed that idea. She agreed that Ted, as sports editor, should know, but Ted had such a big heart he'd give his staff a heads up. It was, after all, right before Christmas. Except this Christmas wasn't going to have an *It's a Wonderful Life* ending with everyone gathered around the Christmas tree throwing money at the *Nortown Journal.* Nope. This Christmas everyone would be updating their resumes, scrambling to get their best clips together, and wishing they'd never started working for this broken-down old paper.

In about one week everyone in this building would sit there listening to Harry explain how and why the Nortown Journal was going to be turned into a shopper and they'd be stunned and scared and disbelieving.

A headline—Coventry Council Collects Kudos—blurred in front of her and she quickly blinked to clear her eyes. Alliteration. Cute. Jaimie's phone rang and she picked up, almost wishing it was someone bitching about not getting their paper. These people loved their paper. If it was a couple hours late, they were on the phone complaining. God, she'd miss this place.

"Jaimie McLane."

"Are you the girl who was asking about Joshua Tate?"

Jaimie felt a flash of irritation. The Joshua Tate story would never be written. Three notebooks full of crap, including the stuff about his father being in prison. What was the point now? "I am. What can I do for you," she said, lazily grabbing the nearest notebook and pen.

"My name is Beatrice Moran. I was talking to Mr. Babcock from across the street and he said a reporter had been around a few weeks ago trying to find out a bit more about Joshua Tate. Or maybe it was longer. You spoke with my husband and, of course, he forgot to mention it. How long ago were you here?"

"About a month," Jaimie supplied.

"Well, I must not have been home because of course I think I could have helped you out a bit. I winter in Florida so I wasn't here when that boy got murdered. But I saw his picture on the television and I think that's the same boy I used to see cross my yard all the time with that other boy. The Schiffer boy. I know the family because their oldest mows my lawn and shovels for me when I'm in Florida so the house looks lived in. You never can take any chances nowadays."

"The Schiffer boy?"

"Oh, yes. The two of them used to cross my yard. I thought that little boy could tell you more about Joshua Tate than anyone. I know the family and I'm sure the mother would let you talk to him. Alex, I think his name is. Did you stop by there?"

"I'm not sure. Quite a few families weren't home that day." This *was* something she'd been looking for, something to make Joshua Tate seem like a real little boy, a friend who could say whether he liked Mountain Dew or watched Sponge Bob. It wasn't the greatest story in the world, but she could finally write a bit of the story she'd set out to write.

"How old is Alex. Do you know?"

"Well, I know he just started second grade."

"Seven or eight. Thank you so much Mrs. Moran. Could I have your number in case I have to talk to you?"

She got the number and hung up. Then picked up a phone directory looking for Schiffers in Cedar Heights.

After two rings, a woman answered. "Hello, Mrs. Schiffer. My name is Jaimie McLane from the *Nortown Journal*. I've been working on a piece about Joshua Tate and I've been having a tough time finding kids who played with him. I understand your son, Alex, was his friend?" She held her breath.

"They used to play together sometimes, yes."

"I wonder if I could talk to Alex for a bit. I'm looking to write a story about the type of kid Joshua really was. What did he like to play, eat. Kid stuff. It's the kind of information that can make a story so much better."

A pause. "I suppose that would be all right. They weren't best friends. To be honest . . . Well, never mind. Do you have our address?"

"Two Twenty-nine Mason Drive. Can I come straight over? I'll only stay about a half hour or so." Mrs. Schiffer agreed and Jaimie grabbed her tape recorder, notebook, and pen.

Alex Schiffer was about as cute as a kid comes. He was wearing cargo pants, and an oversized sweatshirt that made him look even smaller than he was. He looked scared, but then most kids looked scared when an unknown adult walked into the room. He sat on the couch, back against the cushions, sneakered feet dangling above the carpet.

"Hey, Alex, did your mom explain why I'm here?"

He looked over to where his mother stood smiling at the entrance to the small living room and nodded. "About Joshua."

"Yeah. I know he was one of your friends. I know this may be hard to talk about, because he was your friend." He began swinging one of his legs, thumping against the sofa. "Lots of people say he was a real good kid, but not that many hung out with him."

"He was kind of weird," Alex said, then darted a look over to his mother, as if knowing he shouldn't say anything bad about a kid who was dead.

"Don't put that in your story," Mrs. Schiffer said, laughing nervously. "Joshua was a nice kid. Smart. Intense. He'd talk to me like an adult, do you know what I mean?"

Jaimie smiled at Mrs. Schiffer and shrugged. "What did you guys do together?"

"I don't know. Hung out. We used to play army sometimes, but . . ." Again that look to his mother.

"Maybe I should just let you two talk," she said, winking at Jaimie.

"You played army?"

"Sometimes. And other stuff."

Kids were tough interviews until they felt comfortable, then you couldn't get them to shut up. Most of the time. Sometimes they never got past one syllable answers. Yup. Nope. I guess. "You ever walk down to the 7 Eleven and get a slurpy?"

He smiled. "Yeah. Joshua would get the blue one. It was so gross. He'd try to drink it all at once and one time he drank it so fast he threw up. I laughed so hard."

"I hate the blue ones," Jaimie said, even though she'd never had one. "What flavor did you get?"

"Cherry. But Joshua would always say I was drinking blood. He was really into blood stuff. When we played army, he'd get bugs and squish 'em with his guys and say it was the guys' guts." He wrinkled his nose, disgusted with the memory. "He really liked to gross kids out. That's why no one liked him." He stopped suddenly, looking guilty and flushing slightly.

"But I bet it was funny sometimes," Jaimie said, hoping to draw him back in.

"Sometimes," he said softly, scuffing his sneakers together.

Jaimie grimaced inwardly, but she knew she'd have to ask about the puppy some time. "Did you ever get to play with his puppy?"

He stared at his sneakers. "Not really."

"What was its name again?"

"Skipper."

"A beagle puppy. Cute."

She saw a hint of a smile on his lips, but he didn't look up.

Alex swallowed. "He used to . . ." And then he got a look in his face that she'd never forget, anger, terror and sadness all emanating from a little boy's brown eyes. "I don't want to talk about the puppy. It was just a stupid dog."

"Okay. Did you play sports together? Skateboard? PlayStation? See, I'm trying to put together a picture of Joshua with words. Right now all I have is sort of a shadowy outline. I need details that will fill in the face. Do you see what I'm trying to do?"

"He wasn't really my friend," he said, sounding like he was starting to get mad.

"I'm starting to think he didn't have many friends. Maybe you were his best friend and you didn't even know it."

"Maybe."

Shit. Something had gone wrong. The kid was laughing a second ago about slurpies and now he was sitting there like he was waiting for the principal to yell at him— pretending to be tough but wishing it was all over. He'd closed up when she'd mentioned the puppy. Maybe he'd liked the dog more than Joshua and he felt guilty about it.

"You didn't like Skipper?"

He twisted his hands in his lap. "He was okay," he said softly.

Inspiration struck her at that moment. She was probably wrong, but she couldn't get that crazy neurotic Geoffrey Fox's cat story out of her head. "It's a good thing Joshua had a dog. I don't think he liked cats."

Alex looked up, curiosity clear in his gaze.

"Wanna hear something crazy? One of Joshua's neighbors thinks Joshua killed his cat on purpose."

"With his bike?" he asked, leaning forward.

Jaimie couldn't stop the chill that spread along her spine and ended with almost painful pinpricks on her scalp.

"You mean he actually did it?" she asked, in a that's-so-gross tone.

Alex made a sick face, a kid who's just tasted liver for the first time. "He told me he did but I didn't believe him. At least not then."

"Alex," she said, quietly conveying to him the seriousness of her next question. "Did he ever hurt Skipper?" Alex just stared at her, his brown eyes getting even bigger, and she knew she was right. "He hurt Skipper, didn't he?"

He pressed his lips together before finally saying so softly she was afraid her tape recorder wouldn't pick it up, "All the time." He looked up at her, his eyes filled with tears. "I don't know why he did. Skipper was so cute. He was just little."

"What kinds of things would he do?"

He moved his head as if he were anticipating a blow. "I don't know. Pull his tail. Poke sticks at him really hard, enough to make his fur come off. Stuff like that."

"Do you think that maybe Joshua killed Skipper?"

His face crumpled for a second before he got control of himself. "Yes."

"You saw him kill Skipper, didn't you?" Jaimie looked up to see if his mother had come back and frantically wondered if she should stop the interview.

"That day, I told him to stop hurting Skipper but he wouldn't. Skipper was yelping and he wouldn't stop doing it."

Jaimie didn't move a muscle, she breathed shallowly, she didn't even blink, because she knew in her gut what Alex was about to say, what he was about to confess to and she wasn't going to do anything to stop it from happening.

"He wouldn't stop." He looked at her, pleading for understanding. He closed his eyes, a little boy so wracked with pain and guilt and horror, swallowed up by it. "He was laughing. Every time he hurt him and I kept telling him to stop. He said I was a pussy. Then he threw Skipper at a tree and he just was laying there making this funny sound and then he picked up a big stick and started jabbing at him and that's when I . . ."

Jaimie heard a small sound and looked up to see Mrs. Schiffer, tears streaming down her face, standing at the entrance to the living room. She rushed over to her son and gathered him into her arms.

"I didn't mean to, Mommy. I didn't mean to kill him. I didn't mean to. I didn't."

"It's okay, it's okay, it's all over," she said over and over, rocking him back and forth as he cried, sobbing, his body shaking with it.

"Could you please leave?" Mrs. Schiffer said over her son's head.

Jaimie stood, uncertain what do to or say for a few moments. "I'm a reporter, Mrs. Schiffer. Your son just confessed to killing Joshua. I am going to write a story, I can't not write one. But I'd like to discuss with you how to handle this so that Alex is protected as much as possible."

She shook her head back and forth. "I can't. I can't think right now," she said, still rocking her grief-stricken son.

"I'll give you a few hours. I'd like to come back with my managing editor and figure out what to do. I'm so sorry." She *was* sorry for Mrs. Schiffer and for Alex, but the reporter in her was doing cartwheels. A journalist could live and die three lifetimes and not get a story this big. "What is a good time? Seven?"

Mrs. Schiffer looked dazed. "I have to call my husband."

"Of course. I'll be here at seven with my boss."

"Okay. Seven."

When Jaimie left, Alex was still crying and Mrs. Schiffer was still whispering everything would be all right.

Chapter 20

Harry looked up when Jaimie came into the newsroom and knew something big had happened.

She walked right into his office without knocking, her face shining, her eyes glowing. She stood in front of his desk, staring at him, grinning, catching her breath, willing him to guess why she was looking like she'd just won the lottery.

"I've got the Joshua Tate killer."

"Goddamn," he said quietly.

She took a breath. "That's not the best part."

"Go on."

"It's a kid. A cute little kid who was just trying to save the puppy's life." She shook her head back and forth as if she couldn't believe what was happening, how incredible this story was.

"Okay, so who else has this?"

"No one."

He knew he must have looked confused because her grin got even bigger. "You don't get it, Harry. He confessed to me. The cops don't even have this," she said, holding her recorder out to him as proof. "Chief Girard is going to shit."

Harry let out a low whistle as the scope of the story hit him. "Okay. Start from the beginning."

She nodded, so excited she almost sat on the floor instead of the chair. "You know I've been working on a Tate story. Well, until now it never materialized. I was hoping to do some sort of feature. Meaty, but nothing earth shattering. So I was trying to find out more about this kid other than he was cute and polite. He didn't have any friends. Except one. This little kid, Alex Schiffer. Eight years old and a second grader at Eldredge Elementary School. Turns out Joshua liked to torture animals. I think he killed some guy's cat over on Cedar. Anyway, Alex and Joshua and Skipper, that's the dog . . ."

"I figured."

A grin. "They're all in the woods when apparently Joshua starts hurting Skipper."

"The dog."

"Right. Alex doesn't like that and wants to stop Joshua, he picks up a stick and whammo. Joshua's dead. And so is Skipper. And Alex, poor kid, must have run home and pretended nothing happened."

"That poor kid murdered one of his friends."

Jaimie shook her head. "No. This kid didn't mean to kill anyone. He was just trying to get Joshua to stop hurting the dog."

"So he says."

"I believe him. Plus I got that stuff about the cat. Alex practically confirmed that story. Joshua was a fledgling psychopath and I think the mother knew it, too. Probably would have grown up to be a serial killer. Plus, we've got the father in prison for abusing Joshua." She paused to catch her breath. "Do you have any idea how huge this is?"

He smiled, fully enjoying how exciting this was for her. It was a huge story. A national story. And they were going to break it. But in order to do that, they had to handle things very carefully. The last thing they wanted to do was to tip off the *Day* or the *Hartford Courant* or anyone else, for that matter.

"I told the mother that we'd come back at seven to talk to her, to tell her how we're handling the story. I told her I had to go with it and as long as it checks out, I think we should."

Harry sat back and steepled his fingers. "What if the kid's full of shit. Looking for attention. Sick of his dead friend getting all the limelight."

"I don't think so. No way. He's not old enough to play me like that. He was scared. And when he finally confessed, the kid was crying, really torn apart. No kid could fake it like that. He's only eight."

"You're right. But I don't see any reason to go back to the house unless you have more questions. Let's just go with what we have." He looked at the clock. "It's five now. You'd better get going."

He fully expected her to rush out of his office and go immediately to her computer. Life would have been far easier if she had.

"No way. I said we were going back and we are."

"There's no reason to go back."

She gave him a steady you're-so-full-of-shit look. "We go back because I said we would. We go back because this isn't New York. This is Nortown."

"No kidding."

He fully believed she would have hit him if a desk hadn't separated them because she positively seethed.

"We have the luxury of time and the moral responsibility . . ."

He couldn't help it, he snorted. Wrong thing to do.

She leaned on his desk, planting her hands firmly on it, rage in every cell of her body. She didn't look sexy, she just looked pissed. "These people have just entered a nightmare that's going to get a hell of a lot worse in the next few days. Let the TV reporters walk all over them. Let the goddamn major papers do it. But I'll be damned if I'll do it. They aren't just sources," she spat. "They're people who are in deeper than they could ever imagine. I was there. I saw a family being torn apart before my eyes. You get your tail to that house and explain to those people what they're in for tomorrow when they buy the paper. If you don't, I quit and I bring my story to the *Day.*"

Jaimie almost regretted that last, but she kept her eyes steady on Harry and wondered what the hell she'd do if he called her bluff. She couldn't read him, never had been able to, but the last thing she expected was for him to smile. He sat there with a grin on his face that was as sexy as it was maddening.

"Lousy bluff, Jaimie. I know you'd never take this story to the *Day.*" He tilted his head and pressed his lips together before saying, "Okay. We'll do it your way. You know these people better than I do. But I can tell you what's going to happen. They're going to beg us not to run with the story. They might have even hired a lawyer to threaten us with a lawsuit. We're going to be walking into a nest of scorpions. So if you think they're going to be grateful that we've come back to discuss how we're going to fairly and accurately report on the fact their son killed a little boy, you, my friend, are delusional."

So what if that was sort of what she'd been thinking. She really hadn't been thinking all that clearly when she'd left the house and the sobbing mother and child. Harry was right. Damn him. Chances are they would have a lawyer on hand who would try to manipulate the story or at least try to get them to hold it until they'd gone to the police. If they hadn't done that already.

* * *

At seven sharp, Jaimie and Harry pulled in front of the Schiffer house, Harry pointing out the Beemer parked in the driveway behind the minivan and the Jetta. The license plate of the Beemer said: DEFENSE. Jaimie smiled.

"It's Scott Wu. I went to high school with his little brother. He's a good guy."

"Is he a lawyer or a football player?" Harry asked sardonically.

"Ha ha." Jaimie got out of the car and slammed the door, heading toward the house without waiting for Harry to follow. His superior attitude was beginning to wear a bit thin. And it wasn't lost on her that one of his predictions—the family hiring a lawyer—had already come true.

The door opened before either had a chance to knock. A man stood there, not Scott and certainly not friendly. But he stepped back and said, "Come on in. Alex is asleep, so you can't talk to him."

"I didn't plan to interview him tonight," Jaimie said softly. "Poor kid's been through enough."

His belligerent expression softened a bit until he looked at Harry.

"Harry Crandall. I'm managing editor at the *Journal*." He didn't hold out his hand for shaking, just nodded his head. Harry looked his New York best. He'd gone home and changed into one of his best suits, a four-buttoned navy, a brilliant white shirt, and blue-and-red-striped tie. He looked like a politician, so Jaimie wondered if that had been such a great choice.

"Brian Schiffer. Let's get this over with."

They walked into the living room, now brightly lit in the way people only did when something unusual was happening in the house. Scott sat on the couch next to Mrs. Schiffer and smiled when Jaimie walked in.

"Hi, Jaimie. I was trying to reassure the Schiffers that, if this had to happen, it was good you're the reporter who's writing the story."

Scott always had been such a suck-up, and Jaimie would have called him on it in different circumstances. "Hi, Scott. Thanks."

"This is bullshit," Brian said, standing in the middle of the room looking like a prizefighter with no one to hit. His tie was loosened at his neck and he looked disheveled and bull-rage mad. "It's all bullshit. Alex didn't kill that kid. I don't care what he said."

Mrs. Schiffer jumped up from the couch and went over to her husband. "Brian, please. If you can't be rational right now, then go for a walk or something."

"How the hell can I be rational when everybody's saying my kid's a murderer?" His voice broke slightly and he swallowed hard.

Mrs. Schiffer closed her eyes. "Brian. Please."

He clamped his jaw tight and threw himself down on the nearest chair, crossing his arms and looking like he was ready to spring up if anyone said the wrong word.

Harry was the first to speak after Brian sat down. "We're going to be as fair and even-handed as possible with the story we run tomorrow."

Scott immediately broke in. "I don't think it's in anyone's best interest that any story run tomorrow. Surely you can't be basing your story on the so-called confession of an eight-year-old boy. I'll have a lawsuit filed before the paper hits the stands." Coming from any other lawyer that would have been irritating, but Jaimie knew Scott well enough to know he didn't mean a word he just said. But he had a couple of very upset clients, so it didn't hurt to make an effort to stop the story.

"We're running the story, Mr. Wu," Harry said, not giving an inch. "I have complete faith in Jaimie's reporting. It's regrettable, but the story will run."

Brian moved restlessly in his chair and for a second Jaimie was certain he was about to catapult out of it and attack Harry. He clutched the arms, putting an impressive dent in the fabric, but stayed put, swearing under his breath.

"What about his name? Are you going to run his name? Or ours?" Mrs. Schiffer asked.

Jaimie tensed, but let Harry answer, praying they agreed on this. It had always been the *Journal's* policy not to release the names of minors unless they were charged as adults.

"Of course not. He's a juvenile. He'll be described as an eight-year-old Nortown boy. That's all. And we won't use your names, because that would also identify him. However, if the courts decide to charge him as an adult, we will use his name. And I can't promise the other media will follow suit. Every newspaper's policy is different. This is going to be a major news story and his picture is going to be on television and, of course, in the newspaper. I'm afraid it's going to be impossible to hide his identity for long. As soon as his identity is made public, the *Journal* will also use it. But we won't be the first." Harry looked at Jaimie and gave her an almost imperceptible smile and her heart swelled in her chest.

"This is a fucking nightmare," Brian said, burying his head in his hands. "Why didn't he tell us? Why?" He gave his wife a pleading look. "The poor kid's been walking around with this inside for what? Eight months?" He turned toward Jaimie. "He's a good kid. Christ, he cried when I killed a butterfly once. He was just trying to get that kid to stop torturing his dog."

"Mr. Schiffer," Scott warned, and shook his head. Scott Wu handed Jaimie a sheet of paper. "This is a statement from the family. By the way, this has all been off the record, right?"

"Right." She gave him a look that told him she knew better, but this time she'd let him off the hook.

"What happens next?" Mrs. Schiffer asked, and Jaimie was pretty sure she'd never felt more sorry for another person in her life.

"We run the story tomorrow. Tonight I plan to call Chief Girard to give him heads up about the story we're running. To be honest with you, I don't know what his reaction is going to be."

Scott interrupted. "I plan to call the chief as soon as the *Journal* leaves and tell him that you've retained an attorney for Alex and that you'll be bringing him into the station in the morning for a statement. The chief will contact the prosecutor and I'll argue that we can bring Alex to the station tomorrow, that he's not a flight risk, that his parents are cooperating. Has Alex had any previous contact with police?"

"No," Brian said, and he shook his head as if he still couldn't believe what had happened.

"As long as you two are cooperative, I can almost guarantee you that Alex will sleep in his bed the whole night."

"You mean there's a chance they could take him tonight?" Mrs. Schiffer asked, new tears welling up in her eyes.

"I'm almost certain it will not come to that. If it does, Alex will be transported to New Haven." He lay a hand on Mrs. Schiffer's arm. "I'm not going to let that happen."

Harry stood. "Do either of you have any questions?"

"Yeah," Brian said, looking up at Harry with pure disgust. "How do you sleep at night?"

"Some nights are better than others. No matter what we write, you're not going to like it. I can guarantee you that," he said, grimly. "All I can promise is that we'll be fair and accurate."

Brian tore his gaze away from them as if he couldn't stand to look at them, and for a second Jaimie wished she'd never knocked on their door, that she could just sweep it under the rug.

Mrs. Schiffer stood and held out her hand, ignoring her husband's sound of protest. "Thank you for coming," she said. "I know you didn't have to."

Harry and Jaimie walked to the car in silence, not saying a word until they'd gotten in and Jaimie started driving away.

"Now I know why I've never done that before," he said.

Jaimie let out a laugh. "It was a bit intense. But I'm glad we did it. Are you?"

"Yeah. I am. You do know that, in the end, you'll be lumped together with the rest of the media. I've written some kick-ass stories and gotten my butt chewed by people who read something in the *Post*. We're all scum to them."

"Some people like us."

"Who? Your mom?"

Jaimie let out a laugh. "Actually, yes. And all the other mothers who look for their kids' names on the honor roll. I bet the Schiffers liked us until today."

"You sure your name isn't Mary Sunshine?"

Jaimie rolled her eyes. "So I am a little idealistic. And I hate most of the media. Really, I do," she said when she saw his look of disbelief. "I mean, what is the news value of a reporter going up to someone whose loved one was just in a plane crash and asking how they're feeling. I actually saw that once. The poor guy was in the airport waiting for his wife and this idiot asks him how he's feeling. It was bad reporting."

Harry chuckled. "You'd never make it in New York."

"I'd never want to go there, don't worry," she said fiercely, trying and failing to ignore the knife he'd inadvertently thrust into her heart.

"Hey," he said, putting a hand on her arm. "I didn't mean that as an insult."

She knew, but it still bothered her. She also knew she couldn't do some of the things big-time reporters did—couldn't and didn't want to. She'd always known she had something missing, that toughness or hardness that made some reporters do anything to get a story. Great reporters were able to separate the story from the people giving them the information. She'd never been able to do that with success. Something perverse made her confess one of her greatest failings, driving home the point she didn't belong in New York or Boston or L.A.

She didn't belong with Harry, she realized with a painful start.

"When I first started at the *Journal* I did the cop beat. Probably was the worst cop reporter the newspaper's ever seen. There was this kid, he hung himself from one of those old Civil War statues in Montville. The editor told me to go talk to the family. Normally we wouldn't report on a suicide. But this was a *public* suicide, so the rules changed. I can remember sitting in my car outside the kid's house trying to get the courage to go interview the parents. I couldn't do it. I gave myself a lecture how it was my job, my job to talk to parents who were facing the worst nightmare of their lives. In the end, I talked myself out of it, convinced myself it was wrong, immoral, of no news value. I lied and told my boss they weren't home. The *Day* reporter had more balls— literally and figuratively—than I did. He wrote a terrific story, got details about the kid that I didn't." She turned in her seat to face him, to drive the point home, to completely self-destruct any idea she had in her head—as small as that thought was—that she might actually go to New York. That he might ask her to go with him. "You know what? I didn't feel guilty about not doing my job. I felt good. Intellectually, I know I screwed up. But I'll never regret not bothering those people that day."

"You think you're the only reporter to get cold feet?"

"No. Did you ever pull something like that?"

Harry looked away. "No. I never had a problem fucking other people's lives up."

"Cold, Harry. Very cold."

"No. Professional."

"So, I'm not professional."

He sighed. "I didn't say that."

"Not directly." What the hell was she doing, picking a fight on what was one of the most exciting nights of her life? Okay, she knew what she was doing. She was pushing him away before he left so when he did go to New York with a peck on her cheek and an "I'll call you" she'd be emotionally ready for it. She knew what she was doing because she'd done it so many times before, except in the past she'd done it to guys she wanted to get rid of. Harry, she wanted. Forever. And it wasn't going to happen.

Hey, kid, there's something crazy going on in this head of mine. New York isn't the same this time around and I've finally figured out why. Sure, the dames are all there, but there's one dame that's not. You, kid. Let's go get hitched.

Oh, Harry, let's! [Cue music]

She drove back to the paper trying to focus on the story,

the lead, the people she still needed to call, the sidebars that would go along with the main story. Thinking about the story was more satisfying than thinking about Harry and New York and being alone. With her cat. "How about a sidebar about the police investigation so far," she said smiling.

"Really jam it up the chief's ass, huh?"

"Why not? He's been a jerk during this entire investigation. Plus, one of his detectives on the case had a good lead and he ignored it. One of my police sources had a feeling about the kid."

"Alex?"

"No, Joshua. I think he thought the kid was a little off. And I think he believed the story that guy told about Joshua killing his cat. I can't use anything with my interview with the guy, but I can use the police report he filed." She let out a laugh of pure happiness and banged the steering wheel with the heel of her hand. "This is going to completely piss off the chief. I wish I could see his face when I make that phone call."

All doubts were forgotten as the adrenaline kicked in. This was an unbelievable coup. Small papers just didn't get this kind of story. Jaimie couldn't help but laugh.

"You're getting giddy."

"I know," she said, dissolving into snorting guffaws. "And I also am aware that two minutes ago I was saying how I couldn't be a hard-ass reporter. But this is different. This is a fan-fucking-tastic story. Man!"

"If he actually did it," Harry said calmly.

Talk about a bucket of cold water. "He did it. Don't you think he did it?"

"Yes I do, Mary Sunshine. But I don't want you writing the story as if it's a foregone conclusion. It isn't. For all we know, tomorrow the kid will recant the story, say he was yanking your chain, making the whole thing up to get attention."

"Naw."

"It could happen."

"Stop saying that," she said, whining intentionally and making Harry laugh. "You're right," she grumbled. "But I planned to write it straight, if you must know. I might be a wimp, but I know how to write a good story."

"Of that I have no doubt."

She looked over to him, and for a split second their eyes met and it seemed they'd connected in a way they never had before, a more intimate way. More intimate, even, than making love in an alley. She turned back to her driving before she rammed the car into a telephone pole.

"What are you going to say when AP calls?"

"They're going to want this one on cycle."

She squeezed the wheel. "You're not going to give it to them, right?"

"What do you think?"

She relaxed. "No. Of course not. Sorry. I'm a little tense about this story." In all her time working for the *Nortown Journal,* Jaimie had only held back a story the Associated Press wanted once, and it was nothing compared to this one. Typically, the AP would request a few paragraphs then put it out after everyone's deadline. But if a story was big, like this one, it requested to send it out immediately.

"This is one of the best stories I've ever worked on, McLane. Do you really think I'd let anyone get this?"

"Really?"

"Really what?"

"This is really one of the best stories you've worked on?" She darted a look over to him to make sure he wasn't pulling her leg.

"It's got some incredible elements. Dead kid, dead dog. We're going to have children's advocates, animal rights activists, every major media outlet in the country converging on Nortown. We're going to have to flood the zone with this one."

"Huh?"

"Flood the zone. Get every reporter in the newspaper working this story. We've got a head start, but as of tomorrow afternoon, we're all going to be working on an even playing ground. I want to kick everyone's ass on this one."

Jaimie thanked God she was driving, because if Harry had been able to see her expression, it would have been downright embarrassing. The neon sign on her forehead was now flashing "I Love You." Harry was electrified by this story, as excited as she was. If they didn't have to rush back and write the story, Jaimie would have pulled the car over to the side of the road and ravaged him.

Jaimie was in the zone, the place writers go when everything clicks. She didn't hear the sports writers yelling when Tom Brady threw his third touchdown against the Jets. She didn't notice when Jennifer offered to write the inside headlines and edit the stories. She didn't see the reporters come and go from meetings, write stories, head to Duffy's with a quick good-bye. All she saw were those words, popping onto her computer as if they had a mind of their own. Because it sure as hell wasn't her mind writing those words. When she was done, Jaimie read it over, jabbing at the keys to make quick changes.

"We're going to miss deadline," Jennifer said.

"Screw the deadline," Jaimie responded, but her eyes

darted to the clock as she looked over the copy, back to her notes, double checking quotes, spellings, events, dates. Jaimie was a slob at home, and her desk wasn't much neater, but she was obsessively organized when it came to her notes. Each notebook was dated, the content indexed on a separate sheet of paper. She flipped through each one, fanning the pages until she got the right quote, the right description. She listened to the tape once to compare it to her notes and to make certain every word he'd uttered was accurately repeated in the story. And while she was being so thorough, the clock continued to tick.

"Okay. I'm calling the chief," she announced, but the newsroom was nearly cleared out. She looked at the clock: ten forty. "Shit. Oh, God. We're going to miss deadline."

"It's extended," Harry said, coming out of his office. Jaimie looked up and saw a Harry she'd never really seen, walking toward her. He seemed more in control, stronger, like an athlete walking out onto the field before a game. He had that we're-gonna-kick-your-ass stride going. Harry's hair was mussed and he had five o'clock shadow, but other than that he looked alert and alive and full of energy. And too sexy to be walking across the rundown, about-to-be-a-shopper *Nortown Journal*. Why was it every time she looked at him she had to be reminded that he was a *New York Times* staffer who because of necessity had to go slumming at the *Journal?*

He had his game face on, pulling Jaimie back to the business at hand. "I just edited Ryan's stuff for the investigation sidebar. It's good. All you need to do is add a couple of current quotes from the chief and send it over to copy. We've got some time before the press guys start getting antsy. I've already told them we're taking this deadline to the limit."

"I'm sure they were thrilled."

"If this thing rolls off the presses too late, I'll get a ration of shit tomorrow from every department in the paper."

She grinned. "Harry, this story is worth it."

"Then I'll let you sit in on the morning meeting."

"Hey, I'm just about to call the chief at home and wake him up with the good news. Wanna listen?" she asked with a rather evil smile.

He leaned on her desk and folded his arms over his chest, looking every inch a modern, better-looking Cary Grant. Too bad she'd never make a good Rosalind Russell.

She picked up her phone and dialed the chief's home number. His wife answered. "Mrs. Girard, I'm so sorry to disturb you this late. This is Jaimie . . ." She didn't get to finish.

"Yeah, what is it? Do you know what time it is? This better be good, McLane."

"Sorry about the time, Chief," she said, then mugged a grin at Harry who sat there smiling and looking happy as hell. "I thought I should call and tell you about the story we're running tomorrow on page one."

"I already heard all about it from Scott Wu and I turned the case over to the juvenile prosecutor. And then I called the *Day.*"

Jaimie's face flushed and Harry sat up, his smile instantly gone. "I wonder if you'd like to comment about the fact a reporter solved a case your entire detective unit couldn't?"

"What?" he asked, clearly surprised by the question.

"Alex confessed to me, Chief."

She could almost picture him sitting up in bed, his face going all red. "You can't run a story like that."

"We're running it, along with another sidebar about the police investigation. How's that going, by the way?"

"Don't be a smartass or I will call the *Day,*" he said, and Jaimie almost collapsed in relief. He was such a nasty man. "Okay, McLane, what the hell did the kid say."

"Alex Schiffer alleges Joshua Tate was torturing and killing his own dog and Alex tried to stop him. With a really big stick. Oh, and by the way, Alex also confirmed that Joshua killed Mr. Fox's cat." She heard the chief pull the phone away and swear. "Is that on the record? Chief?"

He let out a sigh. "Okay, McLane. I have no comment except to say that the police department will continue its investigation following up on all leads."

"Do you have any idea about the charges the prosecutor might file?"

"I'm not going to speculate. That's all, McLane." And he hung up, but not before Jaimie heard him spit out "Fuck."

Jaimie put the receiver down and looked up at Harry who was smiling like a guy who'd just won a bet. "How pissed was he?"

"He said a rather choice word when he hung up the phone. Maybe that should be my lead. He also claimed he called the *Day* about it, which is why I nearly fainted, but he didn't. Thank God. And even if he calls now, I don't think they'll be able to get it in."

"Okay. Plug some quotes into Ryan's story and then send the stuff over to me. We've got to get this baby to bed or the press is going to have my balls for breakfast."

Harry started heading to his office at about the same time panic struck Jaimie. What if at four o'clock this morning Scott Wu called and said the kid changed his mind and if one word of the story hit the papers the *Journal* and Jaimie were in for the biggest lawsuit imaginable. What if the story ran and none of it were true? That thought nearly made her physically ill.

"Um. Harry?"

He stopped midstep. "What," he asked, though Jaimie could tell he didn't want to know.

"We're doing the right thing. I mean, you believe the kid, right?"

He walked over to the desk and leaned against it, slowly crossing his arms over his chest looking grim, though she thought his eyes held a hint of amusement. "What do you think?"

"I hate when you do that."

"What?" he asked, all innocent.

"Answer a question with a question. You do that all the time just to get me crazy, don't you?"

"I do?"

She gave him a look and he laughed. "Yes, Lois Lane, we're doing the right thing. The kid admitted it. I heard the tape and I feel safe that he was telling the truth. Our only problem will be if the parents get cold feet and make the kid deny the whole thing. The father just might do that but I don't think the mother will." He planted his hands on her desk and leaned so close she could see the green flecks in his eyes and she had the most incredible urge to lean into him and kiss him. "Now. Will you please send me that story?"

"Okay." She let out a puff of air. "Okay."

Jaimie watched Harry walk into his office and swing his chair around to his computer. The screen flashed up her story and before he could read a word, she was in his office and pulling up a chair to sit next to him. His fingers flew over the keys.

"What are you changing?" she demanded.

He turned slowly, as if he hadn't realized she'd barged into his office. "I thought I'd give you a by-line on this little gem of yours," he said.

"Oh. Sure. I thought it was a good idea for me to be here just in case you have any questions."

He grunted something then turned back to the story. It took thirty teeth-grinding minutes to edit the main story. He made only minor changes, and Jaimie felt she had to question each one. She had to admit he had the patience of a saint.

He leaned back and stared at the screen when he was done. "That is one hell of a story," he said. "Holy shit, Jaimie. This is what it's all about. Damn."

"It's okay then?"

"Okay?" He swung his chair around and beamed at her. "It's sending this paper out with a bang, I'll tell you that."

The joy flew out of her, sucked hard like a vacuum to her gut. "For a few minutes, I forgot. I actually forgot this is all going to end in a couple of weeks." Her eyes burned with unshed tears.

"Come on, Jaimie, don't get all maudlin on me." He was still smiling, as if by smiling at her he could make it all go away.

"You don't get it Harry. This is my life. Maybe I'm romanticizing this place, but the *Journal* is the heart of this city. We don't have much, but we had our own little paper. It was the only place that really covered what was happening in Nortown, the only paper that made room for stupid stories about kid's plays or a new sidewalk."

"The *Day's* putting in a bureau, the town will get coverage," he said, sounding almost desperate to cheer her up. "And if you're bureau chief, the coverage might even be better. Maybe they'll even make room for those hokey fiftieth anniversary pictures you like so much."

A tear spilled over and she let out a soggy laugh. "My grandparents got in the *Journal* five years ago. They clipped it out and framed it." She rested her head on his shoulder. "I'm tired," she said in apology as more tears fell, staining his white dress shirt. "The paper's shutting down, you're going to New York and I'll miss . . ." She stopped herself. "I'll miss this place. I don't even know for certain I have a job."

"You will," he said, and she gave him a watery smile, thinking she just might kiss him for being sweet and letting her cry when he should be down in the pressroom making sure the front page looked okay. "After this story, I think you can write your ticket."

"Maybe I should get a real job like Nate."

He shook his head. "I'd give you a week before you were bored out of your mind."

"Hey, maybe I'll apply at the *Times*," she said, and felt him stiffen, and felt her heart completely breaking at the proof he didn't want her with him. He didn't love her. "Naw, I'd just end up humiliating you by upstaging you all the time and that's not a very nice thing to do to a friend." The word "friend" seemed to echo in the room.

"No. I suppose not." He brought a hand up into her hair and kneaded her scalp lightly. She'd blown it straight today and wished she'd left it curly. Yeah, right, like he'd fall in love with her if she'd just kept her hair curly. He might fuck her against the desk, but he'd keep his heart where it was. She pulled away.

"Let's go down to the press room and check out the front page."

"What kind of shampoo do you use?" he asked, and she looked at him as if he'd gone insane.

"Do you have a hair fetish?"

He laughed. "Let me smell your hair again," he said, as if he were conducting a scientific experiment.

Jaimie shook her head. "Harry, you really need to get over my hair. Come on, smell it on the way to the pressroom. I want to see that front page."

Chapter 21

Harry half sat at her desk, she sat in her chair with the computer off, facing everyone in the newsroom. The mood was jubilant thanks to their front page and it made Jaimie sick to know that in about five minutes no one was going to be congratulating her on a great story, they were going to be out of jobs and extremely unhappy. Kath was trying to telepathically get her to tell her what was going on, but Jaimie shook her head. Every eye was on them and they all looked more curious than anything else. What bad thing could happen during one of the paper's shining moments?

Harry stood. "By tomorrow morning, this newspaper is going to be in the national spotlight," Harry said grimly, but no one seemed to notice.

"Yeah Jaimie," Kath called.

"Unfortunately, that's not why I called this meeting. Two months ago, we learned that the *Journal* was in serious financial difficulty. So as some of you may have noticed, we began selling more ads, publishing more special sections, increasing circulation, jazzing up the front page, in an effort to meet our financial goal. Then Hampton's announced its bankruptcy. Hampton's was the paper's largest advertiser and when it failed, it left the *Journal* far short of its target." He stopped, not for effect, but to take a deep breath. "Paul and Martin Mayer, the owners of this paper, have decided to sell to Penworth Media."

No one in the room seemed to know the significance of that news because they all waited expectantly for Harry to tell them what was going on.

"Penworth specializes in shoppers. Its plans are to take over the *Journal* January one. The editorial staff will be laid off in its entirety."

"You mean we're all out of a job? The paper's folding?" Kath asked incredulously, looking at Jaimie whose eyes begged her friend to understand her silence.

"Everyone in this room will be out of a job, including myself and Jaimie," Harry said.

"How long have you known?" Ryan, the new cop reporter, asked angrily.

"Two weeks. They've known for two weeks because that's when I got the story about Hampton's closing," Barry DeSilva said. "Why didn't you tell us then?"

Jaimie stood up. "Personally, I was hoping for a miracle. And the fact is, this paper is going to be around for another four weeks and I didn't want to see a mass exodus that would force us to shut down sooner than we wanted to. I know it sucks but I want you to know that everyone did everything humanly possible to keep this paper going."

"How can Paul do this?" Kath asked, her throat closing as she fought angry tears. "How can they do this when the *Journal* just broke a huge national story?"

"It all comes down to money," Harry said. "The paper hasn't been making enough for years, but this year it's particularly bad. Martin felt it was time to sell. I'm afraid there's nothing anyone can do."

"Martin sucks," Kath said.

"This whole thing sucks," Ted said, coming forward. "You guys have both known for two weeks? What kind of jobs are my guys going to get in the middle of the holidays, in the middle of the football and basketball seasons?"

"We're all going to feel the pinch," Harry said, and Jaimie's heart went out to him. He was staring at fifty pairs of very angry eyes.

"That's bullshit. You have a job waiting for you."

"Ted, I . . ." He stopped because Ted, and the rest of the sports staff, suddenly left the newsroom. That seemed to mark the end of the meeting, with reporters slowly making their way back to their desks. Jaimie followed Harry back into his office.

"That was fun," Jaimie said, tilting her head to see how Harry was doing. "You okay?"

Harry took a deep, shaking breath. "That was the hardest thing I've ever had to do."

"They're all mad now, but they're smart, too. They know we didn't have a choice." He gripped the back of his neck. It was an achingly familiar gesture, one he'd used when he was beginning to get one of his horrible headaches. "Harry, are you okay? Really?"

He looked puzzled for a second, then realized what he was doing and let out a small laugh. "No, I'm not okay," he said, pulling his hand away from his neck. "I just told a roomful of people three weeks before Christmas that they're jobless. Ted was right, I have a job."

Jaimie furrowed her brow. "You mean for sure you have a job? The investigation exonerated you? When did this happen?"

He smiled sheepishly. "I got a call about twenty minutes before you walked in with the Joshua Tate story. All

I have to do is formally accept. So, at least one of the editorial staff is employed."

"Ted was just upset."

"I know. We'll all be okay." Harry gave Jaimie a smile and watched her go back to her desk. He wasn't certain if he'd ever felt so helpless in his life as he gazed out over the newsroom. When had all this become so vitally important to him? He shouldn't feel this bad. He should be relieved that it was over, a clean-cut ending to a rather desperate time in his life. But all he could think of was having a beer with Ted at Duffy's, playing softball, making love to Jaimie. The past months weren't supposed to be fun or challenging or devastating. They were just supposed to be easy, a rest stop in his real life. Nothing about being in Nortown had been easy. And now leaving it wasn't going to be easy, either.

Martin Mayer was about to tee off when Gary Hamilton, one of his golf buddies, drove up in a golf cart.

"I think you might want to head back to the clubhouse," Gary said, his raspy two-pack-a-day-voice sounding loud in the early morning air. It was a beautiful day for golf and Martin didn't want it to shit the bed before he'd even had a chance to do it on his own.

"Why?" he asked, irritated and looking longingly at the first tee.

"Your paper is the lead story on the *Today* show."

"What? Why?"

Gary shrugged. "Something about a murder. They did a promo locally so you've got time to catch the story if you come on back now."

Martin looked again at his ball, glimmering white

against the pristine grass, and swore. "Yeah. Hold on. You guys go on ahead," he said.

"Hey, Gary. You want to be our fourth? Martin won't care if you use his clubs, will you Marty?"

They knew damn well he'd mind.

"Don't worry. I came prepared," Gary said, indicating his bag.

"See you in the club later," his partner said, dismissing him with a friendly smile. That pissed off Martin but he didn't let it show. He didn't like that he was interchangeable with Gary, whose game might be a little better but whose voice was enough to make your game worse.

"Right." Martin rode the cart back to the clubhouse, wondering why the hell that piece of shit paper could be in the news. Maybe Paul went berserk and killed his staff, he thought malignantly. That'd get his loser brother to sell the good-for-nothing place. Actually, the paper did help pay for his mortgage, his wife's gambling habit, and his three kids' college loans. But once he sold it, he'd be debt free.

Martin went into the lounge where some guys were already knocking back a couple and staring at the television. It wasn't even seven in the morning.

"National news come on yet?" he asked Marcy, the blond bartender he'd hit on three years ago without luck.

"Next. They got the guy who killed that kid up in Connecticut. You know, the one with the puppy."

The *Today* show music cued up and Matt Lauer's voice came on: "An eight-year-old boy confessed to killing Joshua Tate, the little boy found dead next to his puppy. Good morning. It's a gruesome story that's taken a bizarre twist. One of Joshua's friends confessed to a reporter that he killed Joshua to prevent the boy from killing his own dog. If the details outlined in the *Nortown Journal* are true, this will turn out to be one of the most disturbing child killing cases in recent history. We have Jaimie McLane, the reporter who interviewed the eight-year-old, now."

"That's my paper!," Martin said, jabbing a finger at the television. "That's my reporter. Jaimie McCain."

"I thought they said McLane. Yeah, McLane, see?"

"McLane. Right. She's my employee."

Marcy stared at the screen with renewed interest. "You own a newspaper?"

He nodded vigorously. "Damn good one, too."

Jaimie stared at the camera wanting to kill Kath, who stood to her side out of sight, mugging as if every word Jaimie uttered came directly from God. At first, it was incredibly weird to see that camera, very high tech and visual in this archaic world she'd become used to. When the crew walked in, they'd loved the place, the same way people who summered in the Hamptons loved Vermont. "Talk to the camera as if you're talking to a person. Just relax." She'd given the woman a quick smile and a nod, feeling far less nervous than she would have thought.

"Here we go. Watch my signal Miss McLane." She didn't need to, she heard Lauer do the entry and was as ready as she'd ever be.

"Did you have any idea when you started interviewing the little boy that he was at all involved in the boy's death?" he asked.

"No. All along I felt there was more to the killing than anyone knew, but I didn't go into the interview looking for anything other than some color on Joshua. I felt the best way to get to know him was to talk to his closest friend."

"According to your story, the boy said he killed Joshua to save the puppy. Do you buy that?"

"I do. A neighbor told police months before the murder that Joshua had tortured and killed his cat, but the police took no action," Jaimie said, trying to ignore the snort of approval from Harry. "I believe this kid was telling the truth. It was heartfelt and wrenching and very difficult to witness. His mother and father are devastated."

"What was their reaction?" Matt asked.

"At first, disbelief. But then came the sorrow, anger, the horror that their son had been carrying this awful secret inside him for months. They were overcome."

"What are the police saying?"

"Not much right now. They're still investigating the boy's confession, making certain it's legitimate. No charges have been filed, but they are expected today or tomorrow. The District Attorney is still weighing what charges to bring. I do know that the boy will not be charged as an adult."

"Well, Miss McLane, congratulations on the story and thank you."

Jaimie nodded, the camera light went off, and she breathed for the first time in what felt like an hour. The shitheads in the newsroom clapped, Harry the loudest.

"That's it? They're done? I think I'll do TV reporting. How's my makeup?" She grinned and struck a pose. "Where is my coffee. People, people, I need my coffee." Jaimie laughed. "Can I take off this suit now?"

"You've still got three more interviews," Harry said. "CBS, ABC, and FOX."

"TV reporters. Can't they get the story themselves?" she groused, but she actually thought it was pretty neat appearing on network TV. What a hoot.

"You are the story, Jaimie," Kath said, delighted that her

friend was standing in the spotlight. After grudgingly forgiving her for keeping the fate of the paper a secret, Kath had helped her pick out her outfit, put on makeup, and fix her hair until Jaimie felt like a red-headed Barbie.

Harry watched, impressed at how well she was doing under pressure. And he was pretty certain other people would be impressed, too. She did TV well. Really well. She had the look, the voice, the personality. He didn't know why he'd never thought of her that way before. Maybe he was so used to thinking about her in those frumpy sweaters, slogging through deadline after deadline of mediocre stories, he couldn't think of her as polished network material. But she was.

He looked up at the sports department's television. She was being interviewed by a CBS anchor now, looking straight at the camera, relaxed and conversational without seeming too blasé. She was incredible. Stunning.

"She's doing pretty good, huh?" Ted asked, his mouth full of a huge bagel.

"She's doing amazing. Do you know how hard it is to stare at a camera and talk to it like you're talking to a person? I know. I tried it. I worked for a week at the NBC affiliate in New York as a fill-in and, I suppose, to see how I'd do. I sucked. Big time. I repeated facts, stuttered and babbled. I begged them to burn the tapes and the producer laughed and said she'd already done it."

"Nice."

Harry jerked his chin toward the TV. "She's a natural."

"You think she's gonna get an offer?"

"I think she's going to get more than one." He watched for a while longer feeling so damn proud his throat started to ache. She'd been hiding this amazing talent and he didn't know about it, hadn't even guessed at it. Sure, he knew she was a great writer, but he hadn't known she'd be so poised under fire. In fact, he'd offered to do the interviews for her.

Harry walked into his office and turned on his own set, switching to ABC to wait for her interview with them. She gave the same basic interview, but in a way that made it seem fresh each time. America was going to fall in love with her.

Just like he had.

Chapter 22

He found her at the end of the second night asleep, her red-gold hair tumbling across her back and arms—and the keyboard of her computer. Harry looked at her across the newsroom, his face, lined with weariness, softening.

"Pretty girl," Jennifer said.

Lately, his mother was annoying the heck out of him. Anyone else could have spoken those two words and he would have taken them at face value. Pretty girl. Yes, damn pretty. But he knew his mother too well, could hear the undercurrent in her voice, the hard edge. The fear.

"You start January, right Harry?"

"That's what I agreed to," he said, feeling his stomach clench slightly.

"Who knows, maybe she'll end up in New York after all, working at one of the networks. She cleans up real good." Jennifer chuckled but in a way that made Harry turn and give his mother a hard look.

"Why don't you like her?"

She looked genuinely surprised at his conclusion. "What ever gave you that idea? Of course I like her."

"I'm going back. You can relax. I'm going back to my old job, my old life, my old everything," he said, slashing his hand through the air, surprising himself at how angry he sounded, how angry he felt. When he saw the look on his mother's face, he was immediately contrite. "I'm sorry, I'm tired."

"Apology accepted," she said, sounding hassled, which bugged him even more.

"I'll see you tomorrow afternoon. It's going to be another insane day."

Insane was a mild expression for the day they'd just had. He hadn't been so dog tired since he worked at the *Times* in the aftermath of September eleventh. After the networks disappeared to pretend to get the story, the staff, every pissed off one of them, rallied to cover every possible angle a story of this magnitude could have. Jaimie had interviewed Joshua's father from prison, and it was the off-lead to another story explaining the charges the prosecutor was planning to file against Alex. The parents weren't talking anymore, not surprising given the incredible media explosion. Every major network, along with their satellite dishes and polished and waxed reporters, were hanging out at the police station, as if the real news was going to come from the chief. Idiots.

A radical animal rights activist group was rallying around Alex and already planned a fund-raiser to help pay for his defense. Alex was a hero, a victim, and certainly shouldn't face prosecution for killing a little boy who was hurting his dog. Or so they said. The editorial staff was busy trying to weigh in on the value of human life versus animal life, and Kath did a nice story on what makes a sociopath. Though the story ran with the Joshua Tate stories, his name was never mentioned, so no one could ever accuse the paper of claiming Joshua was a potential serial killer. It was a dangerous story, because what if Alex was the little sicko and Joshua was just a cute kid who got his head bashed in, but they'd decided to go with it anyway. It was an incredible issue, put out by reporters who were facing no jobs and few prospects and Harry was damned proud of them. But there was no one he was more proud of than Jaimie.

After his mother left and the newsroom was virtually empty but for the pagination department at the far end of the massive room, Harry went over to the still-sleeping Jaimie and hunkered down next to her.

She was sleeping with her head facing him, her arms dangling straight down, her face sort of mushed up on one side. She had incredible skin, pale and soft, without a bit of makeup that he could detect. Her lashes were almost white at the tips, making them appear shorter than they really were. He'd never noticed that before. And even though she was an Irish redhead, she only had five freckles scattered across the bridge of her nose. He hadn't noticed that either.

Amazing what he didn't know about a woman he was pretty much certain he loved. He didn't know what she looked like in the morning waking up all drowsy and warm. He didn't know her favorite color, her favorite movie, her mother's maiden name. He didn't have a clue whether she liked fudge or was allergic to peanuts or hated hiking in the woods. All he knew was the thought of going back to New York alone was getting more and more difficult to take.

He hunkered down by her, his arms folded and resting on her desk, his chin on his arms, so he was mere inches from her face. She must have detected the movement because she opened her eyes and smiled. Blue-green. He hadn't known their true color.

"I fell asleep," she said.

"It's been a long day," he said, steering the conversation immediately away from anything remotely personal. "Tomorrow's going to be just as nuts."

"Mmmm," she said, all sleepy.

Women, Harry decided, should not be allowed to Mmmm near a man who is attracted to them. That innocent little letter was doing all sorts of crazy things to his insides because that was the same sound a woman made when a man was doing some interesting things, and the same sound she made when she was doing interesting things to a man.

"So," he said through gritted teeth. "You get any calls from the networks yet?"

"Yup. All three plus CNN. I passed on CNN already. Right now they're in a bidding war on how much they're going to pay me." She sat up, yawning.

"You joke, but that might not be too far from the truth. You were fantastic today."

"That's bullshit. All I did was talk about a story for two minutes that took me six months to work on."

"You made it look easy and I know it's not. At least not for everyone."

She shrugged, dismissing his compliment as nonsense.

"Are you saying that if a network called you right now and offered you a job you'd turn it down?"

"I'm not sure. Probably."

"Okay. You're out of a job at the end of the month. You have to decide right now. There's a bullet to your head," he said, making a gun with his hand.

"Harry." She let out a puff of air. "No, I don't think I'd take it. I'm pretty certain the *Day* or the *Courant* will hire me."

He narrowed his eyes and shook his head. "You are a strange, strange woman."

"No. I'm a snob. I happened to believe the term TV journalist is an oxymoron."

Harry laughed and she smiled at him.

"You know, you laugh a lot more since the investigation was settled."

"I do?"

Jaimie looked away, horrified that she'd gone all dewy-eyed on him again. "Yeah."

"I think there was a part of me that wondered if I really did screw up. The more I thought about those stories, those mistakes, the more I began to doubt myself. It's like a weight's been lifted." He smiled. "You want to wait until we see it come off the press?"

She did, but she shook her head no. She couldn't take being with him so much. These last few days had been murder on her heart and her raging libido. It was as if they'd never been in that alley, never mind-blowingly lost it with each other. They'd never mentioned it, just pretended it was what it was. Great sex. Except for Jaimie, it had been something more. She'd experienced something she was pretty certain few women did. Complete abandon, completely throwing away caution. No, that wasn't it, because she hadn't been cognizant enough to throw away caution. It had just been him and her and feelings, hot, throbbing, incredible feelings.

"I'm really tired," she said, not quite lying but hiding from the truth just the same.

"Okay. See you tomorrow then." She watched as he headed toward his office, her heart hurting.

"Harry?" He stopped and turned. "Are you staying until the bitter end or heading out before Christmas?"

"I'll probably stay until the end. I'm starting the first week in January."

"Oh."

"So. Yeah. I'll be here."

She forced her mouth into a smile. "Great." Leave,

now, Harry, because I don't think I can take this friend stuff too much longer.

"Goodnight."

" 'Night."

When Jaimie got home she gave in to a good cry, mostly because she was tired and the story and the paper ending and Harry leaving were sucking her dry. Max jumped on her lap and kneaded her thighs, digging in deep, until she laughed at the irony of bearing excruciating physical pain when she felt as if her heart were being mashed. "You're such a comfort, Max," she said, giving him a rub behind the ears and putting the cat into instant ecstasy. Max jumped off her lap, rubbed her legs once, then disappeared under her bed covers. She found a lump in her bed every night, and every night she smiled and wondered how the hell the cat got enough oxygen to breathe. She smiled, thinking about her cat and the lumpy bed, and then started crying all over again, because someday, the lump would be gone and she'd have nothing to smile about and she'd look for that lump for a long time before it finally sank in that her cat was dead.

And then she was crying about Harry again, and how lonely she was and goddamn it why didn't he love her. Maybe good sex was enough. Good sex could go a long way to make someone happy.

"But he's going to New York," she sobbed, padding off to the bathroom in search of toilet paper to blow her nose. She looked in the mirror and grimaced.

"Blick. Honey, you look like hell." And that made her laugh and snap out of her funk. She could always get another cat. And maybe, someday, she could get another Harry. She just hoped it happened before she hit menopause.

* * *

The telephone jarred her awake at seven in the morning, a time of day Jaimie rarely saw with eyes open. She pushed an empty water cup off her cluttered nightstand and dragged the receiver to her ear on the third ring.

"Hello?"

It was Kath. "Turn on your TV. NBC's interviewing Martin next."

"Okay. Thanks. See you later." She let the receiver lay by her ear and could feel herself sinking.

"You're awake, right Jaimie? Jaimie!"

"Yeah, yeah. I'll call you," she said, feeling and sounding more awake.

Jaimie heaved herself out of bed, feeling drugged and numb from stress and lack of sleep. Her head felt like she'd been drinking all night—no-sleep hangover. She'd had them before and they weren't a lot of fun. Grabbing the remote, she flopped back into bed, wishing she didn't care what Martin had to say so she could go back to sleep. She'd only met him a handful of times and hadn't been overly impressed. He was a lawyer, the successful brother, the one everyone in management was trying to please even though most had never met him.

"You must be very proud of your staff," the reporter said.

His staff. What a joke. He hadn't stepped foot inside the newsroom in at least three years. Martin hadn't changed a bit. He still wore a bad hairpiece and had a tan so dark it looked creepy.

"I am. Very proud. We've got a small staff and a small budget but the talent we have on board is impressive. Our managing editor is a Pulitzer Prize-winning reporter from the *New York Times*."

"Yeah, and he's about to go back to the good life," Jaimie muttered.

"Harry Crandall," the reporter supplied. "We've been told that you plan to sell the newspaper at the end of the year to a company that publishes small shoppers with little editorial content. Is that true?"

Jaimie's eyes widened and she let out a hoot, and changed her opinion instantly about TV reporters. They were geniuses. She watched as Martin's face flushed, as he looked around as if someone might save him from his own absurdity.

He smiled, oily and slick. "That's not completely true. I had been in discussions, but nothing is final. In fact, since this story came to light, negotiations have broken down."

Jaimie didn't move a muscle, didn't even want to breathe, because she could not believe what Martin was saying.

"The paper is not going to be sold?" the reporter asked, and Jaimie wondered if someone had gotten to him, whispered in his ear that forty fellow journalists were about to lose their jobs.

"Now why would I want to sell the best little newspaper in the country?" He smiled again and if Jaimie hadn't been quite so happy, that smile might have made her ill.

The phone rang and she picked it up mid-ring.

"Omigod, omigod, omigod," Kath screeched, sounding like a teenager catching sight of Justin Timberlake.

"I know."

"This is fucking unbe-fucking-lievable."

"I know."

"I can't believe it."

"I know. I know. I can't believe he folded like that on national television. Do you realize he's going to have to keep the paper? I can't believe it. I can't."

"Oh no!" Kath said. "I accepted another job."

"No. You didn't tell me."

"I'm sorry. But you didn't tell me the paper was going under, either. We're even."

Jaimie's heart fell from cloud nine to cloud eight. "So. You're leaving."

"I don't know. It wasn't a great job. And I really don't want to move. The money was about the same and the circulation is actually a little less than here . . ."

"So you're staying."

"Yes!" she screamed, putting Jaimie firmly back on cloud nine.

They were quiet for a few seconds before Jaimie said, "I'll never get back to sleep now. And I need to sleep."

"Try."

"Maybe I will. No one else was awake, I'm sure." She'd never sleep if she worried about the phone ringing.

"Take your phone off the hook."

"I'm so glad you're staying, Kath," she said, her throat and eyes burning.

"Me too."

Jaimie hung up the phone and lay in bed for a long time happy and tired, but still doubtful Martin meant what he said. Accolades were one thing, but he was one guy who always looked at the bottom line.

She stared at the phone and wondered if she should call Harry. He was probably asleep. And, really, what did it matter to him whether or not the paper was sold? She knew he'd felt bad about it, but it didn't affect his life personally the way it had everyone else's. He'd still go back to the *Times* regardless of what happened to the *Journal*.

And she could stay in Nortown forever. She waited for even a twinge of anxiety over the prospect of never leaving, but all she felt was happy.

Chapter 23

Jaime was running on empty. For three mornings in a row she'd gotten up at the crack of dawn to stand in front of a camera to tell the NBC anchors what their own local reporters should already know. Then she'd worked until two in the morning trying to get the paper out, write stories, edit everyone else's stuff. It was crazy and exhilarating and the best time she'd ever had. But these early mornings had to stop. She had more than enough on her plate between trying to stay ahead of the other media and trying to discover whether Martin was just showboating for the media.

She felt as if her head might explode if a single bit more information was stuffed into it. Her phone rang for the hundredth time that day and she was seriously tempted to throw it to the ground.

"Jaime McLane," she said, motioning the cop beat reporter over to her side.

A woman introduced herself as Melanie Michaels from NBC and she talked for a while, small talk, until Jaime thought she might hang up on the woman.

"Listen, I really appreciate the opportunity to help you guys out with this story, but I've got a newspaper to run and I just can't do double-duty anymore. I'm working on no sleep so I doubt anyone would want to see my bags in the morning anyway." She smiled at Ryan then rolled her eyes and opened and closed her hand: jabber, jabber.

"Let me get right to the point then. We'd like to offer you a position."

"Really." She held a finger up to the reporter and turned slightly away, her heart racing madly.

"We'd like you to start at the first of the year. We'll need you to come down to New York to sign the contract and go through some company policy details, but other than that, it's a done deal. So, can you start the first of the year?" Then she started talking benefits and money and Jaimie had to stop herself from whistling. She had a pretty good feeling Ms. Michaels expected her to stammer and say yes, what a wonderful opportunity, but Jaimie didn't.

"I'll have to think it over. When do you need to know?"

"I'm afraid we're not moving on salary," she said, some ice entering her tone.

"It's not the salary I'm concerned with. It's more than adequate." Nearly three times her current salary was plenty adequate.

"If you have another offer . . ."

"I don't."

Jaimie could picture the woman's head spinning around in confusion. She was, after all, representing NBC, offering a dream job to a nobody who had to *think it over?*

"I'll get back to you on Monday. That will give me the weekend to think things through. Would that be all right?"

"It would be cutting things a bit tight," she said, not sounding a bit friendly. Likely she was going to have to go back to her boss and tell them the redhead from Nortown hadn't said yes.

"I'm so sorry, but I don't have time to pee, never mind consider a life-changing decision right now. Why don't you give me your number so I can call you on Monday?"

Melanie did and Jaimie hung up, completely blown away. She'd thought Harry was having fun with her, telling her she'd get a network offer. It was ridiculous. Almost as ridiculous as the amount of money they said they were going to pay her. Then again, it was expensive living in New York.

Jaimie shook her head. She could not think about this now. It was too crazy and too far out to even consider.

She turned back to Ryan who was still waiting patiently. "This is a fantastic story, Ryan. But I changed your lead a little bit. Is this okay?"

Ryan leaned over and they both got immersed in the story, job offers and New York slipping completely from her mind.

"Martin offered me a substantial raise to stay," Harry yelled into her ear. There was no need for subtlety; it was so noisy in Duffy's, Jaimie barely made out his words.

"You're kidding. What did you say," she asked, putting her mouth close to his ear—a benefit of the noise.

He grinned and shrugged, like it was a big mystery what he said, and she gave him a light jab to his bicep. She loved it when he smiled, his face got these long lines near his mouth that might have been dimples when he was a little kid and his handsome quotient rose about ten points. She had two beers in her, and, like everyone else in the bar, was feeling no pain. Not because of the alcohol, but because of Martin's announcement he had no intentions to sell the *Journal*. The mood, to say the least, was jubilant.

It had been an incredible week, it was five days from Christmas, the paper had been in the national spotlight and had consistently beaten every other news source covering the story, including the *Day.* They hadn't planned an official Christmas party, mostly because everyone thought it would be a waste of money for a paper that didn't have enough of the green stuff to start. But after Martin's announcement, a party was quickly thrown together, Duffy's unofficially taken over by the paper, and the good times were rolling.

The cover band took a break and the noise level dropped significantly, eliminating the need for yelling. "Come on, Harry, you can tell me. Did you tell Martin to pound sand?"

He smiled again. "Actually, I told him I'd think it over."

"You're cruel," she said, liking this little bit of vindictiveness directed toward a guy she couldn't stand—even if he had decided to keep the paper going.

"I'm actually considering it," he said, moving his mouth so close to her ear she could feel his breath, warm on the side of her neck. Heat like she'd only experienced a few times before, and only with Harry, shot through her body. And then, her heart began pounding as her brain, which seemed to be directly connected to her heart lately, sorted through the reasons why he'd stay. One, the money, which was absurd because there was no way a skinflint like Martin would offer Harry enough money to stay. Two, he didn't want to go back to New York, which was highly unlikely given that every moment of his existence at the *Journal* was predicated on him going back to New York.

Three, he wanted to stay. Because of her, which were only her delusional thoughts at work.

"You see, kid, I just can't bear the thought of being without you. And you can't bear to see me go. I'll admit it if you do. I just think we're a good team, you know, kid?"

She clung to him, looking up into his granite-gray eyes.
"Oh, Harry, are you saying what I think you're saying?"
"Yeah, kid. Marry me." Camera pans out, show rock-
ing chair moving back and forth in the wind, and . . . cut.

She really was a pathetic human being. Jaimie gave him a dazzling smile, an I-really-don't-care-what-you-choose smile, and said, "Harry, I hate to do this to you, but I'm afraid I'm going to have to one-up you. Now, you're going to find this rather ironic." Jaimie laughed. "NBC offered me a job," she said leaning toward him so no one else would hear. Then she fell into a fit of giggles. "Wouldn't it be funny if I ended up in New York and you ended up in Nortown?" she rested a hand on one of his shoulders and laughed some more.

"That wouldn't happen," he said.

"Oh, I know," she said, slightly mad he really wasn't seriously considering staying, and even moreso that he knew, in the end, she wasn't going anywhere. Not that she couldn't. She could. She could say yes to NBC and sell her house and look for an apartment and start a whole new life away from friends and family and a newspaper she'd helped build. She could do it. Easy as pie. "But wouldn't it be funny? Your mother would have a heart attack," she said, still smiling but not feeling it.

He gave her the strangest look just then, one she couldn't even begin to interpret. She only knew it didn't give her a warm fuzzy feeling inside. If it had been anyone else but Harry, she might have even felt a tingling of something close to fear. "What did you tell them?" he asked, as softly as the noisy room would allow.

"That I'd think it over and let them know on Monday." He looked away from her, and seemed mad about something.

"What's wrong with you?"

"Nothing. Only you've told me about a hundred times that you'd never leave Nortown."

She shook her head in confusion. "I never said never. And who said I was going to, anyway. I said I was thinking it over. Who wouldn't?" And then it hit her. He didn't want her to go to New York. She suddenly felt like such an idiot, a royal, paint-me-a-fool idiot. "I don't know why you should care either way."

"You don't?"

"Hey guys," Sharon said, looking happy and glowy from her pregnancy. Then, apparently sensing the iceberg between Jaimie and Harry, said, "Am I interrupting something?"

"No," they said in unison.

"You two talk about babies and stuff. I'm going to talk to your husband," Harry said, making what Jaimie thought was a poor attempt at a smooth exit.

When he was gone, Sharon asked, "What was that all about?"

"I think we're all just a little stressed out with all that's been going on."

"You've been stressed. You should have been in our house the past two weeks. Ted was a wreck. I've never seen him so upset. I kept telling him to get his resume out but he wouldn't. It was as if he was frozen or something. He couldn't bear the thought of moving, even to Hartford, so I think he was pretending that none of it was going to happen. And then," she said, with a huge smile, "it didn't."

"You look great."

"My clothes are starting not to fit," she said, as if that

was the most wonderful thing that could happen to a woman. "I can't wait to get into maternity."

Jaimie was only half listening as her eyes wandered over to where Harry stood, looking tense and mad. Looking like he had when she'd first met him. Hard as a rock and just as friendly.

"Is Harry leaving for New York soon," Sharon asked, and Jaimie was embarrassed she'd gotten caught staring.

"I think so. I'm going to get another Heinie. You want a seltzer or soda?" She didn't want to talk about Harry or New York. She didn't even want to be in this bar celebrating anymore.

Harry watched as Jaimie talked to Sharon. She was wearing a sleeveless black ribbed turtleneck and faded jeans that fit so very nicely. She was talking to Nate, who was probably regretting his decision to leave, and she looked so happy to see him, if Harry had been a different kind a guy, he might be filled with raging jealousy. She was probably telling Nate she got an offer from New York, and he was standing there dying inside, praying she'd accept it but knowing there was a chance she wouldn't. Any other journalist would jump at the chance, but not Jaimie. He wished he could seriously consider Martin's offer, but he couldn't. How could he give up the *New York Times* for a small-time nothing newspaper? When Martin made the offer, his chest had squeezed tightly and he wasn't sure if he was feeling panic or fear that he might actually consider it. Parts of staying here seemed right, somehow, as if fate had pushed him here, pushed him to Jaimie, and then given him the perfect chance to change his life forever. Martin had offered, made a bunch of promises Harry planned to get in writing before he signed on the dotted line, and he'd thanked him. Harry had told Martin he'd give him a decision Monday, but in his heart, he knew he'd never accept. Even though it was breaking his heart.

But now hope, fierce and hot, filled him. She'd be a fool to turn it down, he knew that. She couldn't turn it down, not when it meant they could have a chance, not when she could finally leave Nortown and start living. He couldn't stay, she knew that. But she could leave.

"Somethin' huh?"

Ted came up behind him and slapped him on the back. "Martin's turn-around?"

"Yeah," Ted said, taking a swig from a Sam Adams. "I was shittin' bricks, my man."

Harry knew it wasn't the money he was worried about. "You like it here so much?"

He shrugged. "I don't know. I've been here for fifteen years, met my wife here. I thought when I was a kid I'd have worked all over the country by now. But here I am, about fifty miles from where I started. I didn't want to leave, sell the house, move Sharon away from her family. Especially now. And I would have gotten flak for it because I don't make squat and dragging Sharon off to another job where I wouldn't make squat wouldn't wash well with the 'laws.'"

"This place is a dump. Nortown, too."

Ted chuckled. "I know. But there's something about it. It's like there's a magnet under the city keeping you here. It grows on you. Just look at Jaimie. She's one of the best reporters I've ever seen and she's not going anywhere."

"You never know," Harry said, purposefully vague, hope flaring painfully in his chest. He wished he could ask her to take the NBC job for him, but what kind of fool would he look like if she patted him on the back and called him her "friend" again. His ego and, God knew, his heart, couldn't take it.

Harry's eyes found Jaimie again, animated, not a care in the world. He prayed he had misread her. Could this woman who'd been weepy for about a month, suddenly say good-bye to the paper she claimed to love?

He started walking toward her, a vague plan buzzing in his head. He had to find out how she really felt about him. He'd be damned if he laid his heart at her feet only to have her pat him on the head and tell him good-bye. He'd also be damned if he did nothing.

"Hey," he said when he reached her. "Let's do a pro-and-con list to help us decide what to do."

Nate said his hellos and sort of drifted away, forcing Jaimie to talk to Harry.

"Okay," Jaimie said. "Me first. Pro: money, prestige, excitement. Con. Gee, I can't think of any because who the hell would want to stay in this shithole? Right?"

She sounded mad and she wasn't looking at him and even though she was saying all the right things, it didn't feel right to him. That was always a bad sign. If he could get her to look at him he could smile at her and she'd have to smile back. "Con," he said. "Um. Leaving behind friends, family, familiar things. Selling your house."

"You said it was a dump."

"It is."

Her nostrils flared and her eyes flashed. "Are you supposed to be helping me here, or antagonizing me? Okay, let's go over your pros and cons. Pro."

He watched her, enjoying their bickering, loving the way she sparred with him. And then he thought he saw her eyes glitter suspiciously before she turned away. Then she turned back and looked directly at him without a hint of emotion.

"There aren't any pros for you to stay here, are there?"

"I've made . . . friends," he said, battling with himself over how much he should reveal. "My apartment's nice."

She looked at him, completely somber. "You and I both know you're going back to New York. But I want you to know that whether I stay or go has nothing to do with you, okay?"

Okay, then, you can take that knife out of my heart any time now. "Sure. Same here."

That seemed to amuse her. "I'm beat. This week's been rough on my REMs. I think I'll head home."

Panic sliced through him. This was not going the way he'd thought it would. She'd practically written it out for him in indelible ink that she was ending whatever they'd had, going her way, expecting him to go his. *Whether I stay or go has nothing to do with you, okay?"*

She really didn't seem to care.

He took her arm and waited until she lifted her gaze to him. "You can't go. It's a Christmas party. Anyway, I thought, for old times sake . . ."

"God, Harry, you take the cake," she said, and started walking away.

He knew immediately what she'd thought—that he wanted one more round of sex. He caught up to her, feeling as if everything were slipping through his fingers. "I don't want one last fling," he said, and grinned, trying to recapture something of what they'd had and not knowing quite when she'd gotten so hostile and he'd gotten so desperate to make her smile. "Though I wouldn't say no." No smile and she tried to pull away. "I just wanted to dance. We've never danced together."

"Harry, we've never even had dinner together. I'm going home."

"Then let's go out to dinner. Then will you dance with me?" He was frantic and sounded it and suddenly didn't care.

"Harry," Jaimie said, turning away, terrified that he'd see her tears. "Let me go."

"No. You have to . . ."

"I don't have to do anything." She yanked again, but he held fast and she didn't want to draw attention to them, so she let him pull her close, her heart hurting so much she wasn't sure how much longer she could hold back her tears.

"You can't just go. Not all mad."

She looked up at him guarding her emotions the best she could. "I'm not mad."

He ducked his head and grinned, all charm. Boy, he could really turn it on when he wanted to, she thought. "You sure?"

"I'm tired," she said, her voice and heart hollow.

And he let her go because he knew he had to be on his way. He had a whole other life back there, a life that didn't have room for a redheaded girl with dreams of her own and a heart with a soft spot for a hard man. He kisses her on the forehead before walking away. She watches, the wind whipping her hair, until he's a speck on the horizon. Roll credits.

Jaimie took a well-deserved day off the next day. She hadn't been lying to Harry last night. She was tired, so exhausted she felt slightly light-headed, even after a full night's sleep. She woke up just before eleven, the sun seeping through her shades just enough to make the room gloomy. Max sat on the bed staring at her and when her eyes opened, the cat let out a small sound, then bounded off the bed to the kitchen to guard over his food bowl.

"What do you think of New York," she called as a threat. An empty threat, she figured. She was too old to move to New York just to spite Harry. She'd have to make a real decision instead. Jaimie lay there, staring at an old water stain on her ceiling that looked like George Washington, and wondered if maybe she should take a chance at the big time. But did that mean all her talk about loving her life and living for the *Nortown Journal* was nothing but bullshit? The prattle of a woman who was secretly scared to take a chance? If it was a secret, then it was a pretty good one, because Jaimie had never felt scared about leaving—probably because she'd never seriously considered it.

"They probably don't take pets in the kind of apartment I'd be able to afford," she called. Max actually came back and stared at her from the doorway, then turned around, disgusted that he had to wait for his breakfast.

"Okay. Pros to taking the job. More money. Change of scenery. Living in New York. Maybe bumping into Harry once in a while. Cons to Nortown." She wrapped her arms around her legs and sighed. The biggest con was never seeing Harry again. "How pathetic is that?" she asked herself. When had she become the kind of woman who made any decisions based on a man? Then again, weren't people supposed to be willing to lose the thing most important to them to win their true love? But what if Jaimie left Nortown and Harry was more annoyed than anything? That sure seemed like the message she was getting, had been getting all along.

She picked up the phone and called her mother, laying out the whole story, the great job offer, her happiness at the paper's resurrection, her complete indecision about going to New York.

"That's a tough one, hon."

"That's why I called you. Plus, there's Harry, the managing editor. I'm pretty sure I'm in love with him."

"Here we go."

"What's that supposed to mean?"

"Only that we're finally getting to the reason for this call."

Jaimie didn't argue.

"How does he feel about you? Have you discussed this with him?"

"Gosh, Mom, that sounds like a great idea. Tell Harry I love him even though I'm pretty sure that would make him run like a man being chased by a horde of desperate women."

"Then you have to make your decision based on the job alone. And the fact that if you move to New York I'll only see you twice a year."

Jaimie grinned. "Thanksgiving and Christmas. Gotcha."

Her mother laughed. "Listen, Jaimes, you know what I'm going to tell you. I don't even know why you called."

"I know. I just need to hear you say it out loud," she said, perilously close to tears.

"Listen to your heart. Right? Isn't that what I always tell you?"

"The old gun to the head advice."

"It works every time. Call me when you make your decision."

"Bye, Mom," she managed to get out before bursting into tears. It felt good to give in to a bit of self-pity. She'd been going nonstop for days, and here she was facing a life-changing decision with a fried brain. And a bruised heart.

She stared at the phone, seeing her mother in her mind. "But what if my heart is telling me two different things?"

The phone rang and she smiled, knowing it was her mother. Poor Mom couldn't stand the thought of Jaimie suffering. She'd probably hung up with Jaimie, wrung her hands, and figured out a life plan for her. "Hi."

"I was wondering how you were coming on your decision?"

His voice made her heart thump and drop into her stomach. Not a nice feeling.

"I called my Mom."

"That help?"

"Not really."

"Want to come over and compare pro-and-con lists?"

God, she wanted to. "Okay. But no funny business."

"Can I at least try?"

Jaimie let out a watery laugh. "No."

There was no decision on his part; there never had been. He'd taken the job at the *Journal* knowing that someday he'd get vindicated and go back to New York, back to his life. No self-respecting journalist would pick the *Nortown Journal* over the *New York Times*. When his mother had told him that, he'd been irritated. But he'd known, deep down, she was right. If he felt a little less than thrilled about going back to his life, it was probably because his old life was gone. Anne was with someone else, his apartment was probably being rented to a Wall Street analyst, his desk at the *Times* had been taken over by someone else. He knew it was the right thing to do, but he couldn't figure out why he felt so tentative, like someone getting on roller blades who hadn't skated in twenty years. It would come back, but would he be as good? Was the fire still there?

If it wasn't, he damned well better find it, because fifty

other journalists were biting at the bit to take his place. His editor was lucky to be getting him back. Still, it was going to be strange being back, like jumping through a time warp into the twenty-first century. He was glad Martin would be updating the *Journal* and even a little sorry he wasn't going to be part of it. Martin had clearly wanted him to stay, offering a salary that, while not matching his *Times* salary, was damned impressive. He'd also promised to spend money on the paper, upgrading the computer system, investing in a better press, expanding coverage. Harry had been tempted, but would decline. Somehow the thought of staying in Nortown while Jaimie went off to New York was too depressing. Poor Jaimie probably agonized over the decision, but he knew in the end she'd have to pick the NBC job. Her moving to New York definitely made going back a bit nicer. Way nicer. Maybe he'd help her find an apartment, some shoebox for two thousand a month. Or maybe he could casually mention how much cheaper it would be for them to share an apartment. And maybe he'd make a rule that once you were in the apartment, you had to be naked.

She knocked on his door and he shook his head hard to get rid of the enticing image of her walking around in all her glorious splendor. He opened the door and thanked God and NBC because he wanted to drag her inside and make love and never let her out of his bed. She was pale and beautiful, her hair loose and curling around her shoulders.

"Don't say a word." He stepped back and motioned her in, smiling at her curious expression.

"I've made my decision," he said.

"Me too. I'm . . ."

He put a finger against her lips. "Don't tell me. We're going to write it down, then exchange papers. Write the name of the city."

She grinned. "Ooo. A little game. Though I have to tell

you, Harry, games are only good if you don't know the outcome." She took off her coat and settled down onto the couch, pulling her brown sweater around her as if she were cold. She looked so adorable in that big ol' sweater, her hair flung behind her, her nose slightly red from the cold. She was going to write New York on that paper. He knew she was, because only a frightened fool would stay. Because he didn't want to think about leaving her behind.

Harry felt like celebrating. He couldn't wait until she opened that piece of paper and read "New York." He wouldn't make a complete ass of himself tonight by declaring his undying love, but he felt dangerously giddy. He'd ask her for dinner first. And a movie. He'd find out what her favorite color was, who she went to the prom with, whether or not she wanted kids. Crazy stuff. Stuff Anne and he hadn't really talked about, or if she had it was to disparage it all. Anne had declared everything domesticated as enslavement. If he knew Anne, she'd probably already hired a nanny and was back at work.

Harry handed her a piece of paper and they each wrote their decision. "Okay. I read yours first." He looked down and saw "Nortown" and felt his stomach do an elevator drop. *Nortown?*

"Nortown?" He stared at the word the same way he'd stared at the newsroom the first time he'd seen it: Incredulous horror. "You're kidding, right?"

She stiffened, her cheeks bloomed. "No. I'm staying."

He shook his head in disbelief. Flabbergasted. Betrayed. Angry. Disappointed. "What the hell are you thinking? How can you turn down a network job to stay here and rot?"

"Well, I guess I know what your paper says," she spat, crumpling it up.

"Hey, I'm sorry," he said, knowing he didn't sound or feel sorry. "But I'm having a real difficult time with this.

So. This is it. Your career, from college to retirement, is going to be spent at this shithole?"

Jaimie was angry and beyond hurt and didn't realize he was just as angry and hurt. He was ridiculing her, the paper, her decision. He was letting her know exactly how he felt with his biting sarcasm and nastiness. "I think I better get going," she said, wanting to leave before she did something really stupid like cry. Or slap his smug, holier-than-thou face.

"I don't understand. Don't leave all mad." His tone was a tad conciliatory. "You're a terrific reporter, Jaimie. And you're being wasted here."

"I don't think of it as a waste. And I'm real sorry for you if you think the six months you've been here were a waste. Excuse me, Mr. New York Times, but it was me and this, what did you call it? Ah, shithole paper that broke one of the biggest stories of the year."

She could tell he was exasperated and part of her understood why. Most people would have taken that job. But she wasn't most people. And she didn't like the fact that the overriding factor for taking the job was that Harry was going to be in New York. It wasn't the job that was so enticing, it was living near Harry, the possibility of seeing him, of maybe making love to him one last time. Maybe even in a bed. And that's why she planned to turn the NBC job down, because she'd be damned if she'd be a woman who sold her soul and heart for a man who was oblivious and uncaring. As clearly Harry was.

He let out a sigh. "I'm sorry. I'm an ass." When she didn't argue, he smiled. "I just don't understand. At all."

"I'm happy here."

"You could be happy there, too."

She shook her head. "I don't think so. And you only live once and I want to be happy. You don't get it and you never

will, but I love what I do. I love this city. My mom's here.
I have a house here. It wasn't an easy decision, I wouldn't
want you to think that. It was one of the hardest things I've
ever had to do." Saying good-bye to you. Letting you go.

*(The couple stands near a misty doorway) Listen, kid,
you know and I know that it's for the best. I'm on to bigger and better things, see? And you, you're a small town
girl with small town dreams. It ain't bad, just different.
(Bend to kiss cheek) I'll miss you kid. (Chuck her on the
chin and turn away.)*

"I'm sorry." He did look miserable, so she cut him a
break.

"Me too. Hey, maybe someday I'll visit and you can
take me to dinner."

"Sure."

It would never happen, she knew that. She stood up,
pulling her sweater around her, feeling about as wretched
as she'd ever felt in her life. "I think I'll head home. Are
you coming in Monday?"

He stood back, looking uncertain and she thought she
saw a flash of sadness. "Yes. I've got to clean up things."

She forced a smile. "Yeah, that office of yours is a pigsty."

Jaimie stepped forward and gave in to an awkward hug.
He patted her lightly on the back before stepping away.

When she was gone, Harry sat down on the couch precisely where she'd sat, feeling dragged out and depressed
and pathetically comforted by the warm spot she'd left behind. She was staying in Nortown. And he was going to
New York. It was what he'd thought would happen all
along, except since her job offer . . . It was the hope it had
brought that was so devastating. He never thought she'd
end up in New York. And he sure as shit never thought
he'd stay in Nortown. And he wouldn't. Not even for her.

Chapter 24

Two days after Christmas, Harry stood looking out over an impressive nighttime view of the Manhattan skyline, letting wash over him the feeling of awe that he got nearly every time he'd taken the time to take a look around. It was so immense, and yet, his little corner of it so intimate. He'd never forget being twenty-five and walking into the *New York Times,* seeing those words emblazoned on the building, wondering if he really deserved to be walking through those doors as a staff reporter. He'd been so full of himself, so damned proud.

Today, when he'd gone up to see his old boss, all that pride had flooded over him with such intensity, he was taken by surprise. Co-workers came up to him and shook his hand, welcoming him back. He shook their hands, smiled and was genuinely glad to see them. He wanted to scream: I'm back, people. I'm goddamn back.

But was he happy?

Shit, when had being happy seemed important? He knew, of course, having been introduced to the if-it-ain't-broke-don't-fix-it mentality of Jaimie's existence. He'd always thought being successful, striving to be the best would make him happy. What was he thinking? He *was* happy. Ecstatic to be back. Wasn't it what he'd wanted for months?

He looked at the skyline with renewed fierceness.

"Nice view, huh?" Anne asked, handing him a glass of Pinot Grigio. "I never get tired of looking at it."

Harry accepted the wine and let out something like a grunt.

"It must be good to be back, right Harry?" She was looking at him in a new intense way and he didn't like it.

"Yeah," he said, and took a sip.

Anne looked incredible. She'd had the baby one month earlier and looked like she always did. Slim and beautiful.

"Pilates," she said with a pleased smile when he'd told her she looked skinny. "It's all about the tummy." She patted her nearly flat stomach. Incredible that the last time he'd seen her she'd been nothing but tummy. Her baby was cute enough. He got a glimpse of her sleeping, but didn't stay too long because Bob was hostile and hovering by the doorway. Anne was getting back to herself, albeit a slightly softer version of herself. As he'd guessed, she already had a nanny and was thinking about going back to work full-time instead of part-time as she'd originally thought.

"Bob wants me to ease into it, but I feel like I'm ready now. And I'm bored to tears. Don't get me wrong, I love Jacey, but, God, my brain is atrophying. I think she's going to be an only child."

Harry laughed. "What does Bob say?"

"Well, since he's got a daughter about three years younger than I am and a son I might have dated if I hadn't met him, he's, to say the least, not objecting."

He turned to look back at the view, feeling an empty ache that had nothing to do with Anne. "Monty wants me to go to Israel," he said.

Anne grasped his arm. "Oh, Harry, congratulations.

That's a terrific assignment. Wow," she said, unable to hide the envy in her voice.

"I don't know if I'm going to take it, but I'm afraid if I don't, Monty will tell me to take a hike."

Anne pulled him around so she could see his face. "You don't want to go? I'll go. Damn, I can't go. I don't want to go, really. Jacey. And Bob. I can't leave now. Shit, Harry, are you nuts? You're on page one every other day. That's the hot spot. What do you mean you don't want to go?"

Harry shrugged, feeling slightly sick at the thought of what Anne touted as such a great assignment. Three years ago, he would have already packed his bags and booked a flight. But now . . . Too much had happened. "Larry was there for ten years. I don't want to be out of the states for ten years."

Anne looked at him as if he were some foreign matter in her soup that she couldn't quite identify. "Harry, you're single. No kids. A great reporter. What's stopping you?" She put a hand to her forehead. "God, what I wouldn't do for that assignment." She bit her lip. "But I can't. Even if I could take Jacey, what would Bob do? He'd need a job." She took a deep breath. "I can't do it."

"Of course you can't, Anne. You have a one-month-old baby. What the hell are you thinking?"

"No, I can't do it. I can't. But you can and you don't want it. That's driving me nuts. Make me understand." She was desperate, pleading, completely bowled over.

He knew why, but he couldn't say it out loud. He wasn't even sure he could fully admit it to himself. Israel was too damn far away from Jaimie. If he was in Israel, he truly would never see her again, whatever they had would be over. He still wasn't sure what they had, but he did know that if he were out of the country, it would die a quick death. Maybe that would be for the best.

"It's a woman. That redhead."

He felt his cheeks redden, an intensely uncomfortable sensation and completely foreign.

"Oh my God. You're in love with her."

He shook his head, but said, "Yes. Maybe. I don't know."

"When we were living together, you used to talk about going to Afghanistan and then to Iraq. You talked as if you were going to the corner store, as if it were nothing. Not even something you should discuss with me to find out how I felt. Now you're thinking about turning down one of the best assignments in the paper and you think *maybe* you love her?"

"It's complicated."

"Does she know how you feel?"

"I said, it's complicated."

Anne shook her head in disgust. "You haven't told her but you think she should know. How? By osmosis? Mind-reading?"

"No," he said with overt patience. "It's just that I'm not sure she feels the same way. She had a chance to come to New York and she didn't. She knew I was going to come back."

"And follow a man she doesn't know loves her? How stupid do you think she is?"

He hated when she was right, but he'd be damned if he laid his heart out for Jaimie only to be gently pushed away. Jaimie had never done anything—other than have really hot sex—to make him think she loved him. "She called me her friend."

"Defense mechanism," Anne said. "A woman who isn't sure how a guy feels will call him 'friend' to get his reaction." Then she chewed on her thumbnail. "Then again, she might have said it to clue you in to how she feels."

"Thanks for your help."

She grinned. "With Bob it was easy. It was so obvious that he loved me that I told him first."

"What'd he do?"

"It was right after you left. I always suspected he had a crush on me but he was married, so I just ignored it."

"Plus you were supposed to be in love with me," he pointed out.

"Oh. Yeah. Anyway, after you left, I got the flu and he came over with soup and medicine and basically took care of me for a day. It was so sweet."

"I thought you hated sweet."

"I like it on Bob. On you it seems forced, like you're only doing something because you think you have to."

He was truly insulted. "That's not true."

"Let's face it, Harry, you're not the warm fuzzy type. You're not romantic and you're not thoughtful. That's what I liked about you."

"Was I that bad?"

"Oh, Harry. I said I liked it about you. It's not bad, it's just not what I need long-term."

He pushed his hand through his hair. "You make me sound like an unfeeling jerk." And he couldn't help but think, is that how Jaimie sees me? He thought about their moments together. There had been that one moment right after he'd gotten news of the investigation when she'd looked up at him with those big blue-green eyes and he'd thought: Oh my God, she's in love with me. But it hadn't happened again so he figured he'd been dreaming. Then they'd had that incredible sex in the alley. That had been his all-time classy moment. Still, it had been good, hadn't it? Or had that been wishful thinking, too?

"You're not an unfeeling jerk. You're just not the most demonstrative guy in the world." She must have seen his look because she said, "And I'm not talking about sex. I'm talking about hand-holding and hugs and, you know, little stuff."

He tried real hard not to roll his eyes. "All that touchy-feely crap you mean."

Anne laughed. "I know exactly how you feel. I used to be the same way. But Bob and Jacey changed all that. It's amazing. I'm amazing myself. So, Harry. What are you going to do about the redhead?"

Harry turned back to the skyline. "Damned if I know."

Jaimie stared at her cat. Her cat stared back. "Little shit. You're no fun. At least a dog would sense my sadness and come and lick my hand." She gave Max a dirty look and the cat continued to stare at her. Maybe Harry was like her cat, loved her, but couldn't show it? Or maybe Harry was like her cat, used her because she was around and forgot about her as soon as she was gone.

Her kitchen door opened suddenly and Kath came in, brown paper bag in her hand. "Did someone call a medic?" she asked, and pulled out tequila and margarita mix.

"You're just in time," Jaimie said, a smile tugging on her lips. "I'll get my blender."

Ten minutes later they were sitting on the couch waiting for *When Harry Met Sally* to start on TNT, a big bowl of popcorn sitting between them. It was one of Jaimie's favorite modern movies. She knew she wouldn't be able to sit through *Casablanca* or *Gone With the Wind* or any other classic movie that ended great, but lousy.

"Has he called?"

"No."

"I wish you'd just tell him . . ."

She held up a hand to stifle Kath's opinion. "We're not talking about this tonight. I'm over it. I really am."

"You sound like Sally saying she's over her boyfriend leaving her when she's totally screwed up about it and doesn't know it."

"She is not screwed up until her jerky ex-boyfriend gets married," Jaimie pointed out.

"So, what are you doing New Years Eve?"

"Working, then sleeping."

"Where's Harry going to be?"

Jaimie let out a sigh. "Why, he's going to be running toward my house just as the clock strikes midnight because that's when he's going to realize that he wants the rest of his life to start right now. With me." She put a pillow over her head. "I told you I didn't want to talk about it."

"What if he did that, Jaime? What would you do?"

She pulled down the pillow. "Are you *trying* to make me cry. Is that it?"

Kath grinned.

"I'd tell him I love him too, that's what I'd do. But that's not going to happen, is it."

"Probably not."

The movie came on and Kath stopped torturing her.

Chapter 25

Jaimie had never, in her life, felt more murderous than she did looking at Martin's lying full-of-shit face. Paul had temporarily, and apparently under protest, moved back into his old office, but it was Martin who sat behind the desk, hands steepled, over his buttoned-down belly.

(Stands with sub-machine gun at her hip, lip curled in a sneer) You dirty scoundrel. You double-crossed me for the last time (rat-at-tat-at-tat).

"Harry told me you planned to spend money on the paper. Get a new press, update the computer system. You're telling me that's not going to happen?"

Paul chimed in, using his placating tone she was really starting to dislike. Intensely. "Jaimie, he made those promises based on a package deal presented to Harry. It was never meant as anything other than that."

"And the paper? Are you still planning to sell it?"

Martin didn't even have the grace to look uncomfortable. "The deal with Penworth hit a roadblock. But I've had other offers."

She wanted to scream, to rip off his bad toupee. She wanted to grab him around his loose-skinned neck and throttle him. "You're selling the paper. After going on national television and saying you wouldn't. Why?"

He gave her a look of superior disgust, as if she were a

naïve child. "I never said I wasn't selling the paper out-right. I said, and you can look at the transcript, that negotiations had stalled. And who gives a fuck what I said anyway. The paper is losing money and I happen to be-lieve, as its owner, that the only person who can make this paper solvent is Harry Crandall."

When Harry had left, Jaimie had thought she couldn't get any more depressed than that. Now, it seemed as if a black cloud were settling in around her. She'd passed up a dream network job on the belief that Martin was going to not only keep the paper going, but turn it into the first-rate publication Nortown deserved. A dream job that would have kept her near Harry.

"Listen, Jaimie," Martin said, leaning forward and giv-ing her an icky fatherly expression. "I understand you're upset. But it's my hope whoever buys the paper will keep the editorial content much as it is. Thanks to your stories, we've gotten more interest in the paper from all sorts of people." He smiled his greasy smile and Jaimie felt sick. He was the kind of guy who was always careful what he said, and she was able to read into what he wasn't saying. He *hoped* the new owner would keep the editorial con-tent. He wasn't selling the paper to Penworth. They'd hit a roadblock. But that didn't mean he never intended to sell the paper.

"You're lying," she said, trying to keep her tone steady. "You've been lying all along. The Penworth deal was never dead, was it?"

He leaned back and gave her a shrewd look. "The deal was dead when I thought I had a Pulitzer Prize-winner journalist at the helm."

"I'm the one who brought in the story, Martin."

"That's true. But Harry's the one who would have brought in the money. Don't take it so personally, Jaimie.

This is a business like any other business. It's all about money."

"You should take a look at my salary. Then you'd know it was never about money to me."

Throughout the meeting, Paul sat there mute, and maybe that hurt most of all. She gave him a look but he wasn't even man enough to look up when she stood to leave. Jaimie walked out of the office before she cried. She was doing way too much of that lately.

Jaimie went back to her desk and stared blankly at that day's front-page layout. She wanted to scream and cry and rant and rave, but she sat there, dry-eyed, feeling foolish. She'd worked her butt off for this stupid paper, for those jerks sitting in Harry's office, and for what? The newsroom was busy, the air still jubilant from the Joshua Tate stories and the news that their jobs were safe. She felt sick inside.

Had Harry known that Martin's proposal was a package deal? Probably not. He still wouldn't have stayed in Nortown, but Jaimie knew he would have told her so she'd be prepared. Her eyes went to the phone, then drifted over to the Rolodex where she'd jotted down the main number for the *New York Times*. Harry said he'd call when he had a permanent number. It had been a week without a call, without even a hello. God, she missed him and hated that she missed him because, chances were, he hadn't spared her a thought. She had no one to talk to about Martin's little announcement. If she told Kath, it would be all over the newsroom in hours, and why send people into a panic before any deal was set. Maybe Martin would find a major media conglomerate that would keep the paper much the same. She couldn't confide in Jennifer because she'd made her opinion of Jaimie's decision to reject the NBC job perfectly clear: "You're out of your mind." But Jaimie had sensed she was relieved, which, of course, made things worse.

She looked over to Ted who was fine-tuning his front page. Financially, it didn't matter if he lost his job, so there was no need to tell him either, especially knowing how upset he'd been the last time the paper was going down. The only person on earth she could confide in was gone. She looked at the clock. Nine. Harry probably wouldn't be at the paper working yet. He wasn't supposed to start officially until January second, three more days. She didn't even know where he was staying. Now that was true love if she ever saw it. When was she going to realize that this thing with Harry was over, that it had never even really been anything more than a sexual attraction for him. He'd never claimed to love her, never even hinted they had a future together other than a vague mention of getting together if she was ever in New York. She lived two and a half hours away from New York City and she'd only been there once, when she was twelve.

"You idiot," she whispered fiercely, and that's when she noticed her message light blinking. She picked up the phone and hit zero so she could talk to the night receptionist, a seventeen-year-old single mother. "You have a message for me?"

"Oh. Yeah."

"I haven't been on the phone."

"Sorry. I forgot to hit the button." Jaimie heard her shuffling paper. "Okay. Harry Crandall called. No message."

After Jaimie swallowed down her heart that had leapt full-force into her throat, she asked, "Did he leave a number?"

"Oh, shit. I mean, shoot. Oh, yeah. I couldn't tell whether this was a two or a seven but I'm pretty sure it's a two. If that's wrong, just switch the twos to sevens and that should be right." She rattled off the number and hung up.

Jaimie stared at that number for a minute as she tried to get her heart in order. Harry called. Probably to chat, an obligatory how-ya-doin' call. She should not put any importance into a phone message. She dialed the number, shamelessly forgetting everything she'd thought about two minutes ago, and got a Marriott operator, who connected her to his room.

He's probably not in. It's New York. The city that never sleeps. He's not . . .

"Hello."

"Harry, it's Jaimie. I got a message here that you called." That was good, not too cheerful, not desperate-sounding. Nothing in that sentence to let him know he'd ripped her heart out of her chest with his bare fist.

"Hey, Jaimie. How the heck are you?"

I miss you and, God, it's great to hear your voice. Is there any chance you could rent a car and get your beautiful butt over to my house tonight?

"Actually, things here aren't so great," she said softly so no one in the newsroom would overhear. "Did Martin ever hint that not selling the paper and making improvements was contingent on your taking the job."

"That prick."

"I agree. But did he?"

"No. But I had a bad feeling about him. He's an opportunist and he had this idea that only I would be able to get the paper in the black. I told him it wasn't true, that any competent editor, given the time and resources, could turn the *Journal* into a great little paper. What a class-A jerk."

"I can't believe this is happening," she said softly,

knowing she sounded pathetic but unable to make herself sound cheerful.

"All I need is to feel guilty about leaving," he said, and something odd in his voice gave Jaimie a little jolt.

"What's happening there?"

"My boss wants me to go to Israel."

"Israel?" The air flew from her lungs. "Wow. Great assignment. How long would you be there?"

"I don't know. Years, I guess. It's a great assignment." He didn't sound excited. He sounded like a kid who's trying to be polite in front of company when he finds out supper is liver and onions.

"You don't sound all that excited about it," she said.

"To be honest, I'm not. Anne wants to kill me for not jumping for joy."

"Maybe I'll take it," Jaimie said. "I may be out of a job after all and I have a feeling NBC isn't going to be answering my e-mails."

"You never know," he said, but she could hear the doubt in his voice.

"I think I do know but I guess it wouldn't hurt to try. So. What are you going to do about Israel?"

"That's why I called. Sort of. I'm going to be in town New Years Eve for Ted's party. I don't have to give my boss an answer until the day after New Years and I thought I'd pick everyone's brain. You going?"

It was a casual enough question, so Jaimie ignored her heart that jumped onto cloud nine and started doing a little dance. "I always go to Ted's New Years Eve parties," she said. "I guess I'll see you there."

"Great. And Jaimie, make sure you bring that brown sweater of yours."

"Ha ha." She hung up and smiled. Well. New Years Eve with Harry. Things definitely were looking slightly better.

Chapter 26

Jaimie stared at the pile of discarded outfits lying on her bed, not quite willing to believe she was going through all this just because Harry was coming to the party. Getting Harry to appreciate her body had never been one of her failings. Getting his heart involved, now that was another matter. Ted's parties were never elegant affairs. Half the people attending were sports writers who, in the winter, switched from cargo shorts to cargo pants or jeans and a sweatshirt emblazoned with the logo of their favorite team or college. Beer was always plentiful, though Sharon always made certain she had at least one or two bottles of wine around just in case the guys brought a girlfriend. Sharon had already hinted that she might not make midnight. She was five months pregnant and feeling cranky and tired.

Jaimie was just cranky and tired. The stress of keeping Martin's plans to herself was wearing at her. She worked six days straight so she could take this day off. Most of the reporters filed their stories early so they could have a holiday and Jennifer agreed to work New Years after Jaimie worked Christmas Eve and Christmas day. Mom was not pleased, but not as upset as Jaimie thought she'd be, which was disheartening. Christmas, before her parents' divorce, had always been so much fun. Maybe it was the fog that drifted over memories that made the holidays fun, when in reality, they couldn't have been that great. She wished her mother had protested a bit more, that's all. She wished she had someone who really cared whether or not she worked Christmas Day. Someone like Harry.

She looked in the mirror trying to gain some perspective. "You love him. He thinks you're a good lay," she said, and then gave herself some credit for knowing it even if her heart still held out hope for more. In a way, Jaimie was proud of herself. She hadn't followed Harry to New York. She'd stayed in Nortown with her scummy boss and indifferent cat instead. Yeah, she should be real proud.

"Well, what do you think, cat? The festive red turtle neck or the shockingly revealing black blouse with jeans?" Max yawned and jumped up on the bed. "Hmmm. Black blouse, you say? Shocking."

She bit her lip. If she wore that blouse with her hair all curly and with makeup on, wouldn't she appear a bit obvious? Maybe. And maybe that's just what Harry needed.

She was not wearing the brown sweater.

Harry, along with every other male in that room, felt his jaw drop when Jaimie walked into the room. "How the hell does she do that?" he said aloud to no one in particular. How could the woman he knew be that woman standing at the entrance to Ted's great room? Her eyes scanned the crowd and when she spotted him she smiled, wide and open and just like the Jaimie he knew. God, what that smile did to him. If she knew, she'd probably run back and get that sweater of hers.

Weekend Jaimie, that strange woman he'd seen only a few times, tonight was wearing sexy tattered jeans and a low-cut, breast-hugging black blouse. She was bonus

Jaimie. He smiled back and watched, trying not to make his raging lust too obvious.

"I see Weekend Jaimie has arrived," he said when she reached him.

"A bit shocking, isn't it?" she said, looking slightly embarrassed, but paradoxically pleased with his response.

"I'm afraid it's going to be impossible to think of you as one of the guys tonight, Jaime," he said, blatantly staring at her breasts. She laughed. That's what he liked about Jaimie, she never got all bent out of shape because he was enjoying what she was obviously putting on display. He'd never forget his first *New York Times* party. A woman from production wore one of those dresses that you can't quite figure out how it manages to keep things covered. Nipple glue, he supposed. He looked, sure he did. Isn't that what she wanted wearing a dress like that? He wasn't rude about it, just . . . admiring. She threatened to call security and then actually talked to the *Times* attorneys about a sexual harassment case.

"She was harassing me and every other guy in the place wearing that dress," he'd said to the very unamused attorneys.

Harry told her the story and she laughed with him. "I knew that sexual harassment story wasn't all bullshit," she said.

They talked about New York and how it felt being back, and they talked about Nortown and what was going to happen to the paper. They must have stood there for an hour talking, the rest of the party muted, nonexistent. It was noisy—the sports writers and their girlfriends were getting happily buzzed—but Harry was completely unaware of anything in the room but Jaimie. Man, it was good to see her tonight. She was in the middle of a story about one of Kath's disastrous dates, pantomiming the way the guy ate his spaghetti with his fingers, when he caught one of her hands.

"What," she said, her eyes shining brightly.

"Your hair. You let it curl. Why?"

"Because I knew you like it that way, Harry, and I'm trying to drive you wild," she said lightly. She shook her head and gave him such a burning look of seduction, it was all he could do not to drag her into one of the house's many bedrooms. "Is it working?" she asked, letting her lashes dip down slowly as if hiding her desire. She was kidding, putting on an act worthy of Norma Desmond, but to him she was the sexiest woman alive.

"You are driving me wild," he said, as serious as he could without sounding like a letch.

"I'm just wild about Harry, and Harry's wild about me," she sang.

"You watch too many old movies," he said.

"I do. It's a horrible thing to do because most of the good ones have wonderfully happy endings. I see enough rotten endings in real life. I like my movies to end happily."

"Like *Casablanca*?" he asked.

She wrinkled her nose. "Loved the movie. Of course, you have to love *Casablanca*. But I didn't like the ending."

"Okay. What's my happy ending?"

She frowned slightly and he had a feeling their light moment was slipping away. "You go to Israel. Win another Pulitzer."

"I'm not sure I like that ending," he muttered. "What's yours?"

"I win the lottery, buy the paper, die at home in my bed when I'm eighty-two."

"Do you ever marry?"

She looked away, pretending, he was sure, to look for someone.

"Do you?" he persisted out of some kind of perverted idea that she'd fling herself into his arms and declare her undying love.

"Harry. I'm thirty-one years old and I've only been in love once. It's New Years Eve and I don't have a date. I worked Christmas Eve and Christmas Day and not even my cat missed me. No, Harry, I don't think I'm going to ever get married. I'm going to die alone in my house while my cat watches unconcerned." He could have sworn her eyes glittered with tears before she turned away, but he wasn't sure. "I've got to go to the bathroom," she said, and turned away.

He'd be gone in a few hours, maybe to Israel, and he might not get the chance to hold her again, to inhale that sweet vanilla scent, to bury his hands in her hair. He caught up to her in the hallway between the bathroom and the kitchen, not the best place for privacy. He pulled her into a room that turned out to be a small office, a blessedly empty office. A small desk lamp was the only source of light in the room.

"You're not going to die alone," he said, pulling her against him. "You could call me and I'd hold your hand."

"Sweet, Harry. But I told you already, I'm not going to be alone. My cat, Max the sixth, will be there." He could hear the smile in her tone. She always smelled so damn good and he breathed deeply, trying to put her scent away, store it in his brain so he could call it out whenever he liked. So when he dreamed of her, it would be there to make it seem more real.

"You always smell so good," he said, and swallowed down the lump that was growing painfully large in his throat. He'd known it would be difficult to say good-bye, he just hadn't known how difficult. He hadn't known his chest would ache, that his bed would seem eternally empty, that his life would be so vacant without her. He hadn't known it would hurt so damn much to feel this way and not to know whether she felt anything the same.

Harry nuzzled her neck and it felt so good, Jaimie wanted to cry. She pulled away slightly. "I think I should go mingle. I haven't even said hi to Ted and Sharon," she said overly brightly.

"No. Don't go. Not yet," he said, gently pulling her close. He didn't make any moves, just held her, moving his hand through her hair and nuzzling her neck. She looked up at the ceiling, willing away the tears. He was going to Israel and she was staying in good ol' Nortown.

"Your sweater," he said, his mouth near her ear, his face buried in her hair. "Did you bring it with you?"

"What?"

"Your sweater smells like you."

"Makes sense." She could hardly think past the feeling of his hand buried in her hair, his mouth on her neck.

"I'd like to have it."

She caught her breath, not because of what he'd said, but because he'd just swirled his tongue around her ear. "You what?"

"I want your sweater. I want to be able to hold it up to my face and breathe you in. I want you with me even though you won't be."

She pulled back and looked at him. "You want my sweater?"

"No, you idiot, I want you. But I can't have you, can I? Not if I'm in Israel and you're in Nortown. So I figured I could have your sweater."

Either he was nuts, or Harry was in love.

Chapter 27

She backed away and chewed on her thumbnail. "Harry, what are you saying?"

He was looking at her strangely, his mind working, she could tell by the way he pressed his lips together.

"That I want your sweater."

"Will you leave off about my stupid sweater?" she said, wrapping her arms around her because all this talk about her sweater was making her cold.

He began to pace like some Scotland Yard detective spelling out a case. "Yes, the sweater. The same sweater you wear in the newsroom every day. The one that makes you look like some sort of bag lady. And for some reason, I can't take my eyes off you. And when I walk by and breathe—and I do—I want to rip it off you and . . ."

Her eyes filled with tears that burned and hurt because she was pretty damn sure she knew what he was saying but she was too scared to come out and ask. "What's your point?"

She flushed and turned slightly away from his intense gaze.

"I'm in love with you," he said softly.

Her eyes began to burn. "Okay."

"Okay?"

Jaimie looked at him, searching his beloved face to

see if she could somehow determine if he meant what he said. "Oh, Harry, of course I love you, too."

And right before her, he melted, he simply deflated, ending up on his knees in front of her, clutching her back as if that was the only thing keeping him from slamming into the floor. He dragged her down to her knees until her eyes were level with his. "I love you, too." He pulled her close, so close she could hardly breathe, and kissed her almost painfully, letting out a sound that tore at her heart. She pulled away, putting a hand on either side of his face as tears ran down hers.

"How long have you known?"

He looked slightly ill. "A while."

"God, are we idiots or what?"

"Idiots," he said, laughing. "You said I was your friend and you sure as hell weren't acting as if you loved me."

"Let me tell you something. I wouldn't make love in a stinking alley with anyone I didn't love," she said, and pulled him close again. "I missed you so much, Harry. I thought you were gone and didn't care and here I was alone and thinking I'd always be alone and you were in New York living it up and . . ."

He stopped her with a kiss. "You talk too much," he said, moving his hands to her hair, looking at her as if she were the most beautiful creature on earth. "What the hell are we going to do?"

"I could take the job at NBC. It probably won't be the same offer but I could try."

"I could take Martin's offer and turn this paper into something," he said, sounding far more sincere than she had.

"You'd do that? That's insane. Plus, your mother would kill me."

He kissed her again. "Let's go back to your house. We can talk later."

They walked to her car hand in hand. Jaimie couldn't ever remember walking with a man like that without feeling foolish. She'd never been much of a hand-holding girl. On the drive home, they didn't talk about Israel or the *New York Times* or little papers that were about to be sold. They talked about how cold it was and whether the kids would get enough snow to go sledding this year. When she drove into her driveway, she smiled at how cute it looked from the outside with the Christmas wreath still tacked to the front door and the candles lit in every window, and she was suddenly and fiercely glad she was in Nortown.

"My house is a little messy," she said, putting the key in her lock. "I wasn't expecting anyone. The clothes on the couch are clean, I just didn't have time to fold them yet." She ran ahead and gathered up a coffee mug and a crumb-covered plate while he tried valiantly not to care how messy everything was. "Just let me move this," she said, hefting up a one-week stack of newspapers and throwing them outside into her recycling bin.

"You're going to have to improve on the slobbery if this is going to work," he said.

"I know. I drive my mother nuts. By the way, this is actually pretty clean," she said, grinning as she draped her arms over his shoulders. "I hope I didn't ruin the mood." She kissed him and he pulled her close.

"Is your bed made?" he asked against her lips.

"You really know how to turn a girl on."

"I aim to please."

Her bed was made, a minor miracle and one he'd never fully appreciate. "Making love on a bed. This will be novel."

"You think we're making love?" he asked as he pulled his jersey over his head then half-folded it and laid it on her bureau.

"It hadn't crossed my mind," she said, scooting out of her pants and kicking them aside.

"You just don't do it for me, baby. Sorry." And he pulled down his pants revealing the fact that she did, indeed, do it for him.

"Then that must be a roll of quarters in your boxers. Odd place for them." She started laughing, loving this side of him she'd never seen. "You're actually pretty funny."

"I have my moments," he said, but he'd gone all serious on her. "You know you scare the hell out of me, don't you?"

"I know. I'll try to go easy on you." She would not think about their future, about their love, about the fact he was supposed to go to Israel. As she hoped, he laughed.

"Okay. You win. Get naked and lie spread eagle on the bed and let me have my way with you."

She took off her bra and panties, shucked off her shoes, and did as he asked. "You may ravish me," she said.

She was glorious lying there, her breasts firm and high, her stomach flat, her hips curving and tapering down to those legs he'd dreamed about having wrapped around him. Her pubic hair was dark red, darker than her hair, beautiful. "You'll do," he said. When she moved, he stilled her. "Let me," he said, and kissed her inner thigh as she melted and let him kiss and lick his way slowly up her body until she was trembling, a fine sheen of sweat covering her.

"You're pretty good at that," she said, her voice shaking slightly.

"I'm inspired."

He slipped a finger inside her and she was so slick and tight, he groaned.

"Can I move yet, because I got to tell you, you're killing me."

He bent and licked her, moving his finger slightly, feeling her hips push up against his mouth, feeling her come.

"You can move now," he said, pushing inside, his heart beating so fast he could swear he could hear it. She moved. Man, did she move.

Jaimie woke up the next morning and listened to Harry's soft breathing, feeling so desperately happy, her eyes burned. Everything came back at once, the pain and joy and fear.

"I wasn't that bad, was I?"

Jaimie quickly dashed away her tears. "I'm happy," she said, and rolled away in an attempt to get up.

"Oh no you don't." He pulled her back against him. "Tell me why you're crying?"

He felt solid and warm and smelled so damned good Jaimie started crying all over again. Because some day she was going to by lying in her bed alone wondering what he was doing, missing him desperately and kicking herself for thinking she'd be happy without him.

"Hey," he said, and pulled her even tighter, which, of course, made her cry even harder.

"I'm crying because I love you and you're . . . you're . . ."

"I'm what?"

"I can't ask you to stay here. I can't. Because someday you're going to wake up and look over at me and wonder what the hell you were thinking."

"Are you saying you want me to go to Israel?"

She turned so she could see him, and her heart melted into a big painful blob. "No, I don't want you to go. But if you don't, it'll always be there, this thing that you could have done. Then it will turn into this thing you should have done. And someday we'd have a fight and you'd say, 'Yeah, and I gave up the job of a lifetime for this crap?' Don't you see what I'm saying?"

His eyes drifted over her face, settling on a tear hanging from her jaw. He flicked it off and rubbed his thumb and index finger together.

"You'd feel better if I went to Israel for a while just to prove how absolutely miserable my life would be without you?"

"What if it's not? What if it's the best thing that ever happened to you?"

He smiled. "You're the best thing that's ever happened to me."

She closed her eyes and shook her head. "Maybe not today and maybe not tomorrow, but someday and soon, and for the rest of your life."

"I always hated *Casablanca*."

She opened her eyes in horror. "Nobody hates *Casablanca*."

"Well, I will hate it if you use that stupid line to get out of marrying me."

Her mouth opened and closed and nothing came out.

"I just proposed." He was scowling.

"But we haven't even been to dinner yet."

"Jaimie," he said, his voice edged with anger.

"What?"

"Would you have dinner with me tonight?"

She smiled. "I can't. I have to work. How about breakfast?"

He let out a growl and kissed her neck until she dissolved into laughter. "What's your favorite color?"

"Green."

"What's your favorite movie?"

"Pre-1960 or post?"

"Pre."

"Gaslight."

"Post?"

Jaimie smiled. "Believe it or not, it's *When Harry Met Sally.*"

"Never saw it."

"Then I'm afraid I'm going to have to leave you right now."

He laughed. "Favorite song?"

She kissed his cheek. "Don't have one. Harry, why are you doing this?"

"Because I love you."

And that was reason enough. For now.

Chapter 28

Anne looked down at her daughter sleeping on her side, dark tufts of hair brushing the bunnies on the crib bumper. "I really don't feel guilty about going back to work," she said as Bob came up next to her.

"Are you supposed to?"

"I'm supposed to be filled with angst anyway. But the truth is, I can't wait. I love being with Jacey, but I'm going nuts." Bob laughed and hugged her from behind. "I don't want to be one of those mothers who the kid never sees. But I don't want to stay here all the time either. I think my brain's starting to atrophy."

"Then go back and work forty hours instead of the eighty you used to do. That's all."

She bit her lip. "I suppose."

"What's going on, Anne?"

She turned in his arms and looked up at him, loving his worn-out face, the deep lines, the gray spikes in his dark eyebrows. "It's Harry. He's not going to take that Israel assignment."

"You're kidding."

"It's because he's in love with the editor of that paper he was working at. Would you do that for me? Turn down a great job?"

"There was a time in my life I would have gone to China if it was a great job, no matter who I left behind."

"That's how I feel. But that doesn't mean we don't love each other, right? If they offered me that assignment would you ask me to stay?"

"Yes. Would you?"

She shook her head. "I don't know."

He held her against him. "I really don't think I'd ask. But I'd hope."

"Anyway, it's silly to talk about because I'm not going anywhere now that we have Jacey," she said, smiling down at the baby.

"If things keep going the way they are with my stock portfolio, I'll be able to retire and stay home with her, relieving you of the guilt of not feeling guilty."

Anne turned in his arms. "You're kidding. I thought your investments took a dive."

"They did. So I got out and reinvested. Biotechs. Nursing homes." He shrugged. "Anything to do with getting old and trying to stay young is hot and can only get hotter. So, baby, we're rich."

"How rich?"

"Let's put it this way, I could retire today and live nicely for about twenty years." He looked at his wife and saw a glint in her eye. "What do you have in mind?"

"Just an idea for an investment. I'll tell you all about it in bed."

On New Year's Day, Harry and Jaimie sat at her kitchen table paper and pencil in hand and tried to figure out what the heck they were going to do with the rest of their lives. Reality was much bleaker after a shower and some strong coffee. All the I love yous in the world wouldn't change the fact that Harry worked in New York and Jaimie worked in Nortown. He didn't want to say it, but to him it was clear who would have to move. The *Journal* was most probably going under, and what was Jaimie going to do then? Work for the *Day?* If she was going to get a new job, she might as well get it in New York. There. Simple. Problem solved.

"You can't quit the *Times*. I won't let you." Jaimie gave him such a fierce expression, he actually believed her.

"Great. I don't want to."

"But what about Israel? I really don't want to live in Israel."

"Agreed. I'm pretty sure Monty will give me another assignment. New York's got plenty of newspapers for you. If NBC backs out, someone else will hire you in a second."

Jaimie looked around her little kitchen. She loved her kitchen. She'd painted the walls bright yellow and the old wooden cabinets stark white. She'd replaced all the handles with white and yellow striped pulls. Harry was asking her to give up her house. Her home. And he didn't seem the least bit grateful. In fact, he was acting as if *she* ought to be grateful.

"What about my house?"

"Sell it. We can use the cash for a down payment on an apartment in the city."

"Just like that?" She gripped the edge of her chrome table, a period piece from the forties she'd found in a thrift store, as if Harry were already trying to drag her away.

"Well, I admit a small place like this will probably take a while to sell. I don't know much about the market here, but . . ."

"No."

Harry stopped mid-sentence, his mouth hanging open. "No what?"

"Why do I have to move?"

"I suppose we could live separately. Call every night. Visit every other weekend. It might be tough on the kids at first, but they'll get used to it. Maybe the kids can live with me."

"Ha ha. I'm just asking you to consider the possibility that we don't move to New York. It wasn't even part of the discussion. You sat down and wrote "New York" on top of your paper as if it were a foregone conclusion."

"Isn't it?" he asked cautiously.

"No, Harry, it isn't. Aren't you the same man who was supposedly seriously considering taking Martin up on his offer to stay?" She could feel the panic growing, not fear precisely, but something else she couldn't put her fingers on, as if she were clutching at a cliff and slowly losing grip. Was she afraid to make a move? Was all this talk about loving Nortown and her job, of the importance of living close to her mother, of staying here because she was happy. Was it all bullshit? Was she really just scared?

"It doesn't make sense for us to stay here," Harry said, sounding perfectly rational and completely callous. "My job pays better, plus you're going to be out of a job."

"Not necessarily. Martin hasn't made any announcements yet. And you said you were considering it." She was starting to talk too fast and her fingertips were beginning to hurt from grabbing the table so tightly.

"You won't go, will you?" he asked, his face growing taut.

Yes, of course I'll go. I'd follow you anywhere.

"I . . . I . . . I . . ." She gave Harry a helpless look.

"You've got to be kidding me." He sounded angry but

he looked hurt and Jaimie looked down at her hands. "You want me to give up everything for you and you won't even seriously consider the move?"

"What? You give up everything? You'd just be giving up a job. I'd be giving up my home, my family, friends, the place I belong, the only place I've ever known. The place I've been happy."

"Happy," he spat. "Don't you mean the place you've been hiding?"

Jaimie was so mad, she saw stars flashing in front of her face. "I'm done talking about this right now," she said through gritted teeth.

"Yeah," he said, looking at her with hurt and anger and pain. "I'm done, too."

He stood up and stopped when he took in her expression. She must have looked like death because he sat down and grabbed her hands, prying them off the edge of the table. He enfolded her fingers into his palms and squeezed, giving her a searching look that nearly broke her heart.

"I'm sorry," she said, her eyes filling with tears, her heart aching in her chest. "I just can't. I can't."

Something changed in his eyes, something that made her hate herself and hate him and life and the fear, the goddamn fear that she hadn't recognized until this very moment.

"I can't do the long distance thing. It's why I couldn't go to Israel. I didn't want to be that far away from you. We don't have a future if you stay in Nortown."

Anger flared. "You won't even consider moving here?"

"Jaimie, do you understand what you're asking me? And yes, I did consider it. And I decided I wanted to go back to New York. Can I tell you something? I was miserable about going back without you but I knew it was right. Then, when you got that job offer, I couldn't believe it. It was as if everything were falling into place."

"And I said no."

"Yeah. You said no." He took her hands and pulled her toward him slightly. "Now you've got to say yes."

Something awful blossomed in her, something dark and scary. "I don't think I can, Harry. God, I hate myself. I can't believe it. I can't." She pulled away and ran from the kitchen, her bright yellow happy kitchen where she'd eat breakfast alone for the rest of her life.

Harry left that day, back to New York, back to where he belonged. Jaimie cried until her eyes were nearly swollen shut. She called in sick the next day and didn't answer her phone. It was if her soul had been ripped out, as if Harry had a strand of herself and the farther he went, the thinner the strand got, until it snapped back, hitting her hard, driving her to the darkest place she'd ever been.

All because she was a coward.

"You piece of shit," she said into the mirror. "You're not happy. You're scared. You're a coward." She screamed the last, hitting her reflection until her hand hurt. The anger wasn't just because of Harry, it was because she realized something about herself she'd never known. And it was devastating to learn. She looked down at her sink and watched her tears drip into the drain. "No."

Jaimie blew her nose and walked to her living room, hands fisted, arms straight down until she reached the phone. She stared at it for about thirty seconds, tortured by doubts, nearly paralyzed by fear. Then she grabbed it up and dialed information. "New York, New York. NBC."

Chapter 29

Two days later, Jaimie was at her desk when Martin and Paul came into the newsroom and announced a meeting for the next morning. One look at Paul told Jaimie all she needed to know: They were selling to Penworth.

"What was that about?" Kath asked after they'd gone back into their lair.

"I'm not sure. But I think all that celebrating we did a few weeks ago was a waste of happiness," Jaimie said, a sharp feeling of dread pressing against her stomach.

"You know something," she accused.

Jaimie shook her head. "I swear I don't know precisely what they're going to announce, but I suspect they've sold the paper." She lowered her voice. "I think they sold it to Penworth."

Kath gasped aloud then quickly tried to stifle it with a hand over her mouth. "That bastard. After going on national television and saying he wouldn't sell to them. I can't believe it."

"I'm not certain what's happening. I'm way out of the loop now. But I don't trust Martin."

"God. After raising everyone's hopes," Kath said, looking around the newsroom at the other unsuspecting reporters. "What a jerk."

"The past few months have been insane. Talk about a roller coaster." Jaimie closed her eyes, willing herself not to lose it in front of the newsroom. "I called NBC and asked if their offer is still good. Apparently some executive who does the hiring is on vacation in Italy and they couldn't give me an answer." She peeked up at Kath to get her reaction.

"Wow. Big move. Does Harry know you called NBC?"

Heat flooded her cheeks. "Honestly, if they called and offered me the job again, I don't know what I'd say. So I haven't told Harry anything. We haven't talked in days." To her horror, her eyes filled with tears.

Kath grabbed her arm and led her to the morgue. "What's going on?"

"Harry asked me to marry him and I told him I couldn't leave and then he left and then I called NBC to prove I could leave but I'm scared to death I won't be able to and that means I'm a complete doormat." By the time she finished, she was sobbing. Kath was a good enough friend to have understood every word she'd just said.

"I was scared to death at first when I got that job offer the first time we thought the paper was going belly-up," Kath said. "And it scared me how relieved I was when Martin the ass said on national television he wasn't selling, the bastard. Looks like I'm going to have to get scared all over again."

Jaimie clutched Kath's arm. "What happens if NBC calls and makes an offer?"

Kath gave her a don't-do-this-to-me look. "You know I can't tell you what to do."

"I wish you would."

"You love him, right? You're still getting that zing?"

"Big time."

"Well, duh."

Jaimie let out a watery laugh and gave her friend a hug. "Thanks, Kath. You're a life saver."

Three days later, Kevin Somerville answered an e-mail from his secretary at NBC regarding Jaimie's phone call.

"Tell Ms. McLane the offer no longer stands."

Jaimie stood in the middle of the newsroom that had been a second home to her for nearly fifteen years. The tiles below her feet were scratched and worn, the fluorescent lights buzzed noisily, and it was cold and dreary and the dearest thing she'd ever beheld.

At her feet were four boxes filled with neatly categorized notebooks she'd probably never open again. She told herself to throw them in the recycling bin, but the reporter in her whispered that someday she just might need them. In her right hand was the last issue of the *Nortown Journal* that would ever hit the newsstands. In all, it wasn't a spectacular issue and perhaps the worst part about it was Paul's lame editorial that ran in the lower left hand corner explaining why the *Nortown Journal* was ending.

"In the end, readers, it all came down to economics," he'd written.

Right. In the end it all came down to his incompetence and his brother's tightfistedness. Jaimie hated the ill feelings that had developed between her and Paul; she felt as if she'd lost a good friend and mentor. His office was empty, stripped of everything that could have reminded her of Paul or Harry. Thank goodness. She didn't want to think about Harry, about her failure, about his, about the questions popping up in her head that if either had really loved the other enough they could have figured something out. At least she'd made that call to NBC, though Harry wouldn't have any way of knowing that. He hadn't called and she hadn't called him. It was purely awful. They'd just said a tight-lipped good-bye. She wished Harry had been here to see this ending, to know how ugly it was, how empty.

The only other person in the newsroom was Kath, probably because she was almost as big a packrat as Jaimie. And probably because, like Jaimie, she didn't want this chapter of their lives to be over.

Jaimie was cleaning out her desk when she heard a noise coming from across the newsroom. She looked up to see Kath slumped on her desk, crying her heart out, her body shaking with the force of her sobs.

"I can't believe it," came her muffled voice. "This isn't happening. It isn't. Tell me this isn't happening." Jaimie was by her side in an instant.

"We've been doing way too much crying lately."

"It's usually you."

"True," Jaimie said, her hand on Kath's back rubbing to give any comfort she could. "We'll be fine. Maybe this is the best thing that could have happened to us. I have an interview Monday with the *Day*." She shrugged. "But my heart's just not in it. Maybe I'll feel better after the weekend. You looking?"

"Sort of," she said into her desk. "No."

Everyone at the paper had gotten four weeks severance, a slight cushion in case jobs were scarce. "I don't even want to work at the *Day*," Jaimie confessed. "I think I liked being the underdog, the poor relation. Who is the *Day* going to compete with now that the *Journal's* gone? The *Nortown Shop-a-Day?*" She let out a bitter laugh.

"I wish we had the money to buy Martin out," Kath said fiercely.

"Yeah. You and I could have pooled our five hundred bucks in savings and asked the bank to loan us the rest of the fifteen million."

Kath wiped her face and forced a smile. "Just keep in touch, will you please?"

"Who knows, maybe we'll both work for the *Day?*"

"You're thinking too small, McLane. If I were you, I'd start interviewing in New York."

Jaimie shook her head good-naturedly, but her stomach knotted up. She had no excuse for staying now. No 'I don't want to leave the paper' plea. Nothing to stop her from putting a "for sale" sign in front of her house and a suitcase in her trunk.

Nothing but fear.

Three days later, she was busy watching bubbles begin to form at the bottom of her spaghetti pan, when Kath called.

"Whatcha doing?"

"Watching water boil. It's really fascinating. And you know what else? I know why I was a slob. It was because I never had time to clean. You should see my house now. Spotless. It's almost creepy."

Kath laughed. "Yeah. I was watching water boil yesterday. Listen, have you seen the *Day* today?"

Jaimie glanced over to the neatly stacked paper in the recycling basket she'd bought two days before. "Yes. Why, did I miss something?"

"Get the business section. Page G-3."

Jaimie got the paper and grabbed the section. "Okay," she said, turning the front page. "What am I looking . . ."

"You saw it?"

Jaimie scanned the article quickly. Some out of state investor was planning to start up a statewide paper to compete with the *Hartford Courant.* "That's interesting," she said, still reading the short article, but feeling the beginning of her blood begin to surge. "Pretty good timing, huh?"

"I know. I already called and got an interview."

"You're kidding," Jaimie said, tucking the phone against her shoulder and shutting off the heat under her pot. She grabbed up a pen and paper. "What's the number?"

The temporary offices of the *Connecticut Independent* were located on the fourth floor of a new office building in downtown Hartford, directly across the street from the *Courant's* editorial offices. The lobby's pristine blue carpet still smelled new. Jaimie scanned the directory, almost surprised to see the words *Connecticut Independent* already added. For some reason, it hadn't seemed real until this moment.

She'd called as soon as she'd hung up with Kath and a woman had set up an interview, and then she'd fought wave after wave of almost debilitating fear. Every time she felt her heart race and her pulse pound, she'd start breathing deeply, talking to herself, trying to calm down. The thought of the fear that was ruling her life was as frightening as the anxiety itself. She had never, not even as a college student facing finals, felt this out of control.

She pressed the elevator button and grimaced when

the door immediately slid open. "Come on, you can do this." She had to do this, because that cushion of money she had was quickly running dry.

A newly made and clearly temporary sign was tacked to the door directly across from the elevator bank, almost as if fate were making every stop easy and impossible to back out of. Tugging on the unfamiliar business suit, Jaimie forced herself to walk to the door, still stunned to be this frightened. Breathe. Breathe. She put her hand on the doorknob . . . and stopped. If she could try for this job, couldn't she do the same thing in New York? Chances were if she got a job here, she'd have to move anyway because the commute to Hartford would be a killer.

If she could do this, she could do anything. Suddenly she realized, she *could* do anything. If she was willing to work for this paper, why not a paper in New York?

Feeling a huge weight lift off her shoulders, she turned the knob and walked in, bracing herself.

"Hi. You must be Jaimie McLane," a smiling and entirely too cheerful young woman said. "I'm Amanda. You can go right in. First door on your left."

"I'm sorry, I'm not interested in this job after all. Could you please tell them I won't be interviewing today. I've decided to go to New York."

The young woman looked startled. "Oh," she said. "Okay, I'll tell him."

Jaimie, feeling better than she had in months, strode out the door and headed to the bank of elevators. She was going to do it. She was going to call Harry and move to New York and live happily ever after.

"Jaimie, where the hell do you think you're going?"

Jaimie's heart nearly stopped and she slowly turned around, her knees shaking. "Harry?"

"If you're in New York, how the heck are you going to be my Nortown bureau chief?"

She looked at him, drinking in the sight of his beautiful face. "I guess that would be pretty difficult."

"Not to mention tough on the kids."

"Oh, Harry," she said, and launched herself into his arms.

"PAPER GETS A FACE LIFT"
AP wire reports:

NORTOWN—A New York investor and chief features editor of the *New York Times*, today named former *Times* reporter and Pulitzer Prize winner Harry Crandall as editor and publisher of the start-up *Connecticut Independent*.

Crandall signed a four-year contract with new owners Anne Levine and Robert Porter. Levine is a staff reporter at the *Times*.

The couple, who are married, outlined plans in a press conference yesterday to open several bureaus statewide in an effort to compete with the *Hartford Courant*, which has held a journalistic stronghold in Connecticut for decades.

"We feel it's a sound investment," Porter said.

The couple also named Jaimie McLane as Nortown bureau chief. McLane helped push the now-defunct *Nortown Journal* into the national spotlight last year when she reported that an eight-year-old Nortown boy admitted killing Joshua Tate. His trial on charges of manslaughter is set to begin early this summer.

Discover the Thrill of
Romance With

Kat Martin

__Hot Rain
0-8217-6935-9   **$6.99US/$8.99**CAN

Allie Parker is in the wrong place—at the worst possible time . . . Her
only ally is mysterious Jake Dawson, who warns her that she must play
the role of his reluctant bedmate . . . if she wants to stay alive. Now, as
Alice places her trust—and herself—in the hands of a total stranger, she
wonders if this desperate gamble will be her last . . .

__The Secret
0-8217-6798-4   **$6.99US/$8.99**CAN

Kat Rollins moved to Montana looking to change her life, not find
another man like Chance McLain, with a sexy smile of empty heart.
Chance can't ignore the desire he feels for her—or the suspicion that
somebody wants her to leave Lost Peak . . .

__The Dream
0-8217-6568-X   **$6.99US/$8.50**CAN

Genny Austin is convinced that her nightmares are visions of another
life she lived long ago. Jack Brennan is having nightmares, too, but his
are real. In the shadows of dreams lurks a terrible truth, and only by
unlocking the past will Genny be free to love at last. . .

__Silent Rose
0-8217-6281-8   **$6.99US/$8.50**CAN

When best-selling author Devon James checks into a bed-and-breakfast
in Connecticut, she only hopes to put the spark back into her
relationship with her fiancé. But what she experiences at the Stafford
Inn changes her life forever . . .

Available Wherever Books Are Sold!

Visit our website at **www.kensingtonbooks.com.**

Contemporary Romance By
Kasey Michaels

__Can't Take My Eyes Off of You
  0-8217-6522-1 $6.50US/$8.50CAN

__Too Good to Be True
  0-8217-6774-7 $6.50US/$8.50CAN

__Love to Love You Baby
  0-8217-6844-1 $6.99US/$8.99CAN

__Be My Baby Tonight
  0-8217-7117-5 $6.99US/$9.99CAN

__This Must Be Love
  0-8217-7118-3 $6.99US/$9.99CAN

__This Can't Be Love
  0-8217-7119-1 $6.99US/$9.99CAN

Available Wherever Books Are Sold!

Visit our website at **www.kensingtonbooks.com**.